"Somebod[...]
of the wome[...]

I turned to her. "Ma'am, where is the law around here?"

"The only law right now is Amos Broughton, and he's not here," she said, with a touch of disgust in her voice. "It seems he's not here much at all anymore."

"Deputies?"

"We had two. One quit and the other is about to. You can never find him when you need him."

"He's probably down at the dress shop, flirting with that young widow woman," the other said. "It's just as well. He has no common sense about him anyway. He'd probably arrest poor old Hawk for public drunkenness, instead of the real troublemakers."

I noticed a little boy lingering back in the shadows of a nearby doorway. Fetching out a coin, I got his attention. "There's another for you if you can find the deputy and bring him here," I said. "Look at the dress shop first."

He took the money and headed off on a run, into the better, vice-free part of town.

"Who are you, sir?" one of the women asked.

"A fool who's getting ready to stick his nose into somebody else's business," I replied. "But given that nobody else seems inclined, I guess it's up to me."

I headed for my saddlebags to retrieve my pistol and gun belt.

Forthcoming

The Sharpshooter: Gold Fever

THE
SHARPSHOOTER
BRIMSTONE

TOBIAS
COLE

HarperTorch
An Imprint of HarperCollinsPublishers

This is a work of fiction. Names, characters, places, and incidents are products of the author's imagination or are used fictitiously and are not to be construed as real. Any resemblance to actual events, locales, organizations, or persons, living or dead, is entirely coincidental.

HARPERTORCH
An Imprint of HarperCollins*Publishers*
10 East 53rd Street
New York, New York 10022-5299

First HarperTorch paperback printing: May 2003

HarperCollins®, HarperTorch™, and ♦™ are trademarks of Harper-Collins Publishers Inc.

Printed in the United States of America

Visit HarperTorch on the World Wide Web at www.harpercollins.com

10 9 8 7 6 5 4 3 2 1

THE
SHARPSHOOTER
BRIMSTONE

⇥ 1 ⇤

SHE FLOATED AWAY FROM ME, LIKE SHE'D SUD-denly turned into nothing. Up off the seat of the railroad car, into the air like a piece of fluff, and then she was gone, speeding toward the front of the car as if she'd just been levitated by a particularly adept stage conjurer. Along with the rest of the passengers, at almost the same moment I found myself also in midair, flung there by the terrible jolt that had shuddered through the train from front to rear. We left the tracks—I could tell the moment that happened—and went tumbling. The passenger car rolled like a bottle on a slanted floor, the air full of flailing arms and legs and grating screams underlain with the horrible sound of the metal and wood rending apart. Then I slammed against something, hard, and it all went away. Blackness wrapped around me and I saw, felt, heard, and knew nothing at all.

Sometime later—a minute or a year, I could not have told you—there was a hand on my shoulder, gripping gently. I felt no pain, no real fear, just a vague sense that something significant had happened. I opened my eyes and saw clouds and sky, then a face that loomed over me, unfocused, a man's face with lips rapidly moving and words pouring out that I could not at first understand. Then hearing and vision clarified together, and I realized he was praying. For me, apparently, asking God to protect and help me and to touch with healing whatever injuries I might have suffered.

He had a broad yet skeletal face, somewhat pale and not at all well-featured. His wide-set eyes were squeezed tightly shut, crinkles all around them. His nose was somewhat flat and wide, and his lips heavy around a lean and hollowed mouth, moving as he spoke in a way that made me think of two writhing worms, one atop the other. But the most notable thing about him was the black cloth tied across his forehead, like an eyeless mask that had been scooted up to brow level. My eyes focused on that cloth, my numbed mind puzzling over it while he prayed for me . . . then someone passing by us bumped him and one side of the cloth fell away.

On his forehead were marks, fleshy lines in a recognizable pattern. Three crosses, side by side, Golgotha-style, just like the images in a thousand depictions in a thousand chapels. They were as clearly visible on his pale skin as if they'd been painted there with overly thick paint. I saw them only a moment, though, for he reacted quickly when the cloth dropped, and turned away from me, pulling the cloth back into place in a hurry. I closed my eyes again, and when I reopened them, he was gone.

There was noise, motion, people moving about frantically, dark shadows dancing all around me. I smelled burning wood and something like tar. There were yells and moans and the sound of a woman crying. I turned my head and saw the woman who'd seemingly floated off from me inside the railroad car. She had blood on her forehead and was trying to get up, but a man was attempting to restrain her. He was telling her she shouldn't move until they knew whether she'd been hurt, but she was ranting on about her late husband's coffin back in one of the boxcars and how she had to get to it to make sure it hadn't been burst open by the crash.

Crash. That's what had happened. The train had crashed, derailed, and tumbled, splintering to pieces, tossing us passengers around like dice in the grip of a great, shaking fist, then dumping us out as the sundered train rolled down the grade. Some of us, anyway. There were probably some still inside what was left of the passenger cars.

I was lying on my back, my neck craned as I watched the widow struggling with her well-intentioned restrainer. Oddly enough, I was very relaxed, separate from all this. The woman was a little out of her head, maybe, babbling on about the coffin and fearful her husband's corpse was sprawled out back there in the boxcar with no dignity. It seemed a minor concern to me. A dead man was a dead man, and death and dignity seldom conjoined. No one knew that better than I.

The sun emerged from behind a cloud. I squinted against the light, then simply closed my eyes and lay there, not hurting, but listless and weak, like a wrung-out rag. Slowly some soreness began to creep upon me, a feeling like having been shaken in the jaws of a huge dog, and I hoped I'd broken no bones. I opened my eyes against the light, lifted my head and looked down my supine form. I saw my boots, and made them move. I lifted my hands and counted my fingers. I was in one piece. My eyes closed again and I relaxed on the sandy Kansas soil and drifted off into darkness once more.

I awakened in the house of a stranger, with a little girl and boy staring at me from the side of the bed. In fact they were seated side by side at the edge of the bed, leaning over with their chins resting on the feather mattress. When I opened my eyes they both yelled in unison and jumped to their feet, running away like I was a monster just escaped from a cage. Befuddled and not at that point even remembering what had happened to me, I watched them fly out of the room and heard their receding voices, yelling over one another: "He's awake! He's awake!"

I looked around. The room was spacious, with a high ceiling and walls ornately papered halfway down, wainscot below that. Treetops outside my window told me I was on the second story, and an excess of frills and flowers spoke of a feminine, perhaps matronly touch. The bed was a four-poster, the posts about as tall as I was, but without a canopy.

I heard the children thundering back up the stairs. Heavier and slower footfalls behind them told me adults were on the way. I pushed myself up in the bed a little, felt a couple of twinges of general, hard to pinpoint pain, and turned my eyes to the door.

The children entered first, not afraid now that they had grown-ups with them. Just behind them was a gray-haired man with muttonchop sideburns, an unkempt look, and pleasant features. A very large woman of about his age but twice his girth came in last.

"Ah, yes indeed, Mr. Wells!" the man boomed out, striding toward me on short, thick legs. He put out his hand. "So glad you've come back around! Knew you would, knew you would . . . just didn't know how fast. Knew you would, though."

Feeling very much like I was dreaming all this, I

put out my hand and shook his. It was warm and soft. "Hello," I said.

"Hello to you, Mr. Wells. Hello indeed! So pleased to have you as a guest in our home! Not under these circumstances, of course—sorry you were hurt—but still so pleased to have you! So pleased!"

"I'm Jed Wells," I said, though they seemed to already know me.

"Oh, yes, we know!" He laughed and glanced around at the fat woman, who was beaming like a very large sun. "We know indeed, don't we, dear!"

"We know," she said. "We do know you, Mr. Wells. Why, Murphy has talked of you and your book for so very long!"

"So very long," the man repeated, nodding.

"Why, I've seen him weep as he reads that book. Just read and weep, read and weep."

The man lost his smile quickly. "Belle, that's enough of that. There's no need to tell everything you know. No need!"

He shouldn't have been embarrassed to have it known my story had brought him tears. It was intended to. It brought tears to me to write it . . . and many more to have lived it.

Belle lowered her eyes and looked ashamed. The man looked at me and regained his smile.

"That's my Belle. The finest wife a man ever had. But she talks, oh, how she talks! Don't you, Belle!"

"I do," she admitted.

"Talks and talks," he repeated. "But the finest wife a man ever had. That's the gospel. That's the very gospel."

Belle beamed again. Meanwhile, I was analyzing my host's repetitious speech pattern. Maybe in my next book I could have a character who talked that way. A particularly annoying character.

"Where am I?" I asked.

"In the home of Murphy Wagoner, mayor of the fine and proud town of Bedford, Kansas! And sir, it is an honor indeed to host you. Indeed it is."

"Indeed," said Belle. "Murphy loves your book."

"Belle, propriety! We are in the company of guests!"

"Oh . . . I mean, Mr. Wagoner loves your book."

"You are Mr. Wagoner, I presume," I said to the man, and my voice cracked badly.

"Belle! Water for our guest!" my host said. She waddled off in a hurry. He shook his head sorrowfully at me. "So sorry. So very sorry! We should have realized you would be thirsted!"

The writer in me idly wondered if "thirsted" was a word. The rest of me wondered what kind of odd household I'd entered. I glanced down at the two watching children, both silent as ghosts. I smiled at them, and they pulled in behind Wagoner for protection.

"Fine children you've got," I said.

"Well, thank you. Grandchildren, actually. Mandy and Dero. Poor little orphans! Their mother was our daughter, their father a sorry, worthless son of a . . . gun who abandoned them and their dear mother. It broke her heart. That was what killed her. A broken heart, yes."

"That and that big old rattlesnake that bit her at the woodpile," Dero contributed, the unexpected intrusion of his prepubescent voice startling me.

"Hush, Dero," Wagoner said. I suppose he must have thought I'd like the romanticized version best.

Belle returned with a pitcher sloshing water and a crystal glass that she poured full and handed to me. I'd not had a more satisfying drink than that one, barring the first pure drink from the first clear spring I encountered when I left behind the prison camp at Andersonville years before. That drink would forever remain in my memory as the best, most cleansing, quenching, soul-satisfying, sacred drink I would ever be privileged to taste this side of the heavenly paradise.

"Thank you, ma'am," I said, handing back the glass. I was beginning to piece all this together. The mayor here was obviously one of my devoted readers, and somehow or other—the train's passenger list, most likely, combined with the publishing house correspondence in my pocket—he'd learned who I was and taken me into his house, stationing his grandchildren at my bedside to await my return to consciousness. Now, here I was, at rest in a stranger's home, swaddled in quilts and admiration, laid up to heal from whatever injuries the train crash had brought me.

I wanted out of there as quickly as possible.

"Kind of you to take me in," I said.

"Sir, it's an honor," the mayor replied.

"An honor," said Belle.

Little Mandy edged out from behind her grandfather. "Are you famous?" she asked.

"Oh, I don't know," I replied, though I knew the truthful answer was yes, and though I preferred to think of myself as well-known rather than famous. I'd never been able to deal with that kind of thing. It was an unexpected side-effect of a novel I'd written not for wealth or fame, but for the purging of my own soul. I'd cleansed out the pollution of my Andersonville nightmare through the pages of that novel. I had not anticipated that thousands upon thousands of others across the nation would make that story their own, turning me—me, who grew up poor on a little Kentucky farm slopping hogs and shoveling manure—into a relatively noted literary figure.

For reasons I couldn't figure out, even a lot of former rebels seemed drawn to my novel, this despite the fact that the Andersonville hellhole prison camp was hosted by their side. But they often held a highly different opinion of its literary and historical merits than did those who had fought in the army of Abe Lincoln.

Wagoner himself had been a Union man, his next comment proved. "Mr. Wells is indeed famous, Mandy," he said. "He wrote a very great novel detailing the courage and misuse of the brave men who fought for our flag and had the misfortune to fall prisoner in rebel hands."

"That's the book they won't let us look at," Dero told his sister.

"Is it a bad book?" Mandy asked with that endearing forthrightness of the young.

"No," I replied before her grandfather could scold her. "It's a good book about some bad things."

"Well said, sir," Wagoner commented after a pause.

"Was anyone killed in the train crash?" I asked, shifting the subject.

"No. Not yet, anyway. One man's outcome is questionable, though they hope he'll pull through. They thought there was a fatality on the scene, but it proved to be a man already dead and in his coffin. He was most unceremoniously dumped out back in one of the freight cars."

"I met his widow," I said. "I was talking to her when we crashed. What caused it?"

"A section of bad track. Very negligent of the railroad," Belle observed.

"Did you lose possessions?" Wagoner asked. "Several had horses in the stable car that were injured. Two were killed. I'm a lawyer by profession. I'd be pleased to help you in any attempt to recover compensation for such losses."

"I have no horse just now. I travel by train and rent horses and buggies where I go, as I need to."

He moved in close, eyes a-glitter, a man seeking much-desired information. "Tell me, Mr. Wells, is it true that you are working on your second novel?"

I didn't want that question. The public answer to that question was yes, and it wasn't a lie. In my baggage—and where was my baggage, anyway? And my rifle?—was a notebook full of scribblings and thoughts and the beginnings of a story. Someday that would become the novel to carry on the story begun in *The Dark Stockade*. But no time soon. I'd not written a fresh word for three months. I had more important duties to fulfill, old and lingering obligations that had been hanging over me for far too many years. Thanks to the success of my first novel, I finally had the means and the time to carry them out.

"I'm working on a book," I replied. "Slowly."

"Oh, I wish you'd go fast. I've read *The Dark Stockade* three times, sir. Three times! I'll probably read it a fourth before the year is out. A moving story. Gripping! Hard to read, harder still to put down once you start it. It's both a wounding and healing experience to read that book. A wounding and healing experience all at the same time."

A wounding and healing experience. Not a bad review, that one, and it actually touched me. I gave Wagoner a small grin and quick nod. "Thank you."

"Is that why you are in our area? Working on your next book?"

"Yes, partly." It was more lie than truth. Though I never knew where I might run across material that would in some form find its way into my writing, I was in this vicinity for other reasons, and private. Nothing it would hurt for Wagoner to know . . . just private, that was all.

"Are you hungry, sir?"

Come to think of it, I was, and told him so.

"Then you shall have food. Come, grandchildren. Let's leave our guest in peace. He needs to rest and heal. We'll go see what victuals we can provide him, eh? Come on now, scurry."

2

WHEN THEY BROUGHT ME THE TRAY, THE WHOLE gang of them together, I was out of bed, dressed in a ragged robe I'd found in the wardrobe, seated in a chair and flipping through an old encyclopedia I'd taken off the little bookshelf in the corner.

"Mr. Wells!" Wagoner declared. "I'm surprised to see you up!"

"I'm not one for lying about much."

"But you're hurt! You should be in bed."

He was right, I suppose. But something in me has always rebelled against the notion of being bedridden, even for a short time. I've always sought to prove to myself that I can overcome whatever was trying to bring me down, no matter how massive or how meager. I suppose that's what helped me survive Andersonville . . . not only survive it, but do the near impossible: escape.

"Will you take your tray in bed or sitting up?" Belle asked. The covered tray in her fleshy hands exuded scents to entice a king.

Dero and Mandy, past their shyness, cleared a little table that stood under the window and pulled it over to me. Belle set down the tray and whisked off the cloth dramatically.

Ah, yes. Fried chicken, fresh buttered biscuits, peas, creamed potatoes, applesauce—this was a meal fit for a man about to be executed.

"Oh, ma'am, you are an artist at the cookstove, that I can see," I told Belle, and she puffed up even bigger and smiled even brighter.

"My dear Belle knows her way around food," Wagoner said.

In more ways than one, her girth indicated. Of course, I didn't say it out loud.

The food was delicious but difficult to enjoy fully because I had an audience. I tried to ignore them, but Wagoner kept talking.

"We've got Doc Phillips coming in to take a look at you in about an hour," he said. "Just to make sure you aren't badly hurt."

"I think I'm fine. This food will take care of what ails me." I winked at Belle and she turned red.

"Still, best to be sure, I always say."

"I suppose." Something flashed back to memory. "Perhaps it isn't needed. I've already been prayed over."

"Really?"

"Yes. A little odd, really. I came around after the crash and he was kneeling over me. Praying. A kind of cloth across his forehead. It fell away and . . . well, you know, maybe it didn't really happen. Sort of loco, now that I think about it." I took another bite and glanced up. Wagoner had a look of intense interest on his face.

"Go on," he said. "What did you see?"

"My memory is that the man had a cloth across his forehead that fell away and showed some markings on his skin. Three crosses, side by side."

"It was the Reverend Killian!" Belle said breathlessly. "Surely it was!"

"Who?"

Her husband answered. "The Reverend Edward Killian. You've heard of him, perhaps?"

The name, perhaps, was vaguely familiar. Or maybe not. "I don't know him," I admitted.

"Well, he's a great preacher. A powerful man of God who works as a traveling evangelist. There's an entire team of assistants and so on who travel with him. The work they do is great. Many saved, many reaffirming their professions. And it's no wonder. The man can preach in such a way that it brings the very brimstone of hell up under your feet! I take it from your writing, Mr. Wells, that you are yourself a man of a certain religious sensibility."

"I'm not the consistent churchgoer I should be, but suffice it to say that sometimes having that which is crooked and evil thrust before you so intensely and so continually as Andersonville thrust it before me tends to turn the mind very keenly to a renewed awareness of that which is straight and good."

"Then you should have a great appreciation for the Rev Killian. He is a good man, a great man."

"The marks on his forehead . . ."

"He keeps them covered most of the time. Some would glory in such divine markings, but not the Reverend. He is a humble man, not prone to display the marks of his righteousness in so public a way."

"Divine markings?"

"Have you heard of those great saints and godly men who are touched with the marks of the cross? Stigma, they call it. Bleeding nail scars on their hands, scars on their sides, thorn marks on their brows?"

"I've heard of it. Mostly appearing on Roman Catholics of very strong and intense faith, I believe. Are you saying that the marks on the Rev Killian's forehead are similar?"

"He seldom talks of it, but at times, in sermons, he has mentioned the peculiar markings that were given to him by the touch of God. Three crosses, the emblem of Calvary. Put onto his brow by God Himself." He paused. "It gives one a chill of awe to consider it."

I returned to my food, not replying. Those marks

had looked like scars to me. Though who was I to say? I suppose that if God chose to mark a man as His own, He could do it with scars if He wanted. The only alternative theory I could come up with was that Reverend Killian himself put those marks there, or somebody else put them there for him, against his will or otherwise. Either way, it was intriguing to think about.

Belle began talking. The subject of Reverend Killian evidently was dear to her, because she had a lot to say about him, about how marvelous a preacher he was, how tenderhearted and good a man, how powerful an influence for good. Why, half the countryside turned out for his camp meetings, even though at the moment he was one county over. Many would ride out on horses, wagons, or the train and camp out for nights at a time just to be part of it. Belle had heard that soon the Reverend would be moving his meeting closer to Bedford. This pleased her. It would be much easier to attend then.

"How did he happen to be there when the train derailed?" I asked as I finished off my meal. My stomach was pleasantly full. The best meal I'd enjoyed in many a day.

"I don't know," Wagoner answered. "Probably he was making arrangements for his next camp meeting location. I heard at the scene of the crash that he had been close enough to hear it and came over to see if he could be of help. He'd do that kind of thing."

Dr. Maddux Phillips was a well-dressed, poised fellow who would have looked at home on Fifth Avenue in New York City, but when he spoke he carried the sound of Alabama strong in his voice. He was maybe five or six years older than I, with gray temples, thinning brown hair, and deep lines on a rather expansive forehead. The lines around his eyes had not come from laughter; he didn't seem the kind to smile a lot.

He checked me over thoroughly and found what I knew he would: no significant injuries, just a few bumps and bruises. I was free to do what I wanted as soon as I felt like doing it.

I'd be out of this house tomorrow.

He was packing up his black bag and readying to leave when he paused and looked up at me.

"You are the Jedediah Wells who wrote the novel of Andersonville."

"I am."

"I read that novel."

There was neither compliment or insult in that sentence, so the only meaningful response I could make was to nod.

He closed and latched his bag, then said, "I was in the war, like you."

Again, all I could do was nod.

Another pause. "I was a Confederate, myself."

"You sound like a southern man. I'd guessed you might have favored the gray."

He was struggling to find words. I'd seen it before, from others similarly situated, and suspected I knew what he'd say. It would go one of two ways: explosive anger or—

"I was proud to fight for the cause of state's rights, and to defend against what I saw as an aggressive invasion of my homeland," he said. "I make no apology, and shall make none, for my own part in the war. I was no warrior . . . I tended the wounded. Saved all I could and watched the others die. There were times, when I heard boys crying for their mothers, dying with their arms and legs gone and their guts torn open by shreds of metal, that I prayed curses on the Yankee bastards who had done it. I considered the Lincolnites and all who fought for them to be hardly human beings . . . evil things, a threat to all that is good."

He looked at me, evaluating. I didn't react. None of this was new to me. I'd heard it all, feelings just as virulent on both sides.

"I don't know why I read your novel. But I did . . . and I can't say, sir, that my most basic views are changed. I believe in the lost cause, lost though it is. But your book did open my eyes—and my mind—and I have made room in my mind for a new understanding, a broader one. I know now that wrong can be done in more than one direction. There were things suffered by you and the others in that place you were kept . . . it shouldn't have been. Shouldn't have been."

This was not easy for him. I spoke. "There were those among the Confederates who wanted to help our situation, and who tried."

"Yes. And I'm glad of that. But even so, I must say—I'm compelled to say—it shouldn't have been like it was. For you, and all the thousands more. It shouldn't have been . . . and I'm sorry. I'm sorry."

He picked up his bag and left the room quickly, without looking back.

⊰ 3 ⊱

SOMETIME DURING THE NIGHT, I WOKE UP THINKING about Killian and those marks. I think I'd been dreaming about it, and maybe that accounted for the odd, distant kind of feeling nagging at my mind. Something about his face, or those marks . . .

I thought back, scanning over the years, the places I'd been. Nothing arose. If I'd met Killian before, I couldn't recall it.

Probably I'd just read about him and his meetings, or half-consciously overheard a conversation about him on a train or in a saloon. Rolling over, I put him out of my mind and went back to sleep.

While I slept, soreness of bone and muscle wrapped itself around me, and it had me in its grip come morning. I rose from my borrowed bed like an old man, did my washing and dressing and shaving at a third the speed I'd normally achieve it, and sat at Belle Wagoner's well-laden breakfast table feeling like Great-grandpap come to visit.

Murphy Wagoner noticed my ginger movements and gave an extended commentary on injury, pain, recovery, and the like. He recounted tale after tale from his boyhood on up in which he'd suffered this accident or that, and noted each time that the worst pain was always a day or two after the incident. He made the same point again and again, and at last I figured out the people of Bedford must have elected him mayor just to make him sit down and shut up.

Though I probably should have lingered to rest, instead I took a temporary leave of the Wagoner household and walked slowly to the Bedford livery about half a mile distant and there rented a horse and tack gear. I tipped the livery boy to saddle the horse for me, then with a grunt and groan swung into the saddle.

The ride to the train station was enjoyable. Fresh air, a crisp and unseasonably cool morning, a sky that looked more like autumn than summer . . . I said a prayer of gratitude that I'd come through that train crash alive and with nothing more than some residual soreness that would probably be gone in a day or two.

At the train station service was conducted with fulsome cordiality. Talk had it that the derailment occurred because of railroad negligence along a stretch of track that had never been properly laid to begin with, and the railroad people knew it was their fault that I and lots of others had very nearly been killed. The man behind the counter was as friendly as a first cousin as I presented myself to claim my goods.

They'd recovered it all. No damage to my leather valise other than a bit of scuffing, and the long rifle was still in its case. I removed it and checked it over. Nothing bent, scratched, or otherwise damaged. The rifle was unloaded, so I checked its workings and found all in order.

"Quite a rifle," the man behind the counter said. "I've not seen such a rifle since the war. There was a sharpshooter fellow I saw a few times who carried such a weapon. Only his had a scope."

I nodded, put the rifle back in its case, and thanked the man without picking up on the conversation. As I looked at him, I saw his eyes dart up very slightly, very subtly, and saw the expression of comprehension come over his face as he noted the very faint crescent scar above my brow. Men who spent their war years with a rifle scope pressed against their eye, kicking back with every recoil and sometimes breaking the flesh, almost always had scars like that. Mine was an unwanted badge of a period I'd as soon forget but of which I was reminded every time I looked in a shaving mirror.

As I left the station I wondered if I had been that sharpshooter he'd seen during the war. A little inquiry probably could have resolved that question, but my sharpshooting days were ones I seldom talked of, and never to strangers. If I ever took a wife, I'd maybe talk to her about them . . . or maybe not. What would be the point? A man can't undo what has already come and gone.

Away from the train station, I opened the rifle case again and checked one more thing: the item stored in a side pocket inside the case. It was the long telescopic scope that went through the war with me, always pampered and protected because it was so essential a tool for the grim job that had been mine. Since the ending of the war, I'd kept it, just like I kept the rifle, but the scope had not been mounted atop the rifle from the day that I'd vowed to "study war no more," as the song put it.

Never again would I peer through that scope. I'd made that vow firmly to myself. Never again. I'd seen too much death through it. Death inflicted by me.

Why did I even keep this scope? Why didn't I just throw it away, or take a sledgehammer to it and make it forever part of a past best forgotten? Why did I insist on keeping it and carrying it around as a reminder of things that had inflicted wounds on my soul that ran deeper even than those inflicted by Andersonville? The latter wounds I'd been able to expose and somewhat excise by writing about them. The former ones I hid away and shielded and hardly acknowledged even to myself.

So why did I keep this hated scope? Maybe it was

my penance to carry it. Maybe I owed that penance to some of those whom I'd watched jerk and disintegrate and die through that scope. . . .

I reached up and lightly rubbed the scar above my eye, put away the scope, and took a long ride on my rented horse, letting the morning pass away.

I despised it when I got this way. Depressed, sullen, prone to waste my time idling along through the countryside. I had a task to do, a man to go see, but I couldn't make myself do it. Hours rolled by, wasted.

At midday I was back in town, eating at a little café, when a man approached me with an inquisitive, hesitant expression that I'd grown used to seeing.

"Pardon me, sir, but are you Jed Wells?"

"I am."

"The one who wrote the book?"

"Yes."

The man chuckled. "I'll be! Well! I'd heard that you were in these parts, and when I saw you sitting there, I thought to myself, that fellow looks just like the picture of Jed Wells that I seen in the magazine. And by gum, it is."

"You've read the book, I guess."

"Well . . . no."

"No?"

"I don't read much. But I do look at the pitchers

in magazines and newspapers and such. And I like to meet famous folks."

Oh, Lord. I wasn't in the humor to waste time like this. Hoping to end it, I put my hand out for him to shake, which he did, so vigorously that my aching body suffered some uncomfortable throbs.

He pulled up a chair and sat down across from me. "You wrote about that prison camp," he said.

"Yes."

"I know a man who went into that camp and never came out again."

Him and thirteen thousand others. "What was his name?"

"Cooter. Rushmore Cooter. He was a good man. My neighbor back in Indiana."

"I'm sorry."

"You didn't know him, I take it."

"No. But there were so many. More than forty thousand men there over the time that sorry hell was allowed to exist."

"They say your book is good. I might read it sometime."

"Well, if you do, I hope you'll find it worth your while." I took my final sip of coffee and stood to go.

"I'd like to buy you a drink," he said.

I wasn't one to drink a lot, and never before sundown. But for some reason this proposition appealed to me. "Well, I'll let you do that," I said. "If you'll let me buy you one in turn."

He grinned and stood. "Come on," he said. "There's a place one street over, down about a block, called the Black Ball. Open almost around the clock. Best whiskey in the state."

"Let's go," I said.

"Will you tell me some about your book?"

I paused. "I'd as soon not, Mister . . ."

"Broughton. Buford Broughton."

I had duties, a man I needed to see—in fact I had come to this part of Kansas specifically to see. But that could wait. Today I was ready to put duty aside, just for a few hours. I was ready to achieve nothing more than a bit of distraction and enjoyment.

I put money on the table and followed Broughton out the door.

4

I FELT A LITTLE ASHAMED OF MYSELF WHEN I AR-
rived back at the Wagoner house that night. Truth
was, I'd not intended to be there for another night
at all. My goal had been to ride my rented horse to
the train station, recover my luggage, then come
say my good-byes and thank-yous to the family and
be on my way. It hadn't quite worked out that way.

What embarrassed me most was that I was a little drunk, and Belle could tell it. She seemed disappointed in me; so did her husband. The children
had been sent to bed early, so they weren't around
to see the hero take his plunge from grace.

"Are you feeling poorly, Mr. Wells?" Wagoner
asked.

"I'm . . . uh, yes. I think I should go lie down."

"Have you been in town all this time?"

"No, no. I've been out and around some. I took
a long ride this morning, enjoying your lovely
scenery around here." Then, in the afternoon, I'd

enjoyed the scenery of three different saloons, with Broughton as my host. I didn't say that to the Wagoners.

"There's supper on the stove," Belle said. "Still warm, if you want some."

"Might I take it on a tray to the bedroom?"

"Suit yourself, sir," Wagoner said.

Some minutes later, as I sat staring at my half-finished supper on the tray in the bedroom, I truly regretted my lapse. The Wagoners were good folk, simple and good-hearted and religious. They'd built up an exalted view of me because of my book, and now I'd disappointed them.

But the day hadn't been a waste. Oddly, it had been good for me. The life I'd lived and the tasks I'd taken on myself were often daunting and intense. Sometimes I had to get away from it all, if only for a few hours.

The real value of the day had come from the unlikely source of Buford Broughton. He brought up the prison camp again, and I learned that he was the nephew of Amos Broughton—and Amos Broughton was a man I had once known well. We'd shared the cramped and miserable quarters of a leaky shebang at Andersonville for a few weeks. I'd lost track of Amos since the war, but today I'd stumbled across it again: his nephew told me he was the sheriff of the neighboring county, living in the little town of Starnes with his wife, and doing quite well the last time Buford had seen him.

I'd be going to pay a call on Amos before I left these parts. It would be good to see him again.

I finished my supper and returned my dishes to the kitchen. Wagoner was there but atypically quiet, reading a week-old newspaper and largely ignoring me as I passed. Belle was not around.

Well, I'd stepped in it with the Wagoners and wasn't proud of it. Come morning I'd make my apologies, and then I'd leave. Should have left already, I guess.

Returning to my room, I undressed and dropped into bed and was asleep within two minutes.

The Wagoners were more congenial come morning, and when I left their home—offering to recompense them for their hospitality and having the proposition strongly rejected—I did so feeling on good terms with my former hosts.

They were good people, kind to take me in as they had, and I'd not forget them. But I was glad to be on my own again and back at my own tasks. I still had my rented horse and saddle. Half the contents of my valise were stuck into one of the saddlebags, with the lightened valise itself dangling off the saddle. My long rifle, in its case, was strapped to the saddle itself. My Colt revolver and its holster, which usually rode in the bottom of my valise, were wrapped up in oilcloth and hidden away in the second saddlebag.

I traveled light, always did, having learned the advantages of that long ago. It enhanced a man's mobility and freedom to be lightly encumbered.

As my lively horse followed a dusty road that paralled the railroad tracks, I felt grateful that the book I'd written mostly to save my own sanity had given me the additional favor of financial independence. I did not need to worry about the cost of the rented items or wonder how I would take care of myself. My life these days was in the financial aspect much easier than the impoverished years of my youth, growing up in the Kentucky mountains and astonishing folks all around by my remarkable marksmanship skills.

A talent, given by God, my father had proudly called my marksmanship. I believed him then, but no more. Not since the war. Not since signing on with the regiment of sharpshooters formed by champion sharpshooter Hiram C. Berdan of New York. I traveled all the way to Vermont to seek and gain membership in that exclusive and proud band of specialists, which my father, dying at that time, had read about in a newspaper that fell off some passerby's buggy. To please him, I'd made the journey, and after a grueling test of shooting skill, earned the right to enlist.

They told me that my father had never been so

proud. He'd talked proudly of his son, the sharpshooter, the very day he died. So they said. I was off
at war when he passed, unable to be with him.

In warfare, my performance as a sharpshooter
had outshone all others. My lethal skill drew the attention of those high in the military ranks. Quietly,
I was given a unique status, separated from any
particular body of command, made a special free-
roaming agent who moved from front to front as
needed, answering directly to the highest military
commanders and applying my skills as a sharpshooter when and where I was told to do so. I asked
no questions when assigned to kill, just carried out
the task, separating myself from it. And thus the
Kentucky boy who'd used his marksmanship in
youth to put meat on the table and win a dollar or
two here and there at turkey-shoot competitions
became a reliable deliverer of human death on behalf of the army of the United States of America.

Perched in trees, hidden in rocks, peering
through my scope out of church steeples and off
rooftops, I'd learned to dispatch men with great ef-
fectiveness and dispassion. With a gentle squeeze of
my finger I'd ended the existence of more men than
I wanted to count. The spasm of the body, the spray
of red, the quick, rag-doll collapse of one alive one
second and dead the next, the consternation of
those nearby my victims . . . these had become fa-

miliar to me, and had taught me what my marksmanship skill truly was.

Not a gift of God, as my father had believed. A curse of the devil. Nothing less than a curse that transformed me into something I'd never dreamed I could become.

Hard to believe, but when I was finally captured by the rebs, there was a moment of relief. Whatever happened now, at least I would no longer have to be an assassin, and I was glad of it.

It was a moment, no more. My capture quickly proved to be nothing more than a transition from one level of hell to another. I'd realized that clearly the moment I passed through the stockade gate of Camp Sumter, the official name of the prison camp at Anderson Station, Georgia, and seen the squalid mass of filthy, wasted, rag-clad humans who swarmed like two-legged maggots through the mud and vileness of that terrible place.

I had been transformed once as a warrior. Andersonville would transform me again, as a captive.

The house was painted a dull yellow, the shutters bright green. I paused long enough before the gate to be sure I was at the right place, then dismounted and tethered my horse to the fence. Passing through the gate, I walked toward the porch.

The man emerged even before I got there. He'd

been watching for me, apparently. Between saloon visits the afternoon before, I'd sent him a wire from Bedford, so he knew I was coming.

"Good day," I said.

"Hello. You are Mr. Wells?"

"Yes, sir. You are Henry Callen?"

"I am. Please come in."

He held up better than many with whom I'd had similar meetings. I talked to him quietly, slowly, giving him time to absorb it all. It was difficult for people to take in the kind of information it was my duty to bring them, so I'd learned to dole it out slowly, and with carefully chosen words.

He dabbed his eyes with a handkerchief he kept clutched in his hands, toying with it while he stared at the floor and listened. Every now and then he would nod, and a time or two even smile as I told him of the great courage and compassion his lost loved one had shown in the prison camp.

"We didn't realize the truth, of course, until after it was over," I said. "It was a fact of life and death in Andersonville that the living took what they could from the dead, for there was little to be had in the way of clothing and goods. When they took the clothes, of course, we realized for the first time that she was a woman. All this time, all through the war and all through the captivity, she'd managed to hide her sex from us. And there were others there like that. Women posing as men, fighting and dying and being taken prisoner with people never knowing the truth."

"I know," he said. "I've heard such tales." He paused and smiled. "Dear old Estelle . . . always rough and rowdy and more like a boy than a girl, even when we were growing up. Tough as a knot, that girl was. She could shimmy up an apple tree three times faster than me, steal twice as many apples in half the time, and eat half a dozen more than I could hold. She outboyed me at everything, and that ain't easy for a little brother to accept when he's growing up. You know it? It ain't. Old Estelle . . . poor, dear old Estelle. My parents worried themselves sick about her, her being so boyish and all. You know how parents worry over their children."

"Of course. But I can tell you this, Henry: if she had some masculinity about her in many ways, there was one way she was pure woman, and that was her tenderness. I saw her share rations with starving men in that camp, even when she was down to skin and bone herself. I saw her talk comfort to suffering men in a way that was like a fresh wind through that foul place. That husky voice of hers—even that didn't betray her secret. Now that I look back, though, I marvel that we didn't figure out that she was a woman. I can't think of any man who could have shown tenderness and kindness the way she did."

"I'm glad to hear it."

"We knew her as Edgar Callen. She talked about you a lot, by the way. Just all the time. She was proud of her little brother. Worried about how you were getting along, if you were making it through the war all right. And when it became evident she wasn't going to come out of that camp alive, she told me to find you after the war and tell you what happened. I vowed to her that I would."

"And now you have. I appreciate it, Mr. Wells."

"Call me Jed. By the way, she's in the book I wrote. Not as herself—I changed the names—but she's there. I tried to do right by her in how I portrayed her. She was a heroine, sir, a true heroine, and she died with all the dignity anybody could die with in such a place. When 'Edgar' passed away, there was a lot of grief. And when we took the clothes and realized the truth, we just marveled over him—over her—all the more."

He dabbed his eyes again and nodded.

"Thank you for coming here and settling my mind on this. For all these years I've prayed to learn the truth about what happened to my sister. I'd always suspected she'd joined the army. She'd even talked, as a girl, of wishing she was a boy so she could be a soldier. Loved those uniforms, the guns, the whole notion of soldiering. I'd tease her about it. 'Estelle, you can't be a soldier—you're a girl!' I'd say such things to her. 'Soldiers have to make their pee standing up, Estelle.' I said that too. You know how little brothers will talk to their sisters."

"I'm glad I've been able to ease your mind."

"You do this for others, I gather."

"Right now it's my task in life. I don't know why it is, Henry, but when I was at Andersonville, I was one of those who people came to, and told things to, and asked favors of. A score or more people in that camp asked me, like Edgar . . . like Estelle did, to find their families and tell their stories when it was all over."

"They must have sensed that you would be one who would survive."

"I think so. You could tell, somehow. You could tell the ones, generally, who would make it through, and those who wouldn't. Though I admit I had thought your sister would be one who survived."

"I heard you escaped that camp."

"Yes. I hid among the dead on the wagon they used to carry off the corpses—the same wagon they also used to haul in the swill that passed for food. I had the help of a guard whose life I'd probably saved by giving him warning that another guard was out to kill him. But I did escape."

"That's in your book too?"

"Yes. Done in the form of fiction, but the story is mostly true, told substantially as it happened."

"I'm going to read that book, Jed."

"Good. Look for your sister in it. You'll be proud of the things she did."

"She'd be proud of you, sir. It's a good thing you're doing, traveling to the families of those who asked you to. It's a saint's service, sure as the world."

"It took me far too long to get to it, Henry. But I didn't have the means, or the time. Not until the book became so popular, and gave me the resources to do this. That's been the best benefit of its success: it provides me the opportunity to finally fulfill my promises to those dying souls back at Andersonville."

"God bless you, sir."

"God bless you too."

⊰ 5 ⊱

I TURNED MY RENTED HORSE INTO A PURCHASED one that afternoon. It was a strong, healthy mount, and I needed a horse, so purchase seemed logical. I'd decided to linger in these parts for a spell, anyway. This was a comfortable place to be, a good place to do a bit of writing. My second novel was too long in coming, as John Battle, my capable but overprodding editor in New York City, was fond of frequently pointing out. The nation was eager for a new tome by Jed Wells, and I owed it to my fellow Americans to produce it. When would I have it completed?

I'd grown adept at putting hîm off. The truth was, I had no idea when it would be completed. I'd worked on it sporadically, jottings on pads of paper, that's about all. Right now I had focused my life on fulfilling those Andersonville promises I'd talked about with Henry Callen. The writing would have to fit in where it could and when it could.

I wired John Battle and told him where I was, and that I was inclined to stay awhile and write. He'd be glad to hear that. Probably leave me alone for a month or so. Not that I really minded his contacts or even his occasional merciless prodding. He was a big part of why my first book had been as good as it was, for I was certainly no writer by training. Raised in Kentucky's mountain country, my formal schooling was minimal. My mother, God rest her, had filled the gap considerably, teaching me on her own, keeping books before me, making me read and read some more. My father would sit shaking his head and expressing his view that it was all a waste of time. Read the Bible and that's good enough, he'd say. The rest is worthless.

But Mother had stuck with it, and I was glad she had. Neither she nor I had any notion back in those days that she was training me for a writer's career. But she and John Battle together accounted for what success I'd attained. The writing that had begun as notes scribbled on what meager scraps of paper I could find in Andersonville had turned into the novel that gave me independence I enjoyed and needed.

I could have taken the train to the town of Starnes, but the crash of the last one I'd ridden had persuaded me that I could do without trains for a spell. And the horseback ride was pleasant. When you've spent the hardest months of your life locked up behind stockade walls, shoulder-to-shoulder with men in the harshest conditions, open space and free movement is highly appreciated.

As I approached Starnes, I noted first the courthouse tower, clad in greening copper and with a bell hanging visibly. The courthouse was small by eastern standards, but big enough to provide an impressive and balancing center to an otherwise nondescript town.

The looks of the town improved, however, the closer I drew. Quite a few brick buildings added a look of permanence amid the predominating wood structures, and the false fronts on the wooden buildings provided an illusion of size once one entered the town itself.

Starnes, Kansas. Just one more typical town on the plains, probably a dull place most of the time. The kind of place where the death of somebody's dog would provide a day's worth of conversation.

I rode around a corner and onto a new street, and suddenly Starnes, Kansas, didn't seem nearly so dull anymore.

The street was lined with saloons, dance halls, gambling dens, liquor stores, and a few places with ambiguous names that implied prostitution. This was a miniature Dodge City!

Well, I had to admire the people of Starnes for one achievement: never had I seen a town so capably encapsulate their vice dens in one area. This street, whose name of Bull Creek Avenue was proclaimed on a sign at its entrance, was a wastrel's paradise. The rest of the town was flowers-in-the-window, granny-on-the-porch storybook material.

Even as I sat in the saddle, looking down Bull Creek Avenue, the street came to life.

Coming around a distant corner and then up the middle of the street, howling and dragging a long chain behind him, was an old Indian man who seemed in great distress. Leaping and barking around his feet were three dogs, worked up into excitement by the Indian's shouts and the hoots and howls of the three drunken rowdies who trailed the Indian.

I saw right away what was wrong with the Indian. The chain dragging behind him was attached to a small trap, probably a beaver trap, and the trap's jaws were clamped hard around his ankle.

"Caught us a redskin!" one of the jubilant rowdies hollered at a man who came out of a saloon, beer in hand, to see what the commotion was about.

The Indian wailed again in pain and tried to kneel to pry the trap off his ankle. The rowdies immediately kicked at him and prodded him with the muzzle of a Winchester rifle one of them carried.

A woman on a boardwalk somewhat behind me said to another, "Why, that's poor old Hawk they're tormenting so!"

"Well, that old Indian is going to suffer a lot of torment if he doesn't change his ways," a second woman said. "All he does is drink and put himself into situations that let these bad fellows have fun at his expense."

"But he's a kindly Indian. He works in my yard for me, just so I'll feed him, and he's always so grateful. I'm going to go down and help him."

"You stay away from them, Gert. That's Jimmy Miller with the rifle. He's loco and mean as Satan. He'd injure a woman as quickly as a man. And that other one with him, can't think of his name, but he's as bad."

"That's Jack Cordell."

"That's right. Jack Cordell."

Where was the local law? I had been told that Amos Broughton, who I was coming to see, was the county sheriff, but perhaps there was a town marshal as well. One or the other surely should come forward to take care of this.

"Head on down the road, Injun Hawk!" yelled the one with the rifle. "Traipse down that trail of tears, old boy!"

This was beginning to get me riled. By now I'd dismounted and was scanning the street again for the law, or in the absence of that, some man of the town with a bit of gravel in him, willing to step forward and help this poor old Indian. How he'd got his foot into a trap I couldn't guess for sure, but I'd be willing to bet he'd been forced to step in it, or maybe tricked into it.

"Somebody help that poor old Indian!" one of the women said loudly.

I turned to her. "Ma'am, where is the law around here?"

"The only law right now is Amos Broughton, and he's not here," she said, with a touch of disgust in her voice. "It seems he's not here much at all anymore."

"Deputies?"

"We had two. One quit and the other is about to. You can never find him when you need him."

"He's probably down at the dress shop, flirting with that young widow woman," the other said. "It's just as well. He has no common sense about him anyway. He'd probably arrest poor old Hawk for public drunkenness, instead of the real trouble-makers."

I noticed a little boy lingering back in the shadows of a nearby doorway. Fetching out a coin, I got his attention. "There's another for you if you can find the deputy and bring him here," I said. "Look at the dress shop first."

He took the money and headed off on a run, into the better, vice-free part of town.

"Who are you, sir?" one of the women asked.

"A fool who's getting ready to stick his nose into

somebody else's business," I replied. "But given that nobody else seems inclined, I guess it's up to me."

I headed for my saddlebags to retrieve my pistol and gun belt.

The weight of my gun belt around my waist was familiar and unfamiliar all at the same time. Seldom did I wear my revolver except when traveling alone through rough country, but there had been a time, after the war, when I wore it nearly continually. An effect of my imprisonment, I believe: behind the Andersonville stockade, men were left powerless, weaponless, at the mercy of harsh captors. When at last I was free, it was a comfort to feel the weight of a revolver on my hip.

During that period, I discovered something new about myself: my natural skill with a revolver was almost equal to my riflery skills. With practice, and if showmanship had any part of my heart, I could have become a trick shooter in some Wild West show.

The one with the rifle—Jimmy Miller, I suspected, because he seemed the more dominant— saw me coming first. He frowned and grinned at the same time, like I was a puzzlement and fool, and got the attention of the other and directed his attention at me.

This gave the poor old Indian an opportunity to

drop to the ground and begin working the trap off his ankle. He was whimpering and terrified, very old . . . a pitiful sight, and it made me all the more eager to deal with this pair of bastards.

Hawk let out a yell. The trap was too strong for his fingers, which I noticed only then were bent and arthritic. It had closed back on his ankle just as he'd almost gotten it off.

I stared Jimmy Miller in the eye. "Bend down and take that trap off his foot," I said.

"The hell!"

"Do it! Now!"

He gaped at me, then at his partner, then back at me. "Damnation, you lanky fool, you trying to get yourself killed?"

I saw his finger creep to the trigger of his Winchester, noted a subtle change in the way his left hand gripped the weapon . . .

So quickly that I doubt they saw more than a blur, I drew my Colt and shot off Miller's trigger finger, and the trigger along with it.

Miller screamed like a woman. He staggered back, the Winchester dropping to the ground. Blood gushed from the stump of what had been his right forefinger.

"God!" he yelled, watching the scarlet fountain stream down his hand.

Jack Cordell swore softly and backed away. He had no weapon and I wasn't as worried about him.

I gave him a glance that could burn a hole through cold iron, and he turned tail and ran, fleet as a foal.

"My finger!" Miller exclaimed. "You shot off my finger!"

"So I did." The truth was, I hadn't planned to do that. It was an instinctive reaction to seeing him about to level that rifle at me.

"Where's my finger?" he cried out. He was on the verge of tears. "Where'd my finger go?"

I nodded toward one of the dogs, which had just made quick work of the severed digit.

"God!" Miller exclaimed again. "A dog ate my finger!"

"Get down there and get that trap off this man's foot."

"Ain't no real man, just a worthless old redskin drunkard!"

I thumbed back the hammer of the Colt and aimed the pistol at his other hand.

"No!" he bellowed, putting his hands behind him quickly, slinging blood as he did so. "No! I'll do it! I'll do it!"

He fell to his knees and scrambled toward the Indian, who was obviously quite taken aback by all this. But behind the pain and fear in his dark eyes, I thought I caught a glimmer of great amusement, maybe outright happiness. He'd certainly not expected anyone to come forth on his behalf, especially as intensely and seriously as I had.

For my part, I was wondering what the devil I was doing here. I'd come to Starnes to meet an old friend, not to play the hero.

Lord, I hoped this didn't get out. If John Battle heard about this, he'd probably crawl down my back. He was always concerned that I maintain the "right" image before the public. Gunslinging in western towns probably wasn't what he had in mind.

So pathetic did Miller look, fumbling around with his bloody hands, trying to pull that trap off the Indian's foot, that I might have felt sorry for him. But it wasn't worth the trouble.

He managed to get the trap off, then looked up at me with a face gone quite pale. "I need to see a doctor," he said. "God, you shot off my finger!"

"You ever cross my path again, I might shoot off the other nine," I said. "Get on with you."

He got up and ran away, stooped over and gripping that hand, glancing back at me with eyes squeezed nearly shut and teeth gritted. He reached the corner, stopped, and turned back toward me. "I'll get you for this, you son of a bitch!" he yelled. "I'll shoot off more'n your damn finger!"

I made as if to run toward him, and he bolted off, around the corner and out of sight. I could imagine him running full speed for the nearest cover, looking back over his shoulder to see if I came running around that corner.

"Drop it, mister!"

I turned and saw a quaking, skinny young man with a badge pinned crookedly on his shirt. He squatted down with a Remington revolver aimed at me, gripping it in two shaking hands. The boy I'd sent to fetch this fellow was off on the boardwalk, watching from behind a porch post, probably hoping the lawman didn't shoot me down before I could pay him the rest of his money.

I gently tossed my Colt to the ground and raised my hands. "Easy there," I said. "You can put down that pistol. I'm not going to cause any trouble, believe me."

"It's against the law to carry sidearms in this town, or to discharge weapons."

"I figure it's also against the law to torment old men like this fellow here." I nodded toward Hawk, who looked up at me with tears in his eyes.

"Thank you," he croaked. "Thank you."

"I don't know what's going on here," the deputy said. He still had that pistol aimed at me, and was shaking so bad I feared he'd discharge it by accident. "And I don't know I can figure it out right here and now. You come with me, mister. We'll lock you up and let you talk to Sheriff Broughton, when he gets back."

A grin crept across my face, but I squelched it because I didn't want this fellow to take anything I did for resistance, defiance, or mockery. "I'll go quietly," I said. "But I need to give the boy there a coin. May I do that?"

"He don't need no coin," the deputy snapped. "Come on. Keep your hands up and move, and don't go trying nothing funny."

"Come by the jail and I'll pay you," I said to the boy. "Put my horse yonder in the livery for me, and I'll pay you more than that. Bring my saddlebags and that rifle to the jail. Turn it all over to the deputy here for safekeeping. You understand?"

He nodded and watched me with eyes wide, maybe unsure whether I was a good man or a villain.

I marched down the street in front of the shaky deputy, my hands up. When the onlookers applauded, I glanced back at him. He looked surprised, then grinned sheepishly, clearly thinking the applause was for him.

I had to grin myself. My sojourn in Starnes, Kansas, was off to a most unexpected kind of start.

I was off to be a prisoner in whatever kind of county jail they had in this place. Whatever it proved to be, I wasn't much concerned. I was sure I'd seen far worse.

6

THE BUNK IN MY CELL WAS HARD, WITH ONLY A blanket on it to soften it up. But the pillow was fairly new, looked like it hadn't been drooled into too much by previous prisoners, and with my head nestled softly in it, I dozed off with great ease.

I'd learned the gift of sleep while in Camp Sumter at Andersonville. When waking hours provide little but misery, a man comes to appreciate the bliss of unconsciousness. The problem at Andersonville was that sleep was often hard to come by. There was eternal noise, hunger that kept one's belly cramping, fights, thieves coming to steal what was yours while you slept, and worst of all, rain. When it came, the rain drenched the wretches of Andersonville to the bone, for many had inadequate shelter, or no shelter at all. Many a man in that sorry place spent his nights in a hollow in the ground, and when it rained, that hollow filled with water.

There was a blessing to the rain, though. It

washed away the stench for a time, and provided much purer drinking water than what could be had from Stockade Creek, which flowed through the camp. That creek served both as water supply and sewage disposal system, and quickly one learned to avoid drinking from it if at all possible. When you could stand it, you lived with the thirst, and when the rain came, you collected all you could and enjoyed it as long as it lasted.

Compared to Andersonville, this little cell in Starnes, Kansas, was like a hotel room.

When I opened my eyes, it was dark. Noise had awakened me. I sat up a little and watched as the same deputy who'd brought me in hustled another prisoner into the cell across the way. The man was drunk and troublesome, and it took some effort for the deputy to get him inside and get the door locked. He'd just gotten the key turned in the lock when the man lunged at him, grappling for him through the bars and managing to get hold of his collar. The deputy aimed his fist between two bars and punched the man in the nose. It took three blows to make him let go. Nose bleeding, the drunk staggered off to his own bunk and collapsed there, cursing and now so preoccupied with his injury that he suddenly didn't even seem angry anymore.

The deputy turned to me, straightening his clothes, and shook his head. "I hate this job," he said. "You got to deal with bilge like that all the time! Not much longer, though. I'm gone from here the end of the week. Not that you care none about that."

I glanced at my watch. Eleven in the evening. "Is the sheriff back?"

"Why, hell, no! He was supposed to handle the night duty this evening for me, but once again he ain't come back when he said he would! So here I am, working all day, and danged if it don't look like I'll have to work all night too!"

"Sorry."

"Hell, why should you care? I'd figure you'd be glad to see a lawman in such a situation."

"When I'd have been glad to see a lawman was today on the street. The only reason I got involved in that was that there was nobody else stepping forward to do it, and nobody could find you right away."

"Well, I came when I knowed about it. That's all a man can do. He can't be two or three places at once, and he sure can't work around the clock, never knowing when he's going to get relief. Hell, I may not make it to the end of the week! I swear, I'd like to kick Broughton square in the backside sometimes, just as hard as I could! Hell with him!"

He left the cell area through the heavy oak door that separated it from the front office. The door slammed, the noise resonating in the enclosed area.

The fellow across the hall was muttering to himself and using his cell blanket to try to stop the bleeding.

"Is it broken?" I asked him.

He cussed at me for about thirty seconds.

"Just trying to be friendly," I said, and rolled over to sleep again.

"Well, I'll be," a voice said through the darkness. "I'll be shot if it really ain't the old sharpshooter himself!"

I opened my eyes and looked up into the face of a stranger. He was standing beside my bunk, looking down at me. He had a coal oil lamp in his hand, filling the cell with yellow light. The cell door stood open.

Across the way, the drunk was snoring very oddly, probably because of his ruined nose.

The man in my cell spoke again. "You've fleshed out a mite since last I saw you. I'd hardly know you."

He smiled, and all at once he was a stranger no more. I rose at once and put out my hand, then decided that wasn't good enough and threw my arms around him. We squeezed the breath out of one another, him trying to avoid burning me with the lamp, then stepped back and eyed one another thoroughly.

We'd both changed. In Andersonville, Amos Broughton had been a wisp of a fellow, skin thin as paper, teeth dark and loose, eyes encircled with darkness. I'd been much the same. It was hard to recognize in one another the men we'd been back when we were fellow inmates of hell.

"Last time I seen you, Jed, you were lying dead on the wagon, corpses all around you. You were the deadest looking one of the bunch."

"It's a ride I'll never forget, Amos. Though I'd like to. I waken sometimes still feeling those maggots crawling on me."

"It got you out, though. You escaped. What was the difference lying with the dead in the wagon or the living dead inside the stockade? We were all proud of you, Jed."

"I couldn't have done it without the help of the guard."

"He owed you. You saved his neck."

That was the truth. By sheer luck I'd stumbled across a plan on the part of one Andersonville guard to kill another—a dispute over a woman, I gathered. Something those of us imprisoned could only fantasize about. Seeing an opportunity to gain favor, I warned the prospective victim and saved his life. As I'd hoped, his gratitude was sufficient to make him agree to a plan for escape that I'd developed. With his help, I was able to hide myself on a wagonload of corpses and be hauled out to the so-called dead house, where the guard covered my tracks as I made my way to the river and a rowboat that had been hidden there for me.

It was the start of a long and surreptitious journey. I survived by stealing first clothing, then food, and hiding in the wilds until I had recovered enough from the deprivations of Andersonville to move about in public without drawing notice. I'd always been gifted in mimicking accents, and took on the persona of George Arbuckle, Georgia farmer. I worked my way northward, eventually reaching my home state of Kentucky by way of East Tennessee, where I was helped by the many unionists who resided there. From even before the outbreak of war, an effective, hidden "Underground Railroad" had been developed that conveyed not only escaping slaves, but also white southern Unionists who sought to go north and join the Union cause. By way of this "railroad," I made it to safety in the North.

Traveling to Washington, I spoke with congressmen and senators, office staff members, newspapermen, anyone who would listen, and described the horrific conditions at Andersonville and the need to trade prisoners with the Confederacy in order to relieve the suffering. At one point I very nearly succeeded in meeting the President himself, but not quite.

My efforts had little effect, but I regretted none of it. I'd done my duty then for my fellow Andersonville prisoners . . . just as I had sought to do it ever since.

Broughton looked at me with a smile on his face and shook his head. "Who would ever have figured I'd see you again like this! Locked up in my own cell! What the devil is this story I hear of you shooting off Jimmy Miller's finger?"

"It's the truth. But it was in my own defense. He was preparing to raise a rifle and aim it at me."

"Did he raise it?"

"He didn't get the chance."

"Then you'll have a deuce of a time proving he was threatening you. Not that it matters. Nothing will come of this. I've already heard the details of what happened."

"So I'm not charged with anything?"

"No. Hell, I ought to give you a reward for shooting Jimmy's finger off. Too bad it wasn't his head."

I noticed something just then . . . a whiff of alcohol on Broughton's breath. I recalled his earlier absence and late appearance to relieve the deputy. Odd, to be in his town and in his company so short a time, and already have evidence that all might not be well in the life of Amos Broughton.

"I got into it with Miller and the other one," I

said, "because they were tormenting an old Indian man . . . and there was no law immediately at hand to deal with it."

"You did the right thing. But you'll need to beware: I hear that Miller shouted a threat at you."

"He did."

"He'll never fulfill it to your face. But he's a backshooting type and tenacious as a hungry rat, so if you've got eyes on the back of your head, use them."

"Who'd you talk to?"

"My deputy filled me in on part of it, and I also talked to a witness when I came back into town. You wouldn't know him, just one of them on the street who saw it all."

"Can I get out of here, Amos?"

"You can. If you want a hotel room, there's a couple of good places here in town. I'd invite you to come stay at my house, but I got me a wife. And I can't be there tonight."

I gathered the few items I'd been allowed to take into the cell and for the second time in my life escaped imprisonment.

My saddlebags, belted pistol, and encased rifle were in the outer office. The boy I'd hired had done what I asked. If he'd done the same with my horse, it was safely in the town livery. I'd investigate first thing in the morning.

"That rifle . . . I looked at it before I came in

here. I'm always curious about rifles and shotguns. That looks to me like a sharpshooter's weapon."

"It is. The same one I carried through the war. A gift from my father, when I signed on under Berdan."

"How the devil did you get it back? They didn't take it when you were captured?"

"When it became clear I was caught, I hid it, in hope that one of our own would recover it. It's a long story, but the rifle was recovered by a friend of mine and held for me. I regained it a year after the war and have kept it ever since."

Broughton looked down at the long black case. "You never talked much about your sharpshooting while we were prisoners."

"I don't talk about it much today."

He looked me over again, head to toe. I suppose I looked as different to him as he did to me. "You've done well for yourself."

"Not so well as you. You've got a wife, a home here in a beautiful part of the country. Maybe a bunch of children, for all I know."

"No children. Well, we had a baby, just one . . . but there was something wrong. We buried her scarcely after we named her. But I've got me a good wife, yes indeed. You'll meet her. Callianne. Her last name used to be Bottoms, so I figure I did her a favor in marrying her. You will be around for a spell, I hope?"

"I thought I'd take some time here. Visit you, do some writing."

"Writing. Yes. Congratulations to you on that book. One of the biggest-selling books in the nation, I heard. It made me proud of you. And proud to know that there's a lot of people who know the way it was for us, because you wrote it down."

"I'm humbled by the success of the book, really. It makes me feel guilty, sometimes. Am I wrong to be gaining personal success based on the suffering of others? There's times I don't know."

"It wasn't just the suffering of others. It was your suffering too. You have the right to write about it, if anybody does. I'm glad you wrote it."

"Thank you. I appreciate those words. What did you think of it yourself?"

"I, uh . . . I ain't read it, Jed."

"Haven't you?"

"No. I . . . I can't, you know. I thought to do it once . . . I just can't." He looked away, blinking fast a couple times. "I just ain't far enough away from it yet to go back into it, you know?"

I did know. We all had our own ways of dealing with what we'd experienced. For some like me, it was done through venting it, thinking it through, and thereby limiting and controlling it. Others— Broughton, for example—dealt with it by burying it, putting it out of sight, and avoiding reminders.

It made me wonder for a moment if Amos Broughton really was glad to see me.

"I can see why you might not want to read it," I told him.

"No offense, I hope."

"Of course not."

7

BROUGHTON RECOMMENDED THE STARNES HOUSE
Hotel, so I checked myself in after waking up the
night clerk napping in the office. The bed was saggy
and had a disturbingly moist feeling to it, but it
didn't really matter right away. I'd slept a lot in the
cell, and planned to spend the remainder of the
night accompanying Broughton on his rounds.

We walked the dark town, talking about life, the
town, Broughton's path into the work of a lawman
after the war. He'd tried a lot of different things—
farming, ranching, running a liquor store—but
nothing had worked out for him at the level he'd
hoped. He ran across the woman he fell in love
with, and married, while he was ranching. While he
was running the liquor store, he ran across something else: a discovery that he loved whiskey a bit
more than most. He admitted it straight out, but assured me it was part of his past. No liquor for two
years now, he assured me.

I could smell the whiskey on his breath while he said it.

"I want you to come to the house tomorrow, have dinner with me and Callianne. She'll be happy to meet you. She read your book, by the way. I wouldn't let her talk to me about it much, but she read it. I saw her wiping away some tears from time to time. After she finished it, she treated me . . . special. I think she knows me better now because of that book."

"I hope that's a good thing."

"It is."

We trudged along in silence. It was about four in the morning. I was rested from languishing in the cell for hours, but Broughton seemed exhausted.

"Do you always have somebody patrolling the town at night?" I said.

"Have to," he replied. "Because of all the saloons and such along Bull Creek Avenue. There can be trouble there."

We were far from Bull Creek Avenue now, on the far side of town. Walking along and checking locks.

He must have read the question in my mind. "Oh, I make my way around to Bull Creek several times through the night. But I've discovered by experience that you don't want to be too visible. It brings out the worst in some of the rowdy drunks to have a lawman around. Makes them try things they wouldn't otherwise. And another thing too: them that are on Bull Creek Avenue are most of the time out-of-town people, here to drink and gamble and carouse. The good folks of this town live in the other parts. They're the ones who run these shops we're walking past, pay the taxes, do the school teaching and the churchgoing and all the other things that decent folks do. I figure it's their welfare I'm most obliged to watch out for. I know for a fact that there are some who go over to Bull Creek Avenue, stir up trouble so that the law has to come, then during that time break out a shop window, empty a safe, clean out a cash box. So I try not to help that game along. No patterns. Patrol at random."

"Your deputy told me he's leaving."

"He is. I had another one here until recently. He left to go work in his brother's mercantile in Great Bend. I don't know what I'll do, to tell you the truth. I've been trying to find at least one replacement, but nobody seems interested."

I don't think he said it to try to draw me in. I don't believe there was any conniving or design to it. But immediately the seed of a notion sprouted uninvited in my mind. I put my heel to it at once and ground away at it, but it remained.

"So you have the night work, and the deputy has the day?"

"For now."

"Your deputy was worried you weren't going to make it in to replace him this evening."

Broughton shot a flaming glance my way. "Had something to say, did he?"

I knew right then I'd stepped onto the wrong ground. "He was afraid he'd have to work all day and all night, that's all. Same thing anybody would worry about if somebody was running late, I guess."

"I had something that had to be done. Hell, he's the one deserting me, leaving me with a whole town to tend all on my own. A whole county, really, though when you got only one town of any size in a county, most all the sheriffing ends up being done there. I got all that bearing down on me, and he's worried because I run a couple of hours late? Pshaw!"

We walked along for a while without words. Broughton seemed more weary by the moment. I wondered how long he'd been up. If he was doing "something that had to be done" earlier, that meant he wasn't resting up in preparation for the night.

Obviously he'd not be able to sheriff this county alone, once his sole remaining deputy was gone.

"You did a good job on old Miller, as I hear it. Very fearless," Broughton said. "Maybe that missing finger will remind him that there's sometimes payback for what you do. Miller's always thought he could do anything. Hey, is it true a dog ate that finger?"

"It's true."

Broughton threw back his head and laughed heartily into the dark sky. "If that ain't just the thing!" he declared. "Dog ate his finger!"

"Could have been worse. I could have shot off his whole hand if I'd wanted to."

"You're quite the man with the guns, Jed. If we'd had you the right weaponry and a good place to hide, you could have picked off every guard at Andersonville, right up in their perches."

It was the kind of thought that engaged our fantasies time and again while we were prisoners. But that was all it was, all it could be at that time.

"Yep," he said, "you did a good job on Miller. You'll need to beware of him, though, should you see him again. But I already told you about that."

"Yes."

We walked awhile longer.

"Amos," I said, giving in to what I already knew was inevitable. "Tell you what. If you don't have any luck replacing your deputies in the next few days . . . maybe I could step in, do the job awhile. If you wanted me."

He stopped and looked at me, though we were in so dark a spot just then that we couldn't really see each other's faces. I wondered what his expression was.

"You mean that?" he said, and he actually sounded moved.

Did I? I asked myself the question, hurriedly and seriously. Yes, I did. "I mean it."

"Jed, that's the finest thing anybody has offered to do for me in God knows how long."

"It would have to be temporary. I'm not looking for a lifelong career."

"It would just be until I can find somebody else. And who knows? Maybe I'll find replacement deputies tomorrow and you won't have to do it at all."

"You won't find them tomorrow. You'll be in bed asleep. At least, you better be. You're worn completely out as it is. I can tell it."

"I am worn-out."

"You didn't rest today, and now you're working all night."

"I know."

"Tell you what, Amos. Even though you've still got your one deputy for a few more days, let me go ahead and start tomorrow. Your deputy can train me . . . if he doesn't mind training a man he put in jail the day before."

Broughton laughed again, a tired but happy laugh. He pounded my shoulder. "You're a godsend, Jed. Surely you are! Imagine you coming along just at the time you have, walking up like a ghost from the past. But no ghost. We were ghosts back then, not now."

"That's right. I suppose we were."

"I'll take you up on your offer. There'll be pay for you, of course. With you being so successful and all it won't seem like much to you."

"Whatever it is will be enough. I'm doing this for an old friend."

He pounded my shoulder again. "I'll wait until Leroy—that's my deputy, Leroy Fletch—gets in after breakfast time, and tell him what's happening."

"I don't think Leroy likes me much."

"That's because he only knows you as a fellow who did what he should have been doing in the first place. And you did it better than he could have. Hell, if he'd tried to shoot off Jimmy Miller's finger, he'd probably have shot old Hawk instead. Or some old woman on the other side of town."

"You don't have much confidence in him, it seems."

"He's deserting me. Why should I feel good about him?"

Morning broke and the town stirred to life. Broughton and I made our way back to the office and there met with Leroy, who learned that his former prisoner was now to be his fellow lawman.

That got Leroy and I off to a rather unpromising

start together. Chilling things even more was the fact that Broughton had him adjust his plans and schedule to be on duty come suppertime, when normally he would be relieved by Broughton, so that I could be at supper at the Broughton house, as I'd been invited to do. While this was being worked out, I jumped in to note that I'd be glad to shift the visit to some other time, if that would help out Leroy, but Broughton waved me off. Leroy agreed to the change without much complaining, but I anticipated right then that he'd not finish out his notice, an anticipation that would soon prove itself correct.

Broughton talked to me awhile before Leroy took me under his wing. The sheriff described the basic duties I'd be doing, thanking me again and again for volunteering to help him out, and cast poorly veiled criticisms toward Leroy, comments about reliability, dedication, and so on. It would not have surprised me to see Leroy slam his badge onto the desk and stalk out right then, but all he did was turn red in the face and glare at his soon-to-be-former boss.

Broughton, now thoroughly worn-out and ready to go home to sleep away much of the day, soon dismissed us, sending me out to walk the streets with Leroy, who was clearly glad to leave. I wore my gun belt now, being officially a lawman, even though nothing ceremonial or legal had been

done—no oaths, signed papers, anything of that
sort. Well, I had been handed a badge . . . even if it
looked homemade, like somebody had hammered
it out of metal from a food tin.

Sensing Leroy's understandable grouchiness, I
said little to him to start with. Clearly he wasn't enjoying my company, but after twenty minutes or so
of walking around mostly in silence, he opened up.

"You're a good man to volunteer to help out
somebody like the Good High Sheriff," he said,
putting a sarcastic emphasis on the last three
words. "Old Broughton's lucky that anybody ever
treats him decent, the way he is these days."

"I kind of got the feeling you and him don't get
on the best."

"We don't, not anymore. Too bad. We used to
get on fine. How is it you know him, anyway?"

"We were together during the war."

"Oh, I see. Did you know Broughton was a prisoner at Andersonville?"

"Yes. I was too."

"That right?" He looked at me and suddenly
seemed a little more impressed with me. Obviously,
though, he did not know me as an author. No surprise. He didn't seem the reading type.

"What kind of work are you going into once you
leave this job?" I asked.

"Ranching. I'm going to work with a man I
know who says I can work my way up to being a

full partner with him, and he's got a good business going in cattle."

"I wish you success."

"Broughton don't talk much about Andersonville. I always wished he would. I'm kind of interested in that. Was it as bad as they say?"

"Every bit of it."

"Do you talk about it much?"

"No. I've written about it some."

"Like in newspapers?"

"I wrote a book."

"No! You got a book?"

I nodded.

"I'll be! Then what the devil are you doing taking on a deputy job?"

"Helping out an old friend. It's just temporary until he can hire himself another couple of men."

"Ha! You may have stepped into a tighter trap than old Hawk did! As long as you're willing to help him out, Broughton will just let it all sail. Let it sail like a boat."

"What do you mean?"

"Well, just that he's not made much effort at all to replace me, or Horace, which was the deputy who already left. Here I am in my last week, and he didn't have no prospects at all until you come along . . . but still, he ain't hardly tried to find anybody."

"That's a bit curious. He was worrying earlier

about how he was going to get by with just himself
to do the job."

"Don't make sense, does it! But that's Broughton
for you. Nothing he does makes sense anymore.
Not for the last month or two."

"He wasn't that way earlier?"

"No, no. Oh, he had his ways of getting under
your skin sometimes, but no more than the average
fellow. But the last stretch of weeks—whew! I can't
wait to get away from him!"

I recalled the alcohol I'd smelled on Broughton's
breath, and his obvious lie about not having
touched whiskey for two years.

"Trouble at home?" I asked.

"I don't know. I don't think so. I tell you what I
think it is: religion."

"Religion?"

"That's right. I believe that Broughton's gone
and got himself mixed up with religion in some way
that has just plum messed him up. Them old camp
meetings . . . good things, I suppose, in most ways,
but this Killian fellow . . . I just don't know about
him. I don't know what to make of any man who
runs around with a cloth over part of his face."

This was intriguing, given my earlier random encounter with the Reverend Killian. "Has Broughton
been going to Killian's meetings?"

"That's what I've heard. He's been seen there
several times. And that's plumb over in the next

county! What do you think of that? A sheriff, paid by this county to watch over it, and he's spending time in the next county, listening to some camp meeting preacher! That's why he's running late so much in his work, leaving me to fill in for him, with no way to reach him, nothing. Two nights . . . no, three—three nights he didn't come in at all! You know what tired is, Jed? Can I call you Jed? Tired is when you work all the dang day long and then have to work the night too. A man can't live without sleep!"

Perhaps I was crossing a line I shouldn't, but after a pause, I said, "I think maybe it isn't camp meetings that Amos is going to, Leroy. I smelled whiskey on his breath. . . . Funny thing was, it was while he was telling me about how he's not had a drink for two years."

Leroy stopped in his tracks and stared at me. "No fooling?"

"No fooling. You haven't smelled it on him yourself?"

"My smeller ain't the keenest. Never has been. And besides, I don't get that close to him if I can help it. Since me and him fell out, I just don't like being near him. Drinking! I'll be! I'll be!" He shook his head. "He told me once that he used to be an outright drunkard. If he's gone back to that—"

"I don't know if he's a drunkard, but my nose didn't fool me. He definitely has been into whiskey." As I said this, I wondered how bad a mistake I'd made, impulsively jumping into this job without knowing the entire situation. From this little jaunt with Leroy alone, I had learned enough to realize my old friend had some big and hidden problems. It sounded like the man was falling apart.

"Jed, I've got to say this: get out quick. Tell the Good High Sheriff that your situation has changed and you got to go. You don't want to be working for a man who is caught in the bottom of a bottle."

He was right about that. But this was Amos Broughton we were talking about. A man I'd sojourned with in hell itself. There was a bond there that was bigger than whatever problems he had at the moment. And I was enough of a mystic to believe that maybe I'd been sent here to help him. Things generally happen for a reason, I'd come to believe.

"I'll stick it out for now," I said. "I made Amos a promise. But I'm glad to know the things you've told me. Maybe he needs an old friend around right now."

"All I can say is: you can have him. Lock, stock, and barrel. He's yours. Because I've had my fill of Amos Broughton. Whatever his . . . aw, hell! Look at that!"

He pointed at a flyer tacked to a telegraph post just beside me. In big, blocky letters it advertised the beginning of camp meeting services just days away, right here in this county.

"The Reverend Killian is on the move," I commented. "I guess he's done all he thinks he can over in Russell County."

"Well, at least the Good High Sheriff won't have to travel so far to see his favorite preacher. Maybe he won't leave you in the lurch as much as he has me."

"Is Amos a very religious man?"

"Never has been, in my experience. He goes to church when his wife makes him. Tries not to cuss a lot. That's been the extent of it as far as I know."

"I really doubt he's been attending those camp meetings, then. I'd say he's been out drinking somewhere."

"He was seen at the camp meeting."

"Probably just somebody thought they saw him."

Leroy shrugged. "Don't matter to me, either way. I'm gone from here the end of this week. If not sooner."

⇥ 8 ⇤

BEFORE LONG I BEGAN TO SUSPECT THAT THE LIFE of a lawman in a small town just might be, for the most part, boring. I suppose the exciting times made up for it, but as I walked about town with Leroy Fletch, the prospect of being a deputy for even a short term was just short of dismaying.

I vowed to myself that I would encourage Broughton in any way I could to waste no time in finding permanent replacements.

Though my initial encounter with Leroy had involved me staring down the wrong end of his pistol, I found now that he was not bad company. He was a bit sour, prone to whine, but it was actually somewhat entertaining. After this first day, I supposed, I'd be making my rounds alone, so I decided to make the best of Leroy's company. At midday I offered to buy him a meal at a small café on the corner of Smith Street and Cade Avenue. He gladly accepted.

The roast was a little tough, but flavorful. The

carrots were cooked down to mush, and the potatoes were oversalted. I didn't care, and neither did Leroy.

We left the café with Leroy telling a story about an encounter with Creek Indians his grandfather once had in Arkansas. In mid-sentence he cut off and muttered, "Oh, boy."

I'd already spotted what he had. Jimmy Miller was coming across the street with a white bandage on his hand and a black expression on his face.

"May be trouble," Leroy muttered.

Miller had seemed very cowardly the last time I'd seen him, but he'd apparently gotten mad enough to get over it, or else he was drinking early in the day. With a hurting finger stump, the latter was a good possibility.

He walked up toward me, but stopped about twenty feet away. His glare was that of a dangerously angry man, but his tense stance was that of a man who would probably break and run if I so much as lunged at him.

He began to lift his right hand as if to point at me, then remembered his missing finger and lifted his left hand instead. "You!" he said. "Because of you I've got no finger! Because of you!"

"Actually, it was because you were fool enough to start to raise your rifle at me."

"I didn't do no such thing!"

"All I did was shoot at the trigger of your rifle. If

your finger hadn't been there, you wouldn't have lost it."

"I owe you for what you done!"

"You so much as lift another finger at me, I'll shoot it off too."

"Back off, Miller," Leroy said.

Miller glanced at my gun belt. "Arrest him, deputy. I demand as a citizen that you arrest him!"

"Why?"

"He's carrying a pistol in town, right out in the open!"

"Look at his vest, Miller."

Only then did Miller spot my badge. His dark expression grew even darker.

"The hell! He's a deputy?"

"As official as me. He's got a right to bear a pistol in town."

Miller let out a string of very vile oaths.

Leroy asked, "How about you, Miller? If I searched you right now, would I find a pistol hiding out somewhere on you?"

Miller glared at Leroy, then back at me. He pointed with his damaged hand. "I'll get you, deputy or no deputy," he said. "You'll hear from me! Not when you're looking for it . . . but you'll hear from me. A bullet can come out of nowhere, you know. Just come out of nowhere and sail clean through a man's skull."

I could have laughed at the irony of being the recipient of that particular threat. I knew far better than most about death that came hurtling from nowhere. I'd inflicted so much of it that my dreams would never again be unhaunted.

"It's not wise to threaten an officer of the law," Leroy said. "Particularly in front of witnesses. I heard the threat, Miller. If ever anything should happen to Deputy Wells, we'll know where to come looking."

"You won't be looking. They tell me you're quitting."

"I am."

"Good riddance."

"For once I agree with you, Miller. But there'll be others in my place, and they may not be so kind as me."

Miller looked me in the eye. "You're going to die."

I stepped out toward him so fast he couldn't react, and shot my hand out to grab his throat. Constricting hard, I pulled his face close to mine. Almost nose-to-nose with him, I glared into his eyes and said, so softly that only he could hear it, "One more threat, so much as even one more hard glance from you, and I'll come after you. You understand me? I'll be on you like sweat on a field hand. You don't want to mess with me, Miller. I'm not some old, helpless Indian, and I don't run from anyone."

His teeth were gritted and he made strange sounds in his nearly closed throat. The flesh under his left eye twitched, then his eyes shifted from side to side, looking about to see how many people were in view of his humiliation.

"Am I going to hear from you again?" I asked in the same nearly inaudible voice.

His eye twitched harder and his lip curled in hate. I let up on his throat just enough to let him speak. A long pause, then very quietly he squeaked, "No."

"Good," I said, squeezing back down on his throat again. "Because I don't want trouble with you or anyone else. And you don't want trouble either, because you can't handle it. Every time you look for it, you end up just embarrassing yourself. Have you noticed that?"

He didn't say anything—couldn't—but his eyes were bulging and turning red. I swear the man was about to cry.

What I was doing was dangerous. If Miller had a gun hidden on him, he could dig it out and put a bullet in me point-blank. But I knew he wouldn't. I'd run across his type before. Strutting and cruel when there was someone helpless around to be victimized, like that old Indian man, but cowardly when faced down by anyone with gravel in his craw.

I let go of him and shoved him away in the same

motion. He staggered backward and gasped loudly, wheezingly. He wanted badly to rub his throat—you could just tell it—but his pride wouldn't let him.

"Get out of my sight, Miller," I said.

"In fact," Leroy added, "get out of town. And don't come back, you hear?"

"I—" He stopped, his voice squeaking. He tried to clear his throat but just squeaked again. "I . . . live in . . . this . . ." He sounded ridiculous—a woman on the boardwalk behind me muffled a laugh—and so he didn't try to finish his sentence.

Miller wheeled and stalked away, a man whose ruined pride trailed behind him like a tattered and soiled train.

"I probably shouldn't have done that," I said.

"Maybe not," replied Leroy. "Now, if he does try anything, I can guarantee it will be back-shooting. Not that it would have been anything else, anyway. He's too yellow to face anybody man-to-man."

On the boardwalk behind us someone applauded, a slow, steady clap. Leroy and I turned to see a very short, dapperly dressed fellow with a peach-fuzz mustache and oversized cigar. He was clapping in what struck me as a sarcastic manner. He had a baby face and stocky build and all in all looked like he ought to be at home with mama. His clothes were expensive but shabby, indicating he wore them a lot and maybe didn't have a lot of variety in his wardrobe.

"Well, well, gentlemen, that was quite a show!" he said, slowly ceasing his clapping. "I can't say the scoundrel didn't deserve it—Miller is a waste of good flesh and bone."

"What do you want, Smith?" Leroy asked.

"Why, just checking out a rumor I'd heard, that's all, Deputy Leroy. Can't take rumors at face value when you're in the newspaper business. Not all of them are true."

"I know. For instance, I once heard a rumor that you were born as an actual human being," Leroy replied.

Smith laughed, drew on the cigar, and blew out a perfect smoke ring. He admired it a moment, then advanced toward me with his hand out.

I looked down at him and noted with displeasure that he was pulling a notepad from his pocket.

"Mark Taylor Smith," he said as I reluctantly shook his broad but short-fingered hand. "*Bleeker County Herald*. You are, I presume, Mr. Wells?"

"Yep."

He studied the badge on my vest. "So it's true—one of America's most popular authors is working as a local deputy!"

"Just helping out an old friend."

"And researching a new novel in the process, perhaps?"

"Am I being interviewed here? Because usually I expect to be politely asked if I'm willing to be interviewed before the questions start."

"Not a full interview, Mr. Wells. Just a few questions."

"I can't see that this is of much potential interest to your readers. I'm serving temporarily as a deputy for my old friend Amos Broughton. It has nothing to do with a book."

"I see." Clearly he didn't believe a word of it. "So how long will you continue?"

"I don't know. A few days if need be. Long enough for Amos to replenish his staff."

Smith eyed Leroy through his cigar smoke. "That's right . . . Amos Broughton has trouble keeping help these days . . . good or otherwise."

"Why don't you just go back to your little newspaper office and climb up in your big, tall chair and do some of that brilliant journalism that's carried you so far in your career, little man?" Leroy asked. He thumped me on the shoulder with the back of his hand, then gestured toward Smith. "This little man's papa owns the newspaper, and he still can't get himself no better job than writing up the weddings and death notices, and every now and then trying to write something to get Sheriff Broughton out of office."

"We've always been fair with Sheriff Broughton." Leroy ignored him. "Little man's uncle wants to be sheriff, you see. So the local newspaper does everything it can to make Amos look as bad as possible. Downright shameful."

Smith sighed loudly and rolled the cigar from one side of his mouth to the other. "Believe what you want, Leroy. And keep in mind that I'm fully aware of how you really feel about the good sheriff. The only time you have a decent word to say for him is when I come around."

"Listen to me, stubby: me and Amos Broughton may have our differences, but I got no use for nobody using their newspaper to assassinate a man just so dear old uncle can get his job."

"Why are you quitting, Leroy?"

"Pursuing new opportunities. Who knows? Maybe I'll open a newspaper. A real one. One that tries to be fair and accurate and such as that."

Smith chuckled scornfully and looked at me again. I'd never encountered a less likable individual. Except maybe Henry Wirz, who played the role of Satan in the hell of Andersonville. When the war was through, they put him on trial for the way he'd run the prison, and sent him to the noose as a war criminal.

Smith jotted something in his notepad, put it back in his pocket, and put out his stumpy little hand again. I didn't want to shake it, but did.

"Welcome to Starnes, Mr. Wells," he said. "Come

around the office if you want, and we'll talk about writing."

"Smith can teach you how to write up an advertisement to find a runaway dog," Leroy said.

Smith rolled his eyes. Giving me a smug nod of farewell, he turned and walked away, trailing cigar smoke behind him.

"Leroy, I didn't have you pegged as such a biting wit," I said.

"Smith brings it out in me," he replied. "God, I despise that little fellow!"

"I could tell. But I have to admit I was surprised to see you becoming defensive of Amos Broughton all at once."

"I'd defend the devil himself if Smith started talking bad about him. I just can't help it."

"Will he print something in his newspaper based on this little conversation we had?"

"Probably. And he'll find some way to twist it around to make Broughton look bad." Leroy paused. "It's a shame. Broughton is plenty able to look bad without the newspaper's help."

9

AMOS BROUGHTON HAD MARRIED WELL. IT RE-
quired only an hour or so of visiting and conversation with the Broughtons at their home that
evening for me to see Callianne Broughton for the
treasure she was. She was a pretty, well-spoken
woman on whom the years had left few tracks. Her
disposition was cheerful, her smile ready and appealing . . . but nothing she did could mask the
concern she obviously felt for her husband.

What a supper Callianne had prepared! Beef
roasted in beer, fried chicken on the side, and trimmings of all varieties. Belle Wagoner was displaced
in my private culinary hall of fame.

Broughton had just shared some interesting
news: he had drummed up a strong prospect for a
new deputy. A man named Joe Reid, who'd worked
four years as a deputy marshal in Wichita and two
years before that as a policeman in Chicago. He'd
moved to Kansas to allow his wife to be nearer her
ailing father, apparently had savings or some other

secondary means that would allow him to live on the meager pay of a deputy, and seemed interested in the job mostly because he loved the work. Broughton was in a fine humor about this, and I could understand why. He'd interview Reid in the morning, but he believed it would be mostly a formality. Reid would be offered the job, and he'd already indicated he would take it.

"But I'd like to ask you to consider lingering on for a time, Jed," Broughton said. "I'm still short-handed with just one man."

"I'll stay on," I told him.

"You're a good man, Jed," he said. Abruptly, he pushed back his chair and stood. "If you'll excuse me . . . a little too much coffee." He chuckled. "Can I trust you alone with my wife long enough for me to make a run to the privy?"

"Amos!" Callianne, a bashful woman, reddened.

"Why, I'm just joshing around with Jed," he said. "I can joke with Jed. Well, I'll be right back. Watch yourself while I'm gone, sharpshooter!" He chuckled again and headed down the hall and out of the house.

As Broughton departed, Callianne quickly busied herself carrying dishes into the kitchen.

"Let me give you a hand," I said, standing.

"Oh, you needn't."

"I'm a single man, Mrs. Broughton. I'm used to cleaning up after myself."

We carried plates and silverware into the kitchen and placed them on a big table beside the wash-basin.

"Amos has been so pleased that you came to see him," she said. "And when you agreed to help him out, why, that was all the better."

"Glad to help."

"Amos has a hard job. An entire county to watch out for, with only enough money for himself and two deputies. It really isn't fair."

"No. Typical of rural places, though."

"I suppose. There's so much pressure on Amos, though. He's . . ." She paused. "He's been different lately. Maybe not doing . . . not doing the job as well as he should."

I glanced out and down the hall. No Amos. Callianne's face did not mask her worry now, but it also revealed tension, worry over whether she was saying something to me she shouldn't.

"You're worried about something, I believe, ma'am."

"I'm worried about Amos. He's been different lately. Not at all himself. Have you been able to notice?"

"You have to remember that I haven't seen Amos since we were in Andersonville. I never knew him in a normal life situation. I have nothing to compare his behavior to. But I can tell you that Leroy seems to perceive things much the same as you."

"I'm so concerned . . . and I think he's been drink—"

She cut off abruptly as the door opened and Broughton entered. He was smoking a very strong-smelling cigar, but it did not fully mask the smell of alcohol that came in with him. There was a damp place down his shirt, as if he'd spilled some.

I glanced at Callianne and saw a woman not far from tears. A terrible feeling came over me, worry about my old friend. I wanted the chance to talk to her again, without him around, to mention to her what Leroy had said about Broughton attending the Reverend Killian's camp meetings and his perception that it had something to do with Broughton's decline.

Odd, though. One didn't expect a man who was sneaking off to religious meetings to take to drinking because of it. You'd think that it would influence him the other way.

Amos was talkative, loosened up by the whiskey, I suppose. He talked endlessly, but nothing he said was revelatory or even of consequence. I found a way to mention Killian and his camp meetings, just to see what the reaction was, and there wasn't one . . . not much of one, anyway. Perhaps a brief pause, a flicker in the eyes . . . perhaps not.

But when I looked up at Callianne, she was staring at me in an odd way.

We talked the evening away, Amos seeming little
more than a shallow babbler. It distressed me. Even
though Amos Broughton and I had spent only a relatively small portion of our lives together, I had
considered him a lifelong friend ever since Andersonville. And this evening, being around him for
an extended time, I was able to remember him
better as he'd been when we were imprisoned . . .
remember him on those few good days when,
against all odds, a conversation or a song or a good
joke managed to take us mentally out of that grim
place and make us normal men again. I remembered Broughton as he was on those days . . . and
then even I was able to see that he wasn't now that
same man.

I would find a way to talk to Callianne Broughton
again and finish our interrupted conversation.

My expectation had been to go back to the hotel
and spend the night in that sagging, damp-feeling
mattress, but Broughton would not hear of it. "We
have more rooms here than we need," he said.
"With a house this size, we should have had a big
family, I guess. The point is that there's no call for
you to leave. Spend the night with us and let Callianne fix you a good breakfast come morning."

There was no reason to turn down such a tempt-
ing invitation, and I didn't. I retired already anticipating that breakfast.

The bed was soft and relaxing. Sleep came quickly but was soon interrupted. I woke up, staring at the ceiling and hearing muffled voices. Amos and Callianne were arguing in their bedroom down below mine. I could make out little of what they said, just isolated words: "worried . . . afraid . . . changed . . . whiskey . . ."

Amos Broughton's voice rose, loud and raging. I heard him shout at her, and curse. It was violent enough that I sat up in my bed, wondering if he might strike her.

I heard only the slamming of their bedroom door, though. And Amos's footfalls stomping heavily down the hallway below.

The front door opened and closed.

My room was dark, so I went to the window and peered out around the edge of my curtain.

Amos Broughton was out there in the moonlight, barefoot, clad in trousers and a shirt hanging open. Pacing about, he rubbed the back of his neck, stared at the moon, muttered to himself. He glanced around, then pulled a small flask from the pocket of his trousers and took a drink from it. He corked the flask, then uncorked it at once and drank one more time.

I went back to bed and lay down, worrying about Amos and wondering what would become of it all.

Andersonville had taught me to pray, and I

prayed now. I asked God to look down on Amos and help him in whatever way he needed help, and to help me as well to know what role I could play in the process.

I'd come to Kansas to tell a man about the death of his sister in a war a decade back. But maybe there was a bigger reason I hadn't known.

If Amos Broughton could be helped, I promised myself that I would help him.

Morning brought clear skies and a cool breeze. I held my hat in hand and let the air rush pleasantly against my face while I studied a broadside hanging on the side of the hotel.

The town was covered by them. The Reverend Killian apparently didn't mind spending money with printers. As best I could figure it, most of these signs had been put up during the night.

"You going, mister?"

I turned to see a sandy-haired boy of ten or so looking up at me, big blue eyes in a freckled face, the classic American boy.

"You going to the preaching, mister?" he asked again, pointing at the sign.

"I don't know. Maybe."

"I'm going. I want to see him. My ma says that he's a real special preacher. She says there ain't so good a preacher nor so good a man to be found nowhere else in Kansas."

"He must be quite a fellow."

"Oh, yes, sir. And you can tell it because God has put a mark on him. On his forehead." The boy touched his own brow. "It's a picture of Jesus up there. But he keeps a cloth over it because he ain't afflicted with the sin of pride."

The phrasing had all the sound of something the boy had picked up from an adult, probably his mother. "Actually," I said, "it's three crosses, side by side."

"How do you know?"

"I saw it. I was hurt a few days back in an accident, not bad hurt, but the Reverend Killian said a prayer over me. The cloth fell back for a moment."

The boy's eyes were wide. "I wish I'd seen it!"

"There's not a lot to see. It appeared to me to be scars."

"He prayed over you? You getting well was probably a miracle, sir."

"Well, I don't know. I wasn't hurt much at all to begin with."

"People get healed by him all the time. That's one of the reasons people go to his meetings."

"Do you personally know any who were healed?"

"Well, no . . . nobody except you."

I grinned at my new friend. "My name's Jed," I said, putting out my hand.

"You're a sheriff," the boy said, shaking my

hand and eyeing my badge. "I want to be a sheriff someday."

"Actually, I'm just a deputy, and temporary at that. But I'm sure you'd be a good sheriff."

"Or I might be a preacher like the Reverend Killian."

"Preaching is a noble ambition."

"Or I might be a soldier."

I paused. "Be a sheriff, son. Or be a preacher. If you can help it, don't be a soldier. What's your name?"

"Hiram Mead. My grandpap calls me Hi-ro, though. That's what I like best."

"Good to know you, Hi-ro."

"See you at the preaching, maybe."

"Maybe."

10

BROUGHTON WAS AT THE OFFICE AND IN A VERY good mood. He'd just sent off his interviewee, and all had gone as hoped. The new man would start tomorrow, when Leroy came back for one of his final days and could "train" him in how to enforce law in Bleeker County—which from my own "training" appeared to consist of walking around Starnes, talking bad about Sheriff Broughton.

"Now, if I can just find myself one more man," Broughton told me, "I'll have a full force back again and you'll be a free man, Jed. Of course, you're free to go anytime you want. You don't owe it to me to stay on."

"After that supper last night and that breakfast this morning," I said, "I feel like I owe you a lot. You've got a fine home and a fine wife, Amos."

"Thank you. She's better than I deserve, Jed. A sorry old fool like myself . . . Lord have mercy. I've been mighty blessed to have such a woman, and sometimes I don't always treat her as kindly as I should."

I wondered if he was talking this way because he suspected I'd overheard their argument last night. "If someday I can do half as well as you have, I'd be satisfied," I said.

The subject shifted. "Jed, I've been thinking about Miller and his threat to back-shoot you. I think we've got to take that seriously. He's the kind who might really do it. I'm wondering if I ought to make a call on him and see what the lay of the land is."

"Leroy ordered him to leave town."

"Yeah, but I doubt he'll do it just on a deputy's order. Maybe not even mine. But he's a cowardly soul and I might be able to put the fear of God into him, you know. Make him too scared to actually try anything. I'll take George Washington with me and have a talk with him today."

"George Washington?"

"Yeah . . . the district attorney. A good man, named after the original George. He and I can tell Miller that he's already in big trouble for threatening an officer of the law. We can make him think he's already facing spending half the rest of his life locked up, and that if anything happens to you or any other officer, he'll get blamed for it and be locked up for life, hung, whatever. We'll have that yellow-belly so scared he'll be afraid to go outdoors to piss. You'll not need to worry about him then."

"Want me to go too?"

"No. Best you stay away. You keep an eye out on the town while I'm gone. Then I want you to take this afternoon off so you can work tonight. Would you do that?"

"Surely."

"I was planning to work tonight myself, but there's someplace I need to go."

"I'll be glad to do it."

"Fine." Broughton shook his head. "I'm amazed at the fools in this world, Jed. I'm thinking of Miller in particular, openly threatening you in front of witnesses. Only the greatest of fools announces he intends to commit a crime! If I was going to do a crime, something that would get me in trouble, the way I'd go about it would be just the opposite. I'd say nothing about it, not give a hint to anybody of what I was thinking. I'd make myself the last person anybody would suspect would do the act, and then, when it was done, the odds would be high that nobody would ever catch me. That's the way I'd do it . . . if I was planning to do something."

As I talked to Broughton, I'd noticed from the corner of my eye something that had escaped me before. There was a door on the side of the office behind him. I realized the door couldn't be the back door out of the jail.

"Amos, what's that room there?" I asked, pointing.

"That? Just a room for a jailer to stay in. There's a bunk and a desk and chair. But we haven't had a jailer as such for a good while. The truth is, half the time the cells are empty and there's nobody for a jailer to watch over. So when we have somebody locked up, we just try to let the deputy on duty handle the jailer tasks as well."

That struck me as a precarious approach. A deputy couldn't supervise a town—and in theory an entire county—and also keep watch over an occupied jail.

"Can I see the room?"

"Sure."

He opened the door and I looked the square little room over.

"I'll take it, Mr. Landlord," I said.

"What?"

"I don't like that hotel room I've rented. You let me stay here, and I can keep an eye on the jail for you even when I'm not on duty. I'll take the room in lieu of pay."

"I got to pay you!"

"I don't need the money, Amos. I'm doing this as a favor for you. I do owe you, you know. You remember those Raiders you worked over for me?"

He grinned. "I remember. But that was pleasure as much as anything, Jed. They deserved what we gave them."

What we were talking about went back to Andersonville. Inside the prison, a band of self-serving "Raiders," as they were usually called, victimized other prisoners, particularly new ones, taking from them any possessions they were fortunate enough to bring into camp, even stealing their rations at times. The Raiders set up alliances with corrupt guards and enjoyed a higher standard of living than the rest of the prisoners. They occupied the best part of the grounds, had better shelter, even weapons such as knives. The rest of the prisoners hated them, and justly.

I fell victim to the Raiders early in my imprisonment, and Amos Broughton was among the group that decided enough was enough and made a raid of their own. They retrieved what I and several others had lost, and left the Raiders a little more respectful, temporarily, of their fellow prisoners. Eventually the Raider problem was dealt with through trials held within the prison camp itself, with the cooperation of Wirz and the guards. Several Raider leaders were hanged as a result.

"Maybe they deserved it, and maybe you enjoyed it, but it was me who benefited from it," I told Broughton. "Let me stay here. I can serve as jailer, do a shift as deputy, and I can even do some writing on that table there. If things go well for me with the writing, I might even linger longer than originally planned."

My offer wasn't entirely altruistic. Since I'd become a writer I'd noticed that I would encounter certain places that had the right atmosphere, the right mood, to be writing locales. It could be the oddest places—barn lofts, a corner table in some café, a woodshed. This little room was such a place. As soon as I looked into it I knew I could do some work of quality within its walls.

Broughton shrugged. "Suit yourself, Jed. I doubt I'll be offered any better bargains."

We shook hands, and just then I felt very good about Amos Broughton. The sun was streaming through the windows, the day was fresh and bright, things were going well . . . and Amos seemed like Amos again. So maybe all the worrying and such had been out of place, or at least out of proportion.

I headed to the hotel to check out and bring my limited goods over to my new quarters. As I walked over that way, I noticed another fellow out hanging up more broadsides about Killian's impending local camp meeting. As if the town weren't already plastered with them! A man could collect those broadsides and have enough paper to cover the walls of a house.

*   *   *

When I got back to the jail with my armload of possessions, I received an honor denied to most Americans: I met George Washington.

It was funny, really. He actually looked a little like the Father of the Country. I made no jokes about his name, knowing full well he'd heard them all in his time and probably hated everyone who made one.

"So you two really are going to visit Miller?" I asked.

"Best to prevent a crime than deal with it afterward," Washington said. "Miller is someone you need to take seriously."

"Enough people have said that that I'm convinced it's true," I replied. "I'm glad you're going. I have no desire to take a bullet from nowhere."

"Jed knows a lot about that," Broughton said. "He was a sharpshooter during the war. Don't worry, Jed. George here was a cavalryman out of Pennsylvania. So you probably never killed any of his relatives."

As always when this subject came up, a cold wave of something painful and very personal came over me. I wanted Broughton to shut up right then. But he couldn't know that.

"See that rifle in the long case? That was the very rifle Jed used," he said, pointing at part of my burden.

"No! Might I see it?" Washington asked.

"Later," I said, turning toward my new room.

Something thunked on the floor. Looking down, I saw the scope of the rifle had fallen out of its pocket on the side of the rifle case, which I'd failed to completely button shut. Washington stooped and picked it up.

"The scope?" he said.

"That's right." I wanted to reach out for it, but my hands were full. Taking my goods into the room, I dumped them on the bunk and came out to get the scope. Washington was pressing it to his eye.

"I'll take it now," I said, reaching for it.

He kept it to his eye, peering around the room and out the window, treating it like a toy. With his other eye squeezed closed, he didn't see my extended hand or my grim expression.

I seldom touched that scope. It was a possession I often longed to rid myself of, but couldn't. Through that scope I'd watched too many die, killed by my own hand. I think I could remember them all. . . . One in particular, the last one I'd shot, I remembered far more clearly than all the others. He led me to vow never to put that scope to my eye again—I remembered him vividly and relived it often. I expected that when I lay on my deathbed someday, it would be the final image in my mind before I left the world.

Washington, with no clue that he was doing anything remotely painful to me, removed the scope from his eye, looked it over, and glanced up at me. "Yes indeed," he said. "There's the scar at the eye. See it, Amos? The sharpshooters almost all got scars like that. It fits the size and shape of the scope . . . see?" And he lifted the scope toward my eye, prepared to position it against my crescent scar.

Far too roughly I snatched the scope from his grasp, turning my head away from him. "No!" I exclaimed.

Silence reigned. Washington and Broughton both looked at me, stunned. I felt embarrassed, could hardly hold their gaze.

"Very sorry, sir," Washington said quietly. "I clearly have unwittingly offended you."

"I'm sorry," I said. "There are some memories associated with that scope that I'd like to forget."

Washington nodded. "I understand. My fault. I do beg your pardon."

Broughton chuckled uncomfortably. "Hell, Jed . . . maybe we don't need to visit Miller after all. As quick as you moved when you snatched that scope, I'd say you could just dodge his bullets!"

It wasn't much of a joke, but it broke through the tension. I smiled and shook my head, and Washington chuckled.

"Ah, well, the war, it wounds us all," he said. "Then we get on with living anyway, right, gentlemen?"

"Right," Broughton said. "New let's go have our prayer meeting with Miller. We'll invite him to Sunday school."

"Or to that big camp meeting that's coming," Washington said. "Have you seen all those damned signs?"

"I hadn't noticed," Broughton said. "I don't have anything much to do with camp meetings. Just a lot of squalling and such, usually."

They left me alone in the jail. So Broughton had no interest in camp meetings? Then why was Leroy convinced Broughton had been attending Killian's meetings in the next county? He'd told me that Broughton had been seen there more than once. Maybe it really was just somebody who looked like the sheriff, like I'd theorized.

I didn't really know what to make of it. Entering my room, I put my things into the corner. Placing the scope back into its pocket on the side of the rifle case, I took the rifle and case out to the office and used my copy of the rifle cabinet key to open the cabinet and put the rifle inside. It was a valuable weapon, and I always tried to keep it safely locked up, when I could. I'd probably not need it during my brief term as deputy and jailer. My pistol would be the weapon of choice for that job, and if I were lucky, I'd never need to use it.

11

MAKING THE ROUNDS WAS A PLEASURE ON A DAY such as this one. I walked at a leisurely pace, keeping my eyes open, but for the most part letting my mind take its own path. Though no one who saw me would know it, I was writing while I worked. Not visibly, not physically, but I was doing the mental work necessary before I could actually put words on paper. Plot details and possibilities, alternate versions of the story I planned to tell, and the personality characteristics of characters I would use all danced about in my mind, pieces of a still jumbled puzzle that eventually would fall into place and form something coherent and appealing.

The wind kicked up, and as I passed the mouth of an alley, something blew out of it and wrapped itself around my right leg. I bent and peeled it off. It was one of the broadsides for Killian's camp meeting. The corners were ripped, as if someone had snatched it roughly from a wall somewhere and tossed it down.

Someone approached me as I studied the broadside. It was Smith, the runt of a newspaperman. He had another big cigar burning between those fuzz-crowned lips of his.

"The good sheriff tears those down, you know," he said. "I've seen him do it. I don't know why. It's perfectly legal in this town to hang signs for public events. Even scoundrels like Killian can do it."

Smith had all the credibility of a snake to me. "Now, why would the sheriff care one way or another about some camp meeting preacher?"

"I don't know. You tell me. All I can tell you is what I've seen with my own eyes. I watched him tear three of those posters down yesterday. He'd look around, trying to see if anyone was watching, then he'd tear them down, wad them up, and throw them on the ground. Made quite a mess. You'd think a sheriff wouldn't do such a thing."

"I have reason to doubt your story. The matter of the Reverend Killian came up today, and the sheriff had not a word to say about him. No evident interest in him at all, either direction."

"He's putting on a performance, then. Acting disinterested when he's not. Not only have I seen him tear down the broadsides, but the man who operates our press actually saw the sheriff pull one down, throw it on the ground in an alley, and urinate on it. Does that sound like a disinterested man to you? Of course, who better to pee on than that rubbish Killian? The good sheriff and I are actually in agreement on the worth of that preacher."

"This all sounds like a wild story generated by people who run a newspaper dedicated to putting the sheriff out of office."

"Don't listen to Leroy," he said. "He doesn't understand newspapers or much anything else. We try to be a fair and open publication. The good sheriff is welcome to give his side of anything we print, and he knows it. He always declines the invitation."

"Given the family politics, I can see why you are no friend of the sheriff. But why do you dislike Killian?"

Smith cocked up a brow and drew on his cigar in a way that gave him a perfect expression of haughty wisdom. It had the look of something he probably practiced in front of a mirror in secret. I anticipated a smoke ring, and sure enough . . .

He watched the smoke ring drift up and break apart before he spoke. "Our newspaper expects to print some very interesting stories about the Reverend Killian, as soon as we verify a few more things. There's every reason for good citizens and for law enforcement officers to keep a close eye on that 'holy' man."

"Why?"

"Mark my words, Mr. Wells. Keep your eyes and ears open. There'll be news soon of some sort of crime over in Russell County, òr at least nearby.

Something along the line of a store robbery, a freight office theft, a bank robbery . . . something that brings the criminals a hefty handful of money."

"How do you know?"

"Because there's a pattern. The Reverend Killian goes into a county, sets up a camp meeting, stays for weeks at a time . . . and somewhere along the way, usually right before he uproots, there's a crime. A robbery, usually. Some kind of thief-in-the-night thing, done quite well, with no witnesses, few clues. It doesn't happen everywhere that Killian goes, but it happens at least half the time, maybe a little more."

I laughed. "So you believe Killian preaches holiness while he's plundering banks and freight offices?"

"I don't believe he does it personally. I don't know whether he even has any direct involvement. But somebody's doing it. The thefts usually come when the populace is for the most part at the camp meeting. He can draw them in, you know. Literally, the man can all but empty a town. When that happens, it isn't hard for thieves to strike."

"It could be that some smart thief has simply made the same observation that you have about Killian's ability to draw big crowds, and takes advantage of it."

"Perhaps. There are still some things to verify, as

I said before. Suffice it to say that some of those Killian surrounds himself with are not . . . saintly. Whether he is personally responsible or not, some of his cohorts are."

"Anything the local law should know about, given that they'll soon be gracing Bleeker County with their presence?"

"It isn't my job to do the good sheriff's work for him. Let him figure it out."

And just then something clicked into place in my mind: maybe the sheriff had figured it out. Maybe that was why he was slipping away and attending camp meetings. Maybe the man was investigating!

I wasn't sure it was true, but the thought brought relief. If I was right, then Broughton was more on-the-job than he'd appeared to be. Why the secrecy, though? It wasn't hard to think of possible reasons. Perhaps he was conducting an investigation that was uncertain enough that he thought it best not to mention it even to his deputies. Perhaps he didn't trust Leroy, or even me, to keep our mouths shut. Perhaps he wanted to be sure of himself before he made his suspicions public in any way. It was serious business to link a popular preacher to crime, after all.

"So—when will we get together to have a cup of coffee and talk about the writing trade?" Smith asked.

"I've got a lot to do," I said. "I'm writing when

I'm not helping out the sheriff. Maybe sometime later on."

"You can find me in the newspaper office on Elm. One street over, building with the white columns on the porch."

I'd be sure to come looking. "All right."

He turned away, puffing that stinking cigar. "You keep in mind what I said. There'll be some kind of robbery over in Russell County. Probably just before the camp meeting moves here."

"We'll see."

"We will. Have a good day, Mr. Wells. Oh, by the way . . . there'll be a little story in the edition that prints today about you being part of our community, and the work you're doing for the sheriff."

I wasn't glad to hear it. Any reasonable chance for anonymity I might have had would be gone once that story was published. But it was not a major matter. I was growing used to being known. Most people treated me well. However, a few former Confederates who believed I had libeled the Cause through my writing about Andersonville held me in contempt. Sometimes it was prudent not to advertise my identity.

At noon I took a meal in the same café where I'd eaten with Leroy. I ordered peach cobbler for dessert and was finishing it up with my second cup of coffee when I heard the noise.

A series of pops, off in the distance. Shots, perhaps, or fireworks set off by boys. I frowned and listened for more, but there was nothing.

Leaving the café, I debated about going in the direction I'd heard the noises, but in the end I didn't. I wanted to find Broughton and see how the call on Jimmy Miller had gone.

Some little voice told me I was making the wrong choice, but I ignored it and went on back toward the office.

I had just discovered the office still empty, Broughton not present, when three boys came running up the street toward me, breathless, eyes big.

The tallest and apparently oldest of the boys said, "Are you Mr. Wells, the deputy?"

"I am."

"Come quick! Leroy Fletch sent us to find you!"

"What's wrong?"

"Come quick! He's been shot, and there's another man shot, and another man dead—"

"Leroy is shot?"

"No! No! Sheriff Broughton is shot . . . and the other man . . ."

"Washington?"

"Yes . . . he's shot really bad. And the third one is dead. The sheriff killed him."

"Miller."

"That's him."

"Where was the sheriff shot?"

"In the head. The head."

My knees turned to water.

"Come on," I said. "Take me to him. And one of you—who runs the fastest?—you, then, you go out to where the sheriff lives, and you bring his wife back here."

"She's already on her way, sir. They done sent for her."

They set off on a lope, me following.

I prayed hard for Broughton, harder than I'd prayed for anything in a long time.

⊷ 12 ⊷

CALLIANNE WAS STANDING ALONE OUTSIDE THE house where Broughton had been taken. The shooting occurred three buildings down, at the rugged, poorly painted structure that apparently had been Miller's home.

Miller himself was still there, laid out on the street and covered with a dirty piece of canvas. A puddle of blood had spread out from beneath the canvas and was now congealing in the dirt.

Leroy looked like he'd just crawled out of bed. I went to him.

"How is he?"

"Looks terrible, but he's not hit bad. A bullet grazed through the side of his scalp. It bled a lot and dazed him, but he'll be fine. Washington is a different story. He may not survive."

I stared at the covered corpse of Miller. "I feel bad about this, Leroy. They came here because Miller had threatened me. That makes this my fault."

"Nonsense. The man whose fault this is, is lying under that canvas."

"How did it happen?"

"As I hear it, Miller was involved with some sort of gang planning a train robbery. They were here when here comes the sheriff and the district attorney at the same time. The gang ran, but Miller decided to put up a fight. Poor old Washington was hit before he knew what was happening. Broughton drew his pistol and fought back. Miller came out the worse."

"I heard the shots. I'd just finished my lunch. I should have come to investigate. Good Lord, they left to find Miller this morning. What took so long for them to get here?"

"Miller wasn't here when they first arrived. They went back to Washington's office to talk over some other case Washington was prosecuting, then came back again."

"Who'd you get this information from?"

"O'Riley. The fellow who owns that house there. Broughton dragged Washington over here after the shooting and told O'Riley the whole thing before he passed out. O'Riley knew I was at home and he sent for me. As quick as I got here, I sent those boys to fetch you."

"I want to see him."

"The doctor's still patching him."

I looked over at Callianne. I'd never seen a

woman look so small, frail, and alone. Slowly, I approached her, wondering how much she knew about what had happened, and if she might blame me in some way for it.

"Mrs. Broughton . . ."

She turned a pale face toward me and said nothing.

"Have you see him?"

"Only a moment . . . he looks awful . . . so much blood."

"Leroy told me it wasn't a serious wound. I'm so sorry it happened."

"It was bound to happen. Amos has talked about Jimmy Miller for the longest time, saying that sooner or later he would get somebody killed, or get killed himself."

Hesitantly, I told her what I felt she had the right to know. "He and Mr. Washington came here because Miller had threatened me. They believed they could scare him out of fulfilling the threat. It makes me feel . . . responsible."

She paused, then said, "Don't feel that way. Amos would have done that for anyone. He's worried about Miller for a long time."

Silence held between us a few moments. "Mrs. Broughton, when I was at your house, you were preparing to tell me something when Amos came back in. I've wondered what you were going to say."

"I was going to tell you that I believe Amos has been drinking. Oh, what am I saying? I know he's been drinking. I've found the bottles, smelled it on his breath and his clothes. I could smell it on him when he came back in the house and interrupted us."

"So could I," I admitted.

"He used to drink, before we were married, then he stopped because I made him promise to. But lately he's done it again. I don't know why. I've challenged him about it, and he gets furious. Denies it. It happened while you were staying at our house. I told him I knew he was drinking, and he denied it and shouted at me. You may have heard it."

"No, no. I didn't." The lie was spontaneous, reflexive.

"He denied he was drinking . . . then went outside and drank. I watched him out a window, drinking from a flask." She bowed her head and put a hand on her brow. "He's changed. And it has something to do with that preacher Killian."

I recalled the odd expression she had turned on me when the matter of Killian came up during my visit to the Broughton home.

"What is the connection?"

"I don't know. I wish I did. There's something about that preacher that has obsessed him."

"Mrs. Broughton, it happens that—"

"Please, not 'Mrs. Broughton.' It makes me sound like I'm Amos's mother. Call me Callianne."

"Very well, if you'll call me Jed. What I was about to say was that I'd heard Amos was going out to Killian's meetings. But he never spoke of it to me, never reacted when Killian's name came up. But only today I heard something that might explain it all. I shouldn't say much, because I don't know the facts, but it may be that Amos was sneaking off to those camp meetings for professional reasons."

"What do you mean?"

"He may be investigating a crime. Or a potential crime."

"I don't understand."

"I can't say much, because there may be nothing to what I heard. Suffice it to say there might be something about Killian, or those around him, that is of legitimate interest to an officer of the law."

"But why would that make him drink?"

"I don't know . . . maybe the drinking has nothing to do with Killian."

"I think it does. I can . . . I don't know . . . sense it. He's obsessed with that preacher . . . but he denies that too, just like he denies the drinking."

"I've mentioned Killian's name before him," I said, "and he doesn't react to it. It's hard for me to think of him as obsessed."

"Amos is a good actor. When he doesn't want

something known, he can deny it very convincingly."

"I was told by a man that he saw Amos tearing down one of the broadsides advertising Killian's camp meeting and . . . and treating it in a disrespectful way."

"I can easily believe it. I know that—my God!"

She was looking over my shoulder. Turning to follow her gaze, I was as surprised as she to see none other than Killian himself, trailed by three men wearing black suits and serious expressions, approaching the scene.

Killian paused and looked down at the covered body, then approached Leroy, who was busy trying to keep a steadily growing crowd of gawkers away from the gory corpse.

Killian spoke to Leroy; I could not hear what he said. Leroy shook his head firmly. I suspected that Killian had just requested the right to go inside and pray over the injured.

Killian spoke again to Leroy, who responded with another firm shake of his head. He gestured for Killian to step aside and join the rest of the gawkers. Killian did so, drawing almost as much attention as the dead man.

Killian chanced to look my way. Our eyes locked, and once again I was struck by a sense of distant familiarity with him, that same sense I'd had when I awakened to see him praying over me after the train crash.

"Why is he here?" Callianne asked.

"I don't know. Maybe he's here finalizing his plans for the camp meeting."

"I wish he wouldn't come here. I wish he'd keep himself and his camp meeting away. There's something about him that fills me with a kind of dread."

Oddly, I could understand what she meant.

A man emerged from the house and gestured to Callianne. The doctor, I presumed.

"You come too," she said to me.

"Callianne, you might want to be with him alone."

"No . . . please come."

I glanced over to see if Leroy was managing to control the crowd. So far he was holding his own, though now the newspaperman Smith was pushing up to him, notepad in hand and questions blowing out with clouds of cigar smoke.

Leroy would have to manage on his own. I wanted to see Broughton.

Callianne staggered, as if she might faint, when she saw the body covered by a sheet, head to toe. I actually reached out to steady her as the doctor closed the door.

"I'm so sorry . . . that's George, not Amos," the doctor said. "Amos is going to be fine."

"Oh, God . . ."

"Washington is dead?" I asked.

"I'm afraid so. Amos is in there."

"You go in alone, Callianne," I said. "I'll come in in a minute."

As she entered the other bedroom, I caught a glimpse of Broughton through the door. He was propped up, his head bandaged on one side but otherwise looking fine. The door closed as Callianne rushed to him and embraced him.

A man I didn't know was in the next room, and he approached me with his hand out. I shook it as he said, "I'm O'Riley. This is my house."

"Pleased to meet you, sir. I'm Jed Wells, working as deputy for Amos Broughton."

"Somebody said you wrote some kind of book. About the war."

"That's right."

"I ain't read it, but I probably will. I'm trying to read all I can about that damned war, so maybe I can understand it sometime before the Lord calls me home. I never had to fight, my health being bad, and believe it or not, I managed to make it through the whole dang thing without ever really deciding whose side I was on."

"Consider yourself fortunate."

O'Riley and I talked a little longer. I went to the

window to see how Leroy was handling the crowd. Smith was still giving him headaches, and there were now too many people for him to keep back. The body was surrounded, and braver souls were sneaking looks under the canvas.

"I better go out and help Leroy," I said. But just then the doctor stuck his head around the corner.

"Amos is calling for you," he said.

I left Leroy to fend off the crowd alone and headed around to see Amos.

He looked good, apart from the bandage. I spoke before he had a chance.

"Amos, I feel responsible for this. It was for my sake that you got into this situation."

"Nobody knew it would be this situation, Jed. I figured George and I could handle this with words. Who would have supposed that Miller would pick this time to get brave?" He paused. "George is dead. Dead!"

"I know."

"God. I can't believe it."

"Neither can I."

A muffled knock on the outer door was audible to all of us, but none of us paid attention to it. I heard O'Riley heading to answer the knock.

"What will come of all this, Amos? Will there be any legal repercussions?"

"No. This was Miller's fault, very clearly. And

he's dead. There's nothing to be done but bury poor George and do what we can for his widow. As far as I'm concerned, Miller's remains can be fed to the dogs."

O'Riley appeared at the door of the room. "There's someone here to see you, Sheriff," he said. "Under the circumstances, I thought you'd want this one to come in."

O'Riley stepped aside, and into the room walked the Reverend Edward Killian.

KILLIAN'S ENTRANCE HAD A PROFOUND AND STAR-
tling effect. For my part, I drew in my breath and
found that for a few moments I could not let it out
again. Callianne gasped audibly, and Amos seemed
to freeze. His face became empty and dispassion-
ate, his eyes unblinking.

I wondered why Leroy had let Killian go to the
door, then realized that he probably hadn't. With
the crowd too big for him to control, Killian had
probably just slipped to the door unnoticed,
knocked, and been admitted by O'Riley, whose
look and tone revealed him as a Killian admirer.

"It's the Reverend Edward Killian," O'Riley
proudly announced. "He heard about what happened and wants to come pray for you, Sheriff."

Broughton made some sort of odd sound in his
throat. Callianne got control of her expression and
became cautiously impassive. I simply stared.

Killian seemed taken aback by the coldness with

which he was greeted. He glanced from face to face, and stopped on mine. "I know you," he said.

"You prayed over me after I was in that train accident recently," I said, glancing up at the cloth covering his brow.

"Ah, yes," Killian said. "I remember. You seem well now."

"I'm doing fine."

"Good. Prayer makes a difference." He looked at Broughton. "I know you too, sir. I've seen you at my meetings, I believe."

"You must be mistaken," Broughton said coldly.

"No . . . I'm sure I've—"

"I have not attended your meetings," Broughton said firmly.

Killian let it go. "My error, then. I hope you'll let me pray with you, sir. I chanced to be in town today, readying for a camp meeting that will be hosted in the big meadow south of town, along Starnes Creek. I heard there was a shooting, and came to see if I could be of help."

"If you want to pray, pray. But I'd rather you not do it in here."

"I beg your pardon?"

"You can pray for me somewhere else."

Callianne, very uncomfortable, said, "Amos . . . he just wants to pray for you."

"I said he can do it. But not in here."

Killian seemed authentically stunned, and a realization came to me quite firmly: whatever mysterious obsession Amos Broughton had about Killian, Killian had no counterpart awareness of Broughton. At this moment my impression of Killian was that of a man who had come in for exactly the reason he said, and who was completely puzzled by the rude rejection he was receiving.

"I will pray for you, sir," Killian said, very graciously under the circumstances. "I understand you are the sheriff here. I am a great supporter of those who enforce our laws."

"Good for you. Now give a man some peace."

Killian opened his mouth, then closed it again, seeming to deflate in his bewilderment.

"Why don't you yank that cloth away, Preacher?" Broughton said. "What is it you are trying to hide? If God really did give you those marks, shouldn't you show them off?"

Killian looked more bewildered than ever. He nodded at Callianne, then at me, and turned.

O'Riley, still in the doorway, had to step aside to let the preacher pass. He looked back inside a moment, confusion and anger mixing on his face, then followed Killian out, no doubt to apologize for something that was in no way his fault.

Callianne turned to Broughton. "Amos, why did you treat that man so badly?"

"I don't like camp meeting preachers."

She hesitated, then said, "Tell me the truth,

Amos. I know you've been going to his meetings. Tell me why!"

"I ain't gone to any camp meetings. I don't go to camp meetings."

"Amos, for God's sake, tell me the truth!"

"Are you calling me a liar, wife?"

"I know you've gone to his meetings, Amos. Just like I know you've been drinking. You owe me the truth!"

He stared at her as coldly as he'd stared at Killian. "I haven't been drinking, and I haven't attended any camp meetings. And that's all I'll say on that matter."

Time to go. This was no place for me. "Amos, I'll check back on you later. Don't worry about anything—we'll take care of all your duties until you're better."

"It's just a grazing wound. I'll be back tomorrow."

"Don't push yourself too hard, Amos."

"I'll be there tomorrow."

I nodded, said a quick good-bye to Calliane, and left like there were hounds on my heels.

Despite his promise, Broughton didn't show up the next day, nor the next. His wound, though deep enough to hurt, was not serious. More significantly, his equilibrium was affected. He sent word by a messenger that he would remain at home until he could keep his balance a little better.

It was fine by me, actually. The office was quiet, the jail cells empty. Joe Reid, the new man, came on duty and took his first patrol alone. He required no real orientation to his job beyond being told where things were, given a set of keys, and so on. The similar work he'd done for years in Wichita gave him a quiet confidence that persuaded me Broughton had made a good choice.

In the early afternoon on the second day of Broughton's absence, I encountered Callianne on the street. She had just emerged from the big general store on Kidwell Avenue, carrying a small basket of items over her arm.

"Callianne!" I called as I saw her emerge. She looked up, shielding her eyes against the sun with her hand, and smiled pleasantly as I approached. "May I help you carry that?"

"Thank you, Jed, but it's not heavy. How are you faring without Amos on the job?"

"Fine, fine. It's been quiet, and Joe Reid is a fine deputy. How's Amos doing?"

"He's got his balance back, most of it, anyway. I doubt I'll be able to keep him home past today."

"Thank God he wasn't hurt worse than he was." They'd buried Miller the day before, the funeral attended by only a handful of his few relatives and even fewer friends, many of them drunk right in the church house and reportedly talking virulently about the vengeance they would take on the local law. I was told that the preacher, a local Baptist, was hard-pressed to find anything decent to say about Miller. The Methodist who said words over Washington in a simultaneous funeral on the other side of town had it easier. They buried Washington in the church cemetery, Miller in a family graveyard on the farm of an uncle three miles outside town.

I stood looking at Callianne, wanting to ask her more about Broughton and his late odd behavior, but decided against it. He was recovering, would be back, and it wasn't appropriate to poke my nose in for more news than that. So I just touched the brim of my hat in farewell and told her to tell Amos that we'd be looking forward to seeing him.

As I turned away she said, "Jed . . ."

"Yes?"

"I . . . Amos is . . ." She hesitated, then said, "Amos is so pleased you're helping him out. And I appreciate it too."

I smiled and touched my hat again, then went my way, wondering what she'd been about to say that she didn't. She'd changed course in mid-sentence.

The Amos Broughton who roused me out of bed the next morning was a different man than the one I'd last seen in that bed at O'Riley's house. This Amos Broughton was cheerful, talkative, and seemingly very relaxed. I supposed that the two days off had been good for him.

He quizzed me about events of the last couple of days, had me give him a report on my activities and those of Reid, and informed me that he'd actually read two pages of my book while he was resting. This was unexpected to me, and gratifying, though he admitted it hadn't been easy to be thrown back into the midst of our mutual hellish experience. He'd put the book aside very quickly.

"But I tell you this: I read enough to see that you're a devil of a writer, Jed. Back when you were scribbling notes on every scrap of paper you could find in that camp, I'd never have figured you to be starting out on a career like you've got now."

"Believe me, I didn't expect it either."

Broughton went to his desk and sat down to write a full report about the shooting incident that had killed Miller and Washington. I watched him work and hoped that some kind of corner had been turned and he would be from now on the Amos Broughton of the past, before drinking, before his strange and poorly veiled obsession with the Reverend Killian.

Callianne brought her husband a big tray of food at midday. It was a pleasant surprise for him, and also for me, as I was invited to partake of the bounty, which could have fed four. She said she'd gotten used to doting over her husband during his brief recuperation, but I had the impression that she had mostly come to make sure he was not pushing himself too hard.

Broughton treated her like any wife would want to be treated, thanking her profusely, praising her kindness, and complimenting her cooking skills to me while we ate. Yet I noted that Callianne's responsive smile seemed a little forced, and there was sadness in her eyes that she could not hide.

Broughton had an appointment in early afternoon with a man he was contracting with to keep the jail supplied with firewood once winter came. By the time he left, Callianne had already departed with the leftovers and dirty dishes, so I was surprised when she quickly reappeared after Broughton left.

"I want to speak with you about Amos," she said seriously. "I waited across the street until I saw him leave."

"What's wrong?"

"He's . . . he's . . . I don't know, Jed. It's worse now than it was before."

"Worse? He seems to me to be much more the man I'd expect him to be. Sober and cheerful."

"Yes, but it's all so false. He's putting on a performance, Jed, for you and me and everyone. I know my husband, and he's not acting himself."

"Perhaps not . . . maybe he's just trying a little

too hard to be what he ought to be. But at least he's trying. I think the rest has done him good."

She firmly shook he heard. "No, Jed. Something odd is going on. After he forced out the Reverend Killian the other day, I confronted him very openly. You saw the beginning of it just before you left. What you didn't see was how Amos just closed up within himself the more I pressed him. He closed me off, refused to talk about Killian or his behavior, denied his drinking even though I told him I'd seen him do it, denied he had been acting differently. Then he simply quit talking completely, for hours. When he started talking again, he was like he is now. Cheerful and jolly and so very fulsome. He's been that way for two days. It's a mask, Jed. And I'm almost afraid to know what's under that mask, but I have to find out."

"What do you want me to do? Talk to him?"

"I don't think he'll talk to you or anyone else. Not on any serious level, anyway. Believe me, I've tried over the entire time he was home. But he won't do it. He just smiles and jokes and tries to act like his normal self, and keeps the door closed on me, so to speak."

"So you want me to just keep an eye on him, then?"

"More or less, yes. I just want to know he's all right. I'm afraid, for some reason. I have this fear he's going to do something rash and wrong, and I can't account for it. He hides so much from me . . . maybe he won't hide as much from you."

"I'll keep a close watch on him." As I said it, though, I wondered if Callianne might be misinterpreting her husband. It could be that Broughton was sincerely trying to get himself back on track, and she was just worrying too much. The newly cheerful and energetic Broughton seemed a true improvement over what he'd been before, even if he did overdo things a bit.

"Thank you, Jed," she said. "I do so appreciate your concern for Amos."

"He's an old friend. If I see or learn anything you should know, I'll let you know about it."

"You promise me?"

"I promise."

⚜ 14 ⚜

SMITH SHOWED UP WITH HIS CIGAR AND HAUGHTY attitude about three that afternoon. Broughton was out, I didn't know where, and Reid was scheduled for night duty. I'd just been about to leave the office for a quick foot patrol of the town when Smith arrived, wrapped in smugness and the smell of cheap and burning tobacco.

"Good day to you, Mr. Jed Wells!" he said in that cloying manner of his. "Did you see my story about the shooting incident?"

I had. The paper had printed a small special edition that had hit the streets that morning. I had few complaints with the coverage beyond the fact the newspaper had gone to some pains to paint Broughton's role in the affair in the most negative light, implying that some carelessness on his part had caused the confrontation to escalate to violence. Washington was portrayed in syrupy, overdrawn prose, the classic Good Man, the tragic unfortunate victim of unnecessary violence prompted by a sheriff's zealotry.

I'd also noted that all references to me in the story—which seemed ill-placed in that I'd had virtually no role in the matter at all—were highly, almost embarrassingly, flattering. As I read the story, something I had vaguely suspected about Smith became starkly clear: he viewed me as a celebrated man of letters, a person who had achieved a success with the written word that he envied. As such, he craved my approval. The realization actually made me feel embarrassed for him. I'd encountered the same kind of fawning from fledgling writers a few times before, since I'd become famous. Smith tried to hide his wide-eyed awe behind his brash and obnoxious veneer, but it was there.

"I saw the story."

"What did you think?"

"Not bad, apart from unjustly slandering Amos Broughton a few times. He comes off sounding worse than Miller."

He laughed and nodded. "We do go after the old boy, don't we? But it's for the public good. He really needs to be out of office."

With all the sarcasm I could muster, I said, "I'm sure you're gaining many a star in your crown for your concern for the public good."

He waved his hand dismissively, like it all really didn't matter. "No doubt, no doubt," he said. "But that story isn't why I came today. I'm on to something new. About Killian. Something very solid, something I believe the law may want to know about."

"And what's that?"

"Well . . . I don't know exactly. Not yet. But I'll know within a couple of hours. I've got an appointment to keep, and once that's done, I will have the straight facts about the Reverend Killian and his schemes."

"Why are you telling me this?"

The way this boy looked at me just then, you'd have thought he was a wise old man condescending to accommodate some green upstart. "I like you, Wells. I respect your work, view you as a writer that's not too bad . . . not bad at all. I can't say I favor your associations with Broughton, but given your mutual history, it's understandable you'd have a certain attachment to that poor old incompetent."

"So because you think my writing is not 'too bad,' you've decided to let me in on whatever it is you're up to?"

"Look, Wells, I know this deputy work isn't your true line. I know you're just helping out an old friend. But as long as you're in it, I thought you might like to have a bit of success at it. I have every confidence that what I'll learn later will be enough to let you arrest the Reverend Killian. And if that should happen, that would be one smacker of a story for Very Truly Yours, eh? So what do you say? Will you come with me?"

"What do you expect I'd be able to arrest Killian for?"

"I believe that tonight I'll confirm my theory that Edward Killian and his associates use their camp meetings as distractions to allow them to commit burglaries in nearby towns. As simple as that."

"So then I'd be able to move in and make an arrest, become a big hero. And you'll have a better story because of the arrest. Is that the idea?"

"Something like that." He flipped a cigar ash and tried hard to look taller than he ever would be.

"Sorry. I've got duties here today, and had planned to do some writing tonight."

"You'll be missing an opportunity."

"Go ahead and have your meeting. Publish your story. If there's an arrest to be made at that point, then we'll let the real law enforcement folks handle it."

Smith's smug smile faded a little. "Come now, Wells . . . don't miss this chance."

"Sorry, Smith. I am going to miss it."

He flipped the cigar again, harder, a subtle gesture showing a mounting frustration. "Come, now . . . come on. This could be a major success for you."

"But I'm not looking for major successes as a

deputy. Like you said, I'm just helping out an old friend."

"Then maybe you could use it in a novel. Come on, Wells . . . help me out here! Please!"

This made no sense to me. He didn't need me. How many newspapermen sought to share their journalistic victories with law enforcement officers? If anything, that diluted their own perceived role. The only reason I could think that he'd want to do it was to associate with me in some manner that would be public and permanent. Perhaps he longed to be able to write about his adventure with the famous Jed Wells, fellow writer and all around good friend.

This small-time scribbler was more pathetic even than I'd first thought.

"Sorry, Smith. I have to pass this one up."

For a moment there was a look of true and deep disappointment on his face, the real Smith showing through the mask. Did everyone wear masks around here? Killian with his cloth, Broughton with his deceptive manner, Smith with his brash front put up to hide the unconfident and limited loser he really was? He quickly recovered, though, and looked at me like I was some poor wretch too foolish or deceived to realize what an opportunity I was passing up.

"Well, I suppose it's your choice, Wells. You'll wish later you'd come with me."

"I guess I'll be kicking myself then, huh?"

Smith shook his head and blew out another cloud of smoke. "See you in print, Wells. Take care."

He turned and walked away on his stumpy little legs. He was trying to swagger, but you just can't do it very well when you're that short.

After Smith's departure, I made a quick patrol of the town. Nothing out of order, no sign of crime. Even Bull Creek Avenue was lifeless.

A young fellow I'd never seen before was waiting for me on the jail porch when I arrived. He was moving about in so restless and agitated a manner that I actually wondered if he was in need of directions to the nearest outhouse.

"Can I help you?" I asked him.

"You the sheriff?"

"No. I'm Jed Wells, a part-time deputy."

"You got to come. Somebody's got to come before he kills him!"

"Whoa! Who's killing who?"

"I don't have time to explain it all—he's got him pinned up in the barn, and I swear he'll kill him if somebody don't come! Beulah is trying to stop it all, but she'll not be able to for long, and I'm afraid she'll get hurt!"

It was evident I'd get no clear understanding of

the situation until I saw it myself. This fellow was too worked up to give a coherent account.

"I'll fetch a rifle and you can take me there. Will I need a horse?"

"Yes. It's outside town, three, four miles. Please hurry! We may be too late already!"

If this fellow had left a desperate situation in progress long enough back that he'd been able to ride as much as four miles, he was probably right about being too late. But until I knew for sure, I had to treat it like the emergency it apparently was.

"Wait here," I said. "I'll be ready to go in five minutes."

He talked as we rode, and I was able to get a basic understanding of the situation into which we were traveling.

The boy's name was Charles Gray Jr., and the problem involved his hot-tempered father, Charles Sr., and indiscreet older sister, Beulah. Charles Sr. had caught Beulah in a compromising position with a man out behind the smokehouse—I gathered that Beulah was frequently caught in compromising positions with men out behind the smokehouse and several other places—and Charles Sr. had taken a shotgun after the fellow. The interrupted lover had tried to flee through the Gray barn to escape, but now he was trapped there, holed up with no safe exit. By the time Charles Jr. had left looking for the sheriff, Charles Sr. had not attempted to go up into the loft after the man, mostly because Beulah was pleading so vigorously and pitifully to let the man go. But Charles Jr. had little confidence that his sister would keep their father at bay for long.

"We may find a man dead when we arrive, Charles," I warned him. "Be ready for that. And if that happens, I'll have to bring your father in so the matter can be investigated."

"I know. I know. I hope he ain't killed him yet. I've knowed this would happen sometime or another. Beulah, that girl can't learn from experience. And she can't say no either. It shames the whole family."

We got there quicker than I'd anticipated. It was a typical Kansas sodbuster spread—a plain house, built of lumber shipped in by railroad, with a few sheds, a corral, and a large barn. I was relieved to see a man I presumed was Charles Sr. still outside the barn, with a hefty young woman, no doubt the wayward Beulah, talking to him dramatically, body tense and slightly crouched, red and tear-streaked face pushed out toward her father with her mouth running at full steam.

This all indicated to me that Charles Sr. hadn't yet killed the unfortunate fellow in the loft, and given the time he'd had to do it, I concluded that maybe, down deep, he didn't really want to kill him. This was certainly a good thing. Maybe I could talk that shotgun out of his hands.

"You got a mother around here?" I asked Charles Jr. as we dismounted, me pondering whether I should unboot the rifle I'd borrowed from the office rack—a lever-action Winchester instead of my older, slower-loading wartime rifle—or just go in with my holstered pistol for protection. I opted for the latter.

"My mother's in Cincinnati, visiting her sister. I wish she was here—she can settle Pa down."

I wished she was there too. This kind of thing wasn't something I was used to handling.

Beulah saw Charles Jr. and me before her father did. She said something to him and pointed wildly in our direction.

Charles Sr. turned and raised his shotgun when he saw me.

I stopped and pointed at my badge. "You'd best lower that shotgun, sir . . . I'm with the Bleeker County sheriff's office, and it isn't prudent to raise a weapon on a law enforcement officer."

He lowered the shotgun, but not completely. "Why are you here?" He glared at his son. "Charles Jr., did you bring him?"

"I did, Pa. I don't want you hanging for no murder!"

Charles Sr. raised his voice for the benefit of the

man in the loft. "You betcha there'll be a murder! I'll kill that sumbitch!"

"There'll be no murder here," I said forcefully, walking forward again. "There's nothing gained by that. You give me that shotgun, sir."

"I'll not give you nothing. Except plenty of hell if you try to stop me from what I got to do."

I got within ten feet of him and stopped. This time I spoke much more softly, and in a tone that I hoped was disarming—literally. "Mr. Gray, my name is Jed Wells. I'm a new deputy with Sheriff Broughton, and this is the first call I've had outside of Starnes."

"Well, good for you."

"Mr. Gray, it won't do anybody any good for you to commit a murder here. Especially with me here to witness it. I understand why you're angry, but it's over now. If you'll let that fellow go, he'll run like a scared rabbit, and I doubt he'd have courage to come around here again."

"But I love him!" Beulah wailed. "He's got the kindest, sweetest eyes!"

Charles Jr., just behind me, said, "You love every man you see, Beulah."

"Miss Gray," I said, "if you love that fellow, you'd best keep your mouth shut. The more you talk sweet 'bout that fellow, the more your father will want to shoot him."

My insight actually won me some favor with

Charles Sr. He nodded firmly. "That's right. You're a man who understands, I can see."

"I do. So let me go talk to the man in the loft," I said. "I'll tell him that he's got one chance to leave here, and that if he comes back again, ever, he'll not leave the way he came."

Beulah turned away, wailing, and the fact that she didn't like what I was proposing seemed to give it merit with her father.

"All right," he said after a moment. "You seem like a reasonable man. Go talk to him before I kill him."

"Is he armed?"

"Not that I know of."

"What's his name?" I asked.

"Dead Man Jones," Charles Sr. said, and spat.

"No, really. What is his name?"

Beulah reddened and looked down. "I . . . don't know."

Charles Sr. cussed, and I couldn't blame him. If ever I had a daughter, I prayed she'd be nothing like Beulah, giving herself to a stranger whose name she did not know, just because he had the kindest, sweetest eyes.

As I entered the barn I looked for a back way out. There was only one, a rear double door, and it was chained shut. That explained why the fellow upstairs had found himself trapped once he hid in here.

"You up there!" I said. "I'm with the sheriff's office and I'm here to try to get you out of here alive!"

"I don't believe you!" The voice from the loft was quaking and thin. "Throw your badge up here!"

I unpinned the badge and threw it to the loft. I heard him move around up there but didn't get a glimpse of him.

"This looks homemade!"

"I think it is. Look, it's the badge they gave me, and the only one I've got. You want out of here or not?"

"I want out!"

"Is there a loft window up there, on the back?"

A pause, then, "Yes. It's closed with a big shutter. It's too high for me to jump!"

I looked around and found a short length of rope. "I'm coming up."

He was as plain as a post, a little bit fat and white as a phantom at the moment. He handed me my badge with a trembling hand.

"See if that back window will open," I said. "We'll have to lower you down. If you show yourself out front, old Gray out there will shoot you."

The man blanched a little more and headed for the rear of the loft.

The rear window shutter stuck a little, but opened. The rope was on the short side; he'd have to take a jump at the bottom.

"I'm not good with high places," he said.

"How are you with shotgun pellets?"

His hands pinched tightly around the rope, white and puffy; his body was a leaden weight that threatened to pull me right out of the window. He didn't even make it to the end of the rope before he lost his grip and landed hard. He lay there, wind knocked out of him, staring up at me, then got up and scrambled away, making sure to keep the barn between himself and his would-be killer on the other side of it.

I waited five minutes, then left the barn and told the Gray clan that it was over and he was gone. Charles Sr. cussed and threatened me, Beulah cried and ran toward the barn, and Charles Jr. said thanks.

I mounted and got away from that place as quickly as I could, wondering who that poor fellow in the loft had been, and confident that I would never run across him again. By now he was probably halfway to Canada.

BROUGHTON'S HORSE WAS IN THE LITTLE STABLE behind the jail when I got back. I stabled my own horse, removing the saddle. Broughton's horse was still saddled, indicating he was stopping by only briefly.

I looked forward to sharing with him my story of my adventure at the Gray house. Reflecting on it while riding home, I found it harrowing but also amusing, and was already trying to figure out a way to work it into my next book.

As I hung my saddle over the side of the stall, I caught an unsought glimpse into Broughton's open saddlebag. Sunlight shafting through the cracks in the wall glinted on glass. There was a half-full bottle of whiskey inside the saddlebag.

My mood declined greatly and a new surge of worry for Amos Broughton passed through me. A little anger too. The man had a good life, a wife who loved him, a fine home and honorable line of work . . . why would he want to endanger all that?

When I walked in the office, it grew worse. Broughton was there, with my rifle in hand and the scope mounted. He was peering through the scope, drawing a bead on a knothole, and didn't hear me coming until I'd already entered.

He lowered my rifle, looked like a boy caught stealing tobacco, then shot a feeble, guilty grin at me. His eyes, I noted, were slightly bleary.

"Well . . . hello, Jed. Where you been?"

"Out, doing deputy work. I managed to keep a man from getting shot. What are you doing with my rifle?"

"Just looking at it, that's all."

"You've got the scope on it."

"Well . . . yeah." He quickly began removing the scope and preparing to put the rifle away. "So how'd you keep somebody from getting shot?"

"Never mind. Amos, I don't want you to get out that scope again. And I sure don't want it mounted on that rifle."

He quickly took the scope off the rifle. "Aw, now Jed, I was just—"

"I don't use that scope. That scope has a . . . significance to me. It's not to be used, ever."

"Then why the hell do you keep it?"

"Personal reasons. And nobody but me is to ever touch that scope."

"Now, Jed! Lord have mercy! What kind of nonsense is that?"

I snatched the scope from his hand. "You knew already that I don't want people handling that scope. And why were you looking at my rifle?"

"Because it's a good rifle. I like rifles. I never had a scope in my life, and I wanted to look through that one just to see how it looks."

"Well, now you know." I paused, feeling a little embarrassed because I knew my attitude was odd and hard to understand by anyone not living inside my skin. "It's the war, Amos. It puts burdens on men that are hard to carry, and it seems you can't cast them off. And everyone carries them in different ways."

Broughton was still annoyed at me, and he was a little drunk as well. On a more sober occasion he probably would have kept his mouth shut, but today he went on: "You know, Jed, sometimes you can be a tiring man. Everything with you goes back to the war. The book you wrote, the way you carry this rifle around, this fool thing of keeping your rifle scope but refusing to look through it . . . there's no sense in all that."

"What about you, Amos? You still carry the war around with you too. You can't even bring yourself to read more than two pages of my book because of the memories and so on."

"That's right. But there's nothing nonsenselike about that. But if I carried that book around every-where with me, even though I can't bear to read it and can't stand the memories it brought back, then that would be nonsense. Just like you and this scope."

My temper was up and I wanted to lash back at him—but the truth is, he'd just made a good point. I suppose it did make little sense to carry that scope, even that rifle, around with me. Yet I couldn't conceive of parting with them.

Human nature took over. I sought to turn the attention away from my own oddities and back toward Amos. "How about you, Amos?" I asked. "Is it your own memory of the war that makes you drink?"

"I don't drink."

"I saw the whiskey bottle in your saddlebag just now, Amos."

"You're poking through my possessions?"

"Odd question, coming from a man who I caught with my rifle and scope in hand."

"Your rifle and rifle scope have been locked up in the gun cabinet in my office! I have a right to use that cabinet! You do not have a right to look through my saddlebags. That's private property!"

"Then don't leave your private property with the flap hanging open and the bottle clearly visible."

"That whiskey is there because I use it to purify wounds," he said.

"What kind of wounds? Bodily . . . or the kind that the war leaves inside you?"

Something snapped. Broughton lifted his finger and aimed it at my nose. "Listen to me, Jed. You're a good friend. . . . Even though we've been separated since I saw you hauled away from Andersonville among a pile of dead men, I've always thought of you as like a brother to me, because of the experiences we had together. And I know the war, and Andersonville, both left their ghosts to haunt you . . . but what you've done with them ghosts, Jed, is just feed them. Make them stronger. Writing about it . . . traveling around talking to folks about the things that happened to their kin and loved ones in that hellhole . . . you're just keeping the ghosts alive."

"I don't think so."

"Well, I do. You know what I believe should be done with them ghosts? Kill them! Get rid of them!"

"How do you do that?"

He paused. "Lot of different ways. Depending what the ghost is . . . or who it is."

"What are you talking about?"

"Just that sometimes there's ghosts that are so bad that there's only one way to rid yourself of them, and that's to kill them. Kill them dead."

"Tell me what you mean by that."

"I've said enough."

"No. Tell me what that meant!"

He shook his head, turned and walked out of the office.

Feeling bad about the entire sequence of events that had just transpired, I put the rifle and scope back in the case and locked it away again in the rifle cabinet.

The night duty this time around fell to Reid. He came in and found me writing on my pad back in the little jailer's room. He was a confident fellow, new to this town and this particular job but not to the work of a lawman. We talked briefly. I related my story about the Grays, the shotgun, and the barn loft, getting a good laugh out of Reid—and he went on his way, ready to patrol out on Bull Creek Avenue.

There was a prisoner back in the cells, just a drunk who was sleeping it off and would be freed come morning. The jail was quiet except for his snoring and the whistle of the Kansas wind around the eaves. The words flowed easily tonight, not yet part of a coherent, connected story, just a piece that one day would be, if I was lucky.

I woke up still in my chair. It was about two in the morning, and now two prisoners snored in the back. Reid hadn't bothered to wake me when he brought him in, so I figured it was another drunk. I got up, went back to the cells and looked in. A stranger, reeking of alcohol, snoring on his bunk.

Back in the front office, I noticed that the rifle cabinet was ajar. Right away I saw that my rifle case was not where it had been before. I went to it, picked it up, felt the weight of the rifle still in it and the stiffness of the scope in its own holder.

Seeing the cabinet unlocked had led me to a quick suspicion: Broughton had taken my rifle and scope. Now I felt ashamed at the suspicion. Probably Reid had simply gotten some ammunition out of the cabinet and had failed to lock it. I'd say something to him so he'd not forget again.

Locking the cabinet, I returned to my room and lay down on my bunk, falling quickly asleep again.

I awakened from a dead sleep to a hammering on my window. Sitting up, I reached by instinct for the pistol hanging in its holster from the back of the chair beside my cot, then peered out to see the face of a frantic-looking stranger. I don't think he could see that I held a pistol, because he didn't back away.

"Deputy!" he called in through the glass. "Come quick! There's trouble on Bull Creek Avenue!"

Reid was working tonight; I wondered if the trouble was going on in his absence, or if he was caught in the midst of it. Either way, I had to respond. I leaped up, dressed fast, checked my pistol, and strapped on my gun belt. I was out the door in less than two minutes, the stranger waiting for me there.

"What's the trouble?" I asked him.

"That new deputy . . . they'll kill him, sure as anything!"

Something cold crawled down my backbone. "Is he hurt?"

"He may be by now . . . I ran as fast as I could to get here."

No time for a horse. We ran together toward Bull Creek Avenue. "Who's giving him the problem?" I asked.

"Cleve Miller."

"Miller . . . any relation to—"

"Yes," the man cut in, anticipating the question. "His cousin. He's drunk and vowing vengeance on the law in Starnes, and I think he's determined enough to get it."

"In a saloon?"

"The Big Gate."

I redoubled my speed and left the man behind. Rounding onto Bull Creek Avenue, I noted right away a crowd pressing against the open front door, pushing in as if they were giving away free drinks inside.

I reached the boardwalk but was blocked from entrance by the crowd. From inside the saloon I heard shouts and hoots, and the sound of smashing glass and splintering wood.

"Clear out! Sheriff's deputy!" I hollered at the row of backs in front of me. No one responded.

"Move!" I yelled, right into one man's ear. He glanced around, glaring at me, then ignored me again.

Grabbing him by the collar, I yanked him back and off the boardwalk, sending him stumbling into the street. The man before him got similar treatment while I elbowed a third in the side, all the while shouting out my official status. One man I shoved grabbed me by the shoulder, roughly, and I turned and drove a fist into his bulbous nose. It would now be even larger come morning. He grunted and fell away from me, knocking down another man and actually helping clear the way a little.

The last man blocking the door was a little fellow, and I simply ran over him. Breaking into the saloon, I saw Reid, his holster empty, his clothing tattered, his body postured into a boxing stance, his nose bloody. A big fellow, somewhere between 200 and 250 pounds, was moving in on him, swinging fists that looked as big as Reid's head. Reid ducked one blow, took a second in a grazing fashion that did no harm, then a third at just enough of an angle to save him from being downed.

I drew my pistol to fire into the ceiling, then remembered there were rooms upstairs. So I lowered my aim and fired at the back wall. People on that side of the room yelped and ducked.

My shot didn't even earn me a glance from Cleve Miller. He advanced in again on Reid, still swinging, and this time caught Reid a blow on the side of the head that was forceful enough to knock him to his side on the dirty saloon floor.

I leveled my pistol on Miller and ordered him to desist. He turned, glared at me, then did something that actually embarrassed me a bit: with one big swipe he pulled the pistol from my hand and tossed it to the far side of the bar.

Good Lord, this man was good. And too drunk to have any common sense or caution.

"Finger shooter!" he hollered at me, confusing me until I realized he'd recognized me as the man who'd shot the finger off his late cousin. "Finger shooter hisself!"

He lost interest in Reid and came at me instead. I ducked his first punch, lowered my shoulder and rammed hard into his middle. It was like trying to tackle a deep-rooted tree. He staggered back only a couple of steps, then grabbed me, lifted me, and literally threw me to the floor.

"I'll tear me off a finger to match the one you shot off poor Jimmy!"

He stumped toward me. I kicked my feet up and caught him in the crotch. His eyes bugged and he staggered back. Leaping to my feet, I moved in and gave him four quick blows to the face, one on the chin, three on the nose. He went down on his rump. I spun, bringing out my foot, and caught him in the ear, knocking him to the side and out cold.

The crowd booed. This was not a bunch to take the side of law enforcement.

Reid was up, looking worn-out and battered. "I'd have finished him if you hadn't butted in," he said.

"No doubt about it," I replied, heading for the bar, which I leaped. My pistol was still where it had landed, which surprised me. I guess the fight had been too interesting to allow anyone time to sneak over and steal it.

"Should we take him in?" Reid asked, nodding at Cleve Miller's bulky form on the floor.

"We'd have to carry him."

Reid looked at the big mass of deadweight humanity. His nose dripped blood across his lips, but he ignored it. "I think he's been punished enough."

"Me too. Where's your pistol?"

"Flung into the corner like yours was."

"Somebody return that pistol!" I hollered at the crowd.

No reaction. That pistol was as gone as the third century.

"Let's vacate the premises," I suggested.

Reid did not argue. We left the place with the crowd hissing and cussing at us. A crying saloon girl was kneeling beside Cleve, caressing his meaty head and alternately wailing over him and cursing at me.

"Thanks for showing up," Reid said when we were on down the street. "How'd you know?"

"A man came and fetched me. Don't know who he was."

"God bless him. That fellow's a Miller, you know."

"Yeah. And now we've got even more reason for the Miller clan to hold warm and affectionate feelings toward the Bleeker County sheriff's office."

"And you in particular. You whipped him. Shamed him. He'll not forget it."

"No, I suppose he won't."

It worried me more than I was willing to let Reid see.

"Come on," I said. "Let's go find something to stop that nosebleed of yours."

⇥ 16 ⇤

THE WOMAN AT THE DOOR BORE A RESEMBLANCE TO someone I knew, but I couldn't immediately make the connection. I'd been up an hour and had just turned loose the two drunks from the back. Reid had left a note on the desk telling me that the man he'd locked up needed nothing more than to get sober again, then could go.

The jail was empty now; I was eating a breakfast of cold biscuits, molasses, and coffee.

"Are you Jed Wells?" she said, and as soon as I heard her voice I knew she was surely the mother of Mark Taylor Smith from the newspaper.

"I am, ma'am. Come in."

She had red eyes and a worried manner. I had the impression she probably had not slept. She came in nervously, looking around in a way that told me she'd never been here before. I motioned toward a chair and she didn't seem to notice.

"Coffee, ma'am?"

"No, thank you. Mr. Wells, I'm Lucretia Smith.

My son is Mark Smith, who is with the local newspaper."

"I've met him."

"I know. He talked a lot about you. He said you wrote books. He is very impressed with you. Mark always tries to hide it when he's impressed with people, but I can always tell."

"I'm flattered he feels that way."

"Is he here?"

"No, ma'am."

"Oh. Oh. I was hoping he was here with you. He told me, you see, that he was going to come see you yesterday, and take you with him to talk to somebody who was going to give him a big story to write for the newspaper. Something very important and secret that had Mark very excited."

"He did come by, ma'am, and invited me to go along. I had other duties and declined."

"Oh." She looked away from me, even more worried now.

"Is something wrong, Mrs. Smith?"

"Mark hasn't come home. He was going to be home last night, he told me, but he never came. I sat up all night waiting for him, and he never came."

It seemed to fit a fellow like Smith that he still lived at home and still had a mother that doted over him. But she had a right to be concerned, given what Smith had been going to do.

"All I know is that he said the story had to do

with the Reverend Edward Killian. The camp meeting preacher."

"Oh . . . oh, yes. He's been talking a lot about him lately. Mark believes there is something bad about him."

"Did he tell you who he was going to talk to?"

"Yes. A man named Hamm. Something Hamm. I think maybe it was Morgan Hamm. Or Monroe Hamm."

"Hamm. That helps a lot. That gives me a name I can ask about. Did he say where he was to meet Hamm?"

"No. I have no idea of that."

"Well, it couldn't have been too far away. He was on his way to meet the fellow when he came by, so I figure it was probably somewhere within fairly quick reach of Starnes. Maybe somewhere right here in town."

She said, "I'm afraid. What if someone has hurt him?"

"Has he ever stayed out like this before?"

"No. No. Mark gets sleepy by eleven o'clock. He always is in bed before midnight."

"Don't be offended by this question, Mrs. Smith. Does he drink, or gamble, or have a lady friend?"

"No. Mark is a fine Christian boy. And he has no lady friends . . . there are just no women around here worthy of him, you know. There are so many women who would love to get their hooks into him, but he's very particular."

"Of course." What she'd just said would have been very funny in slightly different circumstances. But it wasn't hard to keep a straight face just now: I too was concerned about what had happened to Smith.

"Ma'am, I'm sure he's fine," I said with much more conviction than I felt. "I'll make you a promise. I'll ask around about him and see if I can find out where he might have gone or who he spoke to. I'll even ride out to the Killian camp meeting site and see if he might have gone there." Given what the topic of his meeting was, I doubted the interview had taken place at the camp meeting site. But I might at least find a lead there on this Hamm fellow.

She still looked horrifically worried, but I sensed I had lightened her burden just a little. "Thank you. Thank you so much, Mr. Wells," she said.

"Just doing what a deputy should, ma'am."

She told me where the Smiths lived. I already knew the location of the newspaper office. Mark's father ran the place, but according to Mrs. Smith was not worried about Mark's absence. He'd told her the boy had probably finally become man enough to spend a night down on Bull Creek Avenue, and that it was about time he did. A man should be a man, he said. Especially when he was young and his passions were high.

It was easy to see where Mark Taylor Smith developed his swaggering attitude about what was manly. I was willing to bet the senior Smith smoked cigars and strutted around, his son imitating him because he thought that was how a real man acted.

"Please let me know anything you find, as quickly as you can," she said.

"I will, ma'am. I promise."

The camp meeting site was visible from more than a mile away. Killian had selected an excellent location, a flat expanse watered by a pure spring and shaded here and there by trees. He'd been at this locale for many days, and it showed in the trampled, grassless earth and the big collection of wagons, tents, and temporary arborlike shelters all around the stage area.

No preaching was under way at the moment. People were cooking meals, fetching water from the spring, washing out clothes in the same. Children ran about, playing and laughing. Quite a few folks, caught up in the religious power of the meeting, were studying their Bibles. A woman's voice, singing an old hymn, carried on the breeze, rising and falling with it.

I admired the setup. Killian's people had developed a very systematic and effective way of setting up mobile camp meetings. The stage itself was a large wagon that carried the pieces of its own roof, which was designed to be set up easily, the pieces simply sliding together and not requiring any nailing. Even the cross-shaped pulpit had a little recess into which its base fit, sturdy and snug.

I rode past a row of wooden outhouses on wheels, sat in place over a latrine trench and marked for male or female use. Never before had I seen rolling outhouses. A clever idea indeed. Somewhere among the ranks of Killian's small staff was someone with the soul of an inventor and engineer.

Out behind the main part of the camp, I discovered something that looked something like one of those rolling Gypsy wagon communities, but without the European impression. These were the homes of Killian and his entourage—cleverly designed wagons that were small homes in themselves. Most were small indeed, chimneyed boxes built on wagon beds and only big enough for a bunk, probably a little table and a couple of chairs, maybe a storage closet or shelf of some kind, and a metal stove, probably tiny. But the one that I assumed was Killian's was much larger. It would take a team of horses to pull this rolling residence—it was narrow but long, with a portable block of heavy wood steps set in front of the door that penetrated one wall. It had several windows with curtains hanging inside, even a slightly pitched roof with metal shingles. I'd seen entire families accommodated by cabins smaller than Killian's home on wheels. I sat astride my horse, letting it nip at the grass while I admired the place.

Some distance away I saw a corral made of posts that stood on bases, with multiple strands of strong rope serving for fencing. I rode over close and examined a light but serviceable stable that stood beside the corral. It was made of timbers cleverly jointed and bolted together. This thing could be taken apart or put together in less than an hour, and hauled about in collapsed form on a wagon when the camp meeting was on the move.

All in all, it was a remarkable and revelatory thing to see, a minor marvel of the frontier. Edward Killian and his group had turned the old American institution of the camp meeting into something very efficient, very portable, very impressive. These folks knew what they were doing.

Yet as I looked at it all, I wondered what kind of life it would be to spend all one's time living in a box on the back of a wagon, moving from backwater town to backwater town, spending every night involved in religious meetings, hearing the same preacher give what were probably the same sermons, the same prayers. . . .

A great spiritual devotion would be required of those who accepted such a life. Unless, of course, the cynical Mark Taylor Smith was right and this was all a front for crime, with Killian or at least some of his staff seeking treasures that were lodged somewhere other than heaven.

As I circled the camp and took it all in, smelling the wood smoke from the campfires of the faithful, seeing the tents and wagons, watching the playing children and hearing the occasional barking dogs, Smith's allegations seemed hard to believe. He was a cynical little man, probably with a worldview much different than that of Killian or those who came to hear him preach. He'd be the kind to assume the worst about a traveling preacher, and I knew already from its treatment of Amos Broughton that his family newspaper wasn't devoted to fairness in journalism.

So organized was this camp meeting that they'd actually laid out the campsite itself with little crisscrossing avenues, not graveled or paved, of course, just open strips of ground running in both directions through the camp. No randomness here! The camp meeting faithful actually occupied squares of land that were the equivalent of makeshift town blocks. There were even signs set up on the various avenues—Glory Street, Bible Avenue, Heavenly Way. I had to grin to myself at the cornpone quality of the signage, yet for what and where it was, and the purpose it served, it was rather clever and provided a structure and organization to the camp that was quite efficient.

I dismounted, tied my horse to a sapling by the spring, and walked into the camp itself, traversing it by way of those "streets" and "avenues." Most people paid me little heed; others nodded hellos, and I tipped my hat to the women and girls. The assorted cooking smells made me hungry. It came to mind that this compacted but organized encampment was everything that Andersonville had not been. This place was here for the good of those it contained; it spoke of health and salvation and life, all the things Andersonville had not been. I found it a pleasant place to be.

But there was, of course, a serious purpose in my being here. As I walked about, I looked for Smith, thinking that he might have made himself part of the camp as a part of his journalistic investigation. I saw no sign of him, though. I worked my way up and down every avenue twice, then gave up looking for him.

Passing around the stage, which I noticed only then was outfitted with a small piano—these folks had thought of everything—I headed back into the community of little residential wagons clustered around Killian's bigger one. My eye was out for either Killian himself or one of his workers; I had a question or two about the Hamm fellow Smith was to have interviewed. Had there ever really been such a man affiliated with the Killian organization?

A door on the back of one of the lesser wagons opened and a man emerged. He wore the black suit typical of Killian's group, but for now the jacket was missing and the tail of his white shirt hung out. He was carrying a skillet and spoon, and went to a rubbish pile and scraped grease out of the skillet, rousing interest from a nearby dog.

I walked over toward him and said hello. He looked up, startled, then grinned at me in a friendly way. " 'Morning, sir! A lovely day the Lord has given us, eh?"

"Yes indeed," I said. "Can't ask for better." I put out my hand; he transferred the spoon over into the skillet so he'd have a free hand to shake with. "My name's Wells," I said. "Jedediah Wells."

"Very pleased to meet you, sir. I'm Nathan Hardin."

"You work for the Reverend?"

"Well, as he puts it, who we really work for is the Lord . . . but he's my employer in the more wordly sense, yes."

"Well, Mr. Hardin, I work with the sheriff's office over in Bleeker County." I pulled back my vest so he could see the badge—and I swear he seemed to go a little pale as he saw it, which surprised me. "We've had a man go missing over there and I thought he might be here at the camp meeting."

"Oh?"

"Yes. His name is Smith. Mark Taylor Smith. Works at a newspaper. Sort of a short man, stocky, young. Smokes big cigars most of the time."

"I can't say I personally know anyone of that description. . . . Of course, there's a lot of people here. And every night many more come in, then go home when it's over. He could be here and I'd never know it."

"I can believe that, sir."

"Sorry I can't be of more help."

"I appreciate your time. I'll take another walk through the camp and see if I chance to spot him."

Hardin smiled; I had the impression he was not comfortable talking to somebody with a badge. Or was that just my own imagination, stirred up by what Smith had speculated about this group?

My next question, held in check for a moment or two, might give me the start of an answer. I waited until Hardin had turned and begun walking back toward his wagon, then said, "Sir . . . one more thing."

He turned. "Yes?"

"You know a man named Hamm? Morgan or Monroe Hamm, I think it is? Used to work for the Reverend Killian?"

This time there was no mistaking it. A darkness rolled across his face, a lowering of the eyebrows and tightening of the posture that was subtle but still very detectable. He glowered at me for half a moment too long, then shook his head. "Never heard of such a man," he said. "The only ham I know is the kind I just fried in this skillet."

Nodding and smiling pleasantly, I touched my hat and thanked him, then turned away.

My father had taught me early in life to trust my instincts. That counsel had served me well in life, from my days as a youthful hunter in the mountains on through my war years and my time at Andersonville, and later as a writer. My instincts right now were ringing out a warning louder than a fire wagon bell. The wild speculations of the missing Smith suddenly had a lot more credibility.

Then came one of those moments that is so perfectly timed, so telling, that one can only believe it came about by the design of some unseen force. Another wagon door opened and another man emerged, and when he came out, he looked right at me and turned as white as the wall of my grandfather's old dairy back home. We stared at each other for a long moment, my expression of surprise probably as undisguised as his, and then he turned quickly and reentered the wagon, closing the door behind him. I heard the click of a lock.

It was the same man I'd helped escape from that barn loft. No mistake. The fellow had far too distinctive an appearance for me to be in error.

Killian himself I could not judge, for I had not been around him sufficiently, but I now knew two telling things about two of his staff members: one was a liar, the other a lecher.

Smith's loco talk about Killian and his group seemed less loco by the moment.

I walked through the camp once more, looking for Smith. Nothing. Returning to my horse, I mounted up and headed back toward Bleeker County. But I would make this journey again today.

Now that I knew something about the kind of men Killian had surrounded himself with, it was time to learn something more about Killian himself.

Tonight, I'd be back to hear a little preaching.

I was halfway back to Starnes when I saw none other than Leroy Fletch riding toward me. He wasn't galloping his horse, but he was pushing it hard. He seemed surprised to encounter me, but did not act like a man with much time for pleasantries and small talk.

"Hello, Jed," he said, talking faster than usual. "I'm going over to Wallen . . . there's been a bank robbery there and my cousin was stabbed."

Wallen . . . a little community in Russell County that was just over the line from Bleeker County, and slightly to the north, if my memory of the big regional map in the sheriff's office was correct.

"Is he alive?"

"Yes, but it was a serious wound. I got a wire about it a little while ago."

"He's a clerk?"

"No. A night guard. The robbery happened last night."

I was thoughtful a moment. "Maybe about the time the camp meeting would have been going on?"

"Well, yes. I suppose so. What's that got to do with it?"

"Maybe nothing. Look, can I go with you?"

"Suit yourself. But I'm moving fast."

"Let's go."

The bank at Wallen had not opened for business and probably would not do so that day. We arrived to find the local town marshal and county sheriff in conference outside the bank, talking to a man in a suit who had the look of a banker.

Leroy had officially ended his status as a Bleeker County deputy the prior day, but the Russell County sheriff apparently didn't know it. He knew Leroy and approached him with his hand out.

"Leroy, I knew you'd come. Good to see you, but sorry it has to be under these circumstances."

"I appreciated you taking time to wire me. How's Martin? Where is he?"

"Martin was cut pretty deeply, but the doctor has worked with him and is very optimistic about him. He'll make it. He's at home right now, I think. The doc saw no need for him to be put up in the infirmary." The sheriff looked over at me, glancing down at the badge on my chest. He put his hand out again. "John Pride, county sheriff. Don't think we've met."

I shook his hand. "Jed Wells. I'm a temporary deputy, working for Amos Broughton."

"Jed Wells ... I've heard that name. Oh, yes! Same name as some bluebelly scribbler who wrote a bunch of lies and exaggerations about Camp Sumter down in Georgia. Just a bunch of libels against the Confederacy."

I glanced at Leroy, sending a message with my eyes: don't say anything. "I heard about that fellow," I said. Some arguments just weren't worth getting into.

"Sheriff, who robbed your bank here?" I asked.

"We don't know. Martin—that's Leroy's cousin, as you probably know—was the only one who saw them, but it was dark and he never got a good look. Dark clothing, he said. Faces blackened up with charcoal. He thought they were Negroes at first, until he struck one of them and the charcoal rubbed off on his hand."

"So this was a break-in after hours," Leroy said.

"That's right. Marshal Kaley and myself are working together to investigate it, and the federal marshal should show up here sometime today, but there's not a lot to go on. Hell, me and Kaley both were down at that camp meeting while the robbery took place. Makes me feel a fool, really. But when you get crowds that size together, you have to be there to keep a watch on things. People get worked up at camp meetings, you know. There can be fights and such. I know a man who lost an eye at a camp meeting. Got it gouged out by a madwoman."

"So we'll probably never know who stabbed Martin," Leroy said.

"Probably not. But thanks to Martin, they didn't get as much as they would have. After they stabbed him, they must have panicked, because they dropped two bags of money on their way out and didn't come back to get them. Maybe you Bleeker County boys can keep an eye out in case they show up in your parts."

"I'll have to leave that to Jed here," Leroy said. "I've left the sheriff's office."

"You're joshing me!"

"No. I'm done with it. Other pursuits now," Leroy said.

Sheriff Pride paused, weighed his words, then said, "How's Amos Broughton doing?"

Leroy also paused before he spoke. "Not the best, in my opinion. He's the reason I'm leaving."

Pride did not seem surprised. "Last time I saw Amos, I believe he was drunk," he said. "It was at the camp meeting . . . I don't recall which night."

More confirmation. Amos was doing the very things he denied—drinking and loitering about the camp meeting.

"I'm going to see my cousin," Leroy announced. "Jed, you coming?"

"I may just walk around the town here a little," I said. "Pretty town you've got here, Sheriff."

"We like it." He turned and went back to his conference with the town marshal.

It was just like Smith had said it would be. Unlikely as his theory had sounded, the timing of this robbery fit perfectly with what he'd predicted. Killian was about to uproot his camp meeting and move it to Bleeker County, and sure enough, a robbery had occurred.

Who'd have ever thought up such a scheme? A camp meeting preacher and his entourage using religious fervor to draw out the faithful from small communities, distract law enforcement officers . . . then striking the local bank or freight office just before they move on, to be out of sight and out of mind.

It was a wild scheme, no doubt about it. But its very audaciousness was what made it work. Nobody would suspect preachers and their assistants of being criminals. There was a natural human tendency to take professed men of God at their word.

But I knew from my experience on the Gray farmstead that at least one of Killian's assistants was no man of God, not unless dallying around behind a smokehouse with a local farm girl was part of being holy. And I was certain that the other Killian associate I'd talked to today at the camp site had lied to me about not knowing the Hamm fellow Smith had gone to meet.

Killian's people were not the kind of men they pretended to be. Very likely Killian was no different than they.

Then my mind flashed the image of Killian's face as he prayed over me after the train accident. That cloth falling away, the scars revealed . . .

And again there was that sense of distant, nearly forgotten familiarity. Something about his face . . . or was it the scars themselves? Something I should know but didn't . . .

It couldn't be. I'd remember something as distinctive as a forehead scarred with the shape of three crosses, if ever I'd seen such a sight before.

Roaming the streets of this town, which was not nearly as pretty as I'd told the sheriff it was, I struggled to put together pieces that refused to fit.

A door marked PHYSICIAN'S OFFICE opened just as I passed it, and a man in a doctor's frock stained with red and rusty streaks came out, nearly bumping into me.

"Pardon me," he snapped, then pushed on past.

Something on my arm caught my eye. Blood! Good Lord! The doctor had rubbed blood off on me when he bumped into me! Disgusted, I pulled out a handkerchief and dabbed it off as best I could.

He noted what I was doing out of the corner of his eye, paused, and said, "Sorry about that." He noted my badge, seemed ready to say something more, but instead just mumbled something under his breath and headed across the street. He entered a café.

I'd turned to continue my walk when a sound reached my ear. It came out the open window of the doctor's office: a human voice, muttering something in a plaintive, childish way, as if through tears.

I knew that voice right away. Going to the open window, I found that the curtains inside were closed. A breeze moved them, though, and I was presented the undesirable spectacle of Mark Taylor Smith pulling on his trousers. He wept and muttered as he did so, and moved slowly, like a very old man.

"Smith!" I exclaimed.

He yelled in what seemed terror, twisted about with his pants only halfway up, and tripped himself. He collapsed onto his rump and yelled again.

Wincing, I quickly entered the untended doctor's office and then the little side room where Smith was dressing. He had scooted back into a corner with his pants still tangled around his legs, and had the expression and manner of a man expecting an executioner.

"Don't worry, Smith, it's just me," I said. Relief

and shock spread across his face. "Where have you been? Your people are worrying about you."

"You came . . . what are you . . . how did you find . . . how did you know . . ."

He was sputtering along like a faulty steam engine, his face red and streaked with tears, his hair wild, his clothing disheveled. His shirt was hanging partly open, and past the bulge of his ample belly I noted a bandage on his side. There was blood on his shirt too. Dried and crusty.

"Smith, compose yourself," I said, reaching down to him. "Let me help you up."

He clasped my hand and I helped him come to his feet. He winced as he rose, then quickly checked his bandage.

"I was afraid I'd broken it open again when I fell," he said, voice still cracking.

"What's wrong?"

"I just got hurt a little."

"What kind of hurt?"

"I don't want to talk about it."

He would not look me in the eye, just stared at his bandage. His left hand came up and he wiped away a tear.

"You've obviously been through something that has scared you, Smith. What's wrong?"

"I don't want to talk about it!"

"Did you meet Hamm?"

He looked at me then, surprised to hear me speak

a name he hadn't told me. "Where'd you hear that name?" he asked.

"Your mother told me. She came to me in hope I would know where you'd gone. She was worried when you didn't come home."

He looked down, embarrassed, maybe, by having his mother come looking for him like he was still a twelve-year-old boy. Just now, frankly, he came across as little more than a boy. No swagger or floating smoke rings.

"Did you meet Hamm?" I asked again.

"I don't want to talk about it."

"Why? Seriously, Smith, what's wrong? Is that a gunshot wound you have?"

"No."

"A stab?"

"I said I don't want to talk about it!" Growing angry now. Hostile.

I nodded slowly, mystified. "Smith," I said slowly, "did you know that the bank here was broken into last night?"

"I don't know anything about anything."

"It was broken into, just like you said, and a night guard was stabbed. By chance he happens to be a cousin of our friend Leroy."

He looked at me from the sides of his eyes. "Is that why you came?"

"In fact, I came to this county both to visit Killian's camp meeting site and ask around a little about this Hamm fellow you were to meet. Your mother said he was once an employee of Killian's, and I thought perhaps I could be steered toward him and find you in the process. On the way home, I encountered Leroy riding toward Wallen because he'd gotten news of his cousin's stabbing. I came on into town with him . . . and lo and behold, I find Mr. Smith! It almost seems providential."

He said nothing, gave no reaction. He was finding something very intriguing about an inkwell on a little desk in the corner.

I let the clock on the wall tick off a few seconds, then said, "Smith, I don't know what has happened to you. But I know you were right about your prediction of a crime in this vicinity before Killian's camp meeting moved on. I believe that you have a stab wound in your side, and I know the guard at the bank was also stabbed. Any connection between the two events, I don't know. Clearly you're not going to tell me anything about Hamm, or whether you saw him. Can you tell me whether you intend to write anything for your newspaper?"

He curled his lip and gave his head a quick shake. "I don't have anything to write," he said.

"Can you tell me why you didn't come home? Your mother will ask you that same question, you know."

"I was hiding. That's all I'm going to say."

My suspicion was that Mrs. Smith would get a

lot further with her son than I was. Perhaps I could talk to her later.

"Are you going home?" I asked.

"Yes."

"Good. Your mother is very concerned about you." I paused, then added, "Your father too, I'm sure."

I didn't like Smith, but I must say that the look he gave me when I mentioned his father was one of the most heartbreaking I'd ever seen on the face of a man. A volume of secret family history was spoken in that single glance, a father too overbearing and distant, a son desperately seeking to please him . . . it could be read in that single, sad glance. Right then I pitied Smith deeply, despite his bad journalism, his unfairness to Broughton, his childishness, his swagger, his big cigar and drifting smoke rings.

Smith finished dressing. I went into the outer office, lingering there in hope that he would emerge in a calmer state and decide to share some information with me. He was indeed calmer when he came out, and more like his old self, but he still was not inclined to be forthcoming with anything helpful.

He looked me in the eye this time. "This whole business has not gone as I hoped. I've got nothing to tell you and nothing to write for the newspaper. I got hurt a little, but I'll be all right. I don't know about the bank robbery or the guard getting stabbed, and I'm not interested in Killian anymore. I'm going home now. Good-bye."

He walked out, pulling a cigar from an inside pocket of his vest. It was crushed, and he tossed it onto the porch in disgust, turned a corner, and went out of sight.

THOUGH SMITH WAS ON HIS WAY BACK HOME, I thought it appropriate to ease his mother's worries as soon as possible, and thus had a telegram wired to her from the local station. MARK FOUND SAFE STOP NOW ON WAY HOME STOP.

Beyond that, I'd leave the details to him. He could explain the bloody shirt and the bandage, if he chose and as he chose.

My mind raced, trying to come up with a theory about what had happened. The simplest option was that Smith had met Hamm, offended him in some way—nothing hard to believe about that— and Hamm had stabbed him and fled. Of course, I didn't know for sure that Smith had a stab wound, but the placement of it, the type of bandage, and his reaction to my mention of stabbing made me relatively certain.

Another possibility was that someone from Killian's group had somehow learned that Hamm was about to tell his story to a newspaperman, and had attacked either Smith alone, or Smith and Hamm together. If so, what had happened to Hamm? Where was he now?

I doubted I'd find out much from Smith himself. His mother, however, was another matter. He might tell her more than he'd tell me . . . and thanks to the telegram I'd just sent, she might feel enough sense of gratitude for my efforts to tell me what her son told her.

Meanwhile, I was more eager than ever to personally witness a Killian camp meeting. Whatever the answers were, they lay there.

I roamed the streets a few minutes more, trying to put the pieces together. Passing the café again, the doctor emerged. He didn't look so rushed and ill-tempered now that he had a meal under his belt.

"Hello, sir," I said as he neared.

"Hello."

"Pardon me . . . might I speak to you a moment?"

He gave me the suspicious look of a man accustomed to being collared for free medical advice. "What is it?"

"I wanted to thank you for the help you gave a friend of mine. Mark Smith."

"Oh. The crier with the stab wound."

"Uh . . . yes."

"Let me ask you something, sir: how do you know I treated him?"

"I heard him through your office window and recognized his voice. So I went in to see him. He's gone now."

"Gone where?"

"Back home."

The doctor looked at me downright harshly. "Who are you and what do you know about Mr. Smith's stabbing?"

"Only what he told me, which wasn't much. As for who I am, my name is Jed Wells. I'm a deputy over in Bleeker County." I flashed my badge.

The doctor wasn't impressed. "Jed Wells, eh? Interesting. There's some politician with that name. Or a writer."

"That's me."

The doctor swore and aimed his forefinger at the end of my nose. "Yeah, and I'm King George the Forty-third. You stay right where you are, sir. I'm going to fetch the law. You're no 'friend' of Mr. Smith. You're the man who stabbed him!"

"Absolutely not, sir. But if you want to consult the law, let's go together."

That threw him a little, but he accepted the invitation. "Come on, then. I know where they are. The bank was robbed last night."

"I know about that. I suppose you think I did that too."

"You never know."

We found Pride and Kaley still at the bank. The

doctor walked up and interrupted their conversation.

"Pardon me, Pride . . . I got a man here who claims to be a Bleeker County deputy."

The sheriff looked at me, then back at the doctor. "What of it?"

"He says his name is Jed Wells."

"So it is. And he is a Bleeker County deputy."

The doctor was struck silent a moment. "Well, you better be sure of it, because he was asking suspicious questions about a stabbing case I treated."

"Stabbing case? The guard?"

"No. There was a second case. A fellow named Smith from Bleeker County."

"Why didn't you report it? You should report stabbing incidents to the law."

"I'm reporting it now."

"Where's the victim?"

"Gone," I said. "His name is Mark Smith. He's a newspaperman over in Starnes."

"Oh, yeah. The newspaper that's trying to put Broughton out of office."

"That's the one."

"Who stabbed him?"

"He wouldn't say. I questioned him."

The doctor didn't look happy to see me vindicated. "This man walked into my office when it was vacant," he said. "I don't like that."

"It wasn't vacant," I said. "Smith was in there.

But he's gone now. He refused to answer my questions and headed back toward Starnes. He's scared to death of something."

"Anything else, Doc?" Kaley said.

"I suppose not." He turned and stalked off.

"Uppity doctor you've got here," I commented.

"I despise the son of a gun myself," Pride said. "Do you think this Smith might have been stabbed in the bank robbery?"

"I don't think so. He'd come here to meet a man named Hamm, either Monroe or Morgan Hamm. I don't really know the first name. Hamm was going to be a source for a story. But now Smith says there'll be no story, won't talk about Hamm, won't say who stabbed him or why. He's on his way back to his mother right now, acting like a scared child."

"And no Hamm?"

"Not that I know of."

"We'll keep a lookout for this Hamm fellow."

"He used to work for the Rev Killian," I said. "I understand he left on bad terms." I chose not to say more. I had nothing more than Smith's unverified word that Killian or his entourage might be behind the bank robbery. Sure, I knew one was a fornicator and another a probable liar, but that was hardly evidence

"Killian . . . there's a man I'll be glad to see go," Kaley said. "The man raises a lot of questions for me. . . . Sometimes I don't even know what the questions are, but there's something there I just don't trust."

I almost spoke up about Smith's suspicions. But I didn't.

Leroy returned half an hour later, a much calmer man than before. His cousin was in no danger, and Leroy was ready to go back to Starnes.

"You coming?" he asked me.

"No. I think I'll stay around for preaching to-night."

"Why? Killian's coming to Bleeker County in the next couple of days."

"Yeah, but I want to see him tonight. I'm the same as Marshal Kaler. . . . There's something about Killian that raises questions for me. I want to see if I can start to find some answers."

Darkness fell slowly, and the camp meeting stirred to life like some nocturnal beast. I positioned my-self in an empty place along "Glory Street," on a slight rise that gave me a good view of the crowd, the perimeter, and the pulpit area.

Initially I found it somewhat exciting to be part of the massive meeting. More people showed up the nearer the starting time drew, every spot filling, the quarters becoming closer, closer. . . .

I felt an inexplicable, growing nervousness. My breathing became slightly labored, and despite a cool breeze, I was sweating.

Music began. A loud piano on the stage began hammering out a hymn; a man in one of those black suits typical of Killian's group stood on the stage, waving his hand and leading the music. It swelled to the heavens, a bit ragged and disjointed, but pleasing in its own way. I watched the song-leader and relaxed, but when I looked across the assemblage of people, that strange tension resumed.

I began to wonder if I was suddenly going loco.

The music went on for twenty minutes, and then, almost like a phantom, Killian appeared. I honestly couldn't see where he'd come from. It was an appearance worthy of a stage magician. But showmanship was no suprise coming from a man with cross-shaped scars on his forehead that he hid behind a dark cloth.

Killian began to preach. His voice was trained and quite audible, though I was a relatively long distance away. The man knew how to project. He sounded deeper, richer in tone than he did when speaking in a close-up setting.

The sermon itself did not strike me as remarkable. The theme was forgiveness—God to man, man to man. The words themselves could have been those of any Protestant preacher, but delivered by Killian, they carried a special force. I could understand the man's success and appeal the longer I listened. And I found it difficult to hear him and believe he personally had any involvement in any crime or duplicity taking place at the hands of his associates.

I listened to Killian, then turned my attention to the crowd again. Looking across them, the crowd pressed close, tents and shanties built by those of the flock who were so faithful to Killian that they had actually taken up permanent residence for the duration of the camp meeting, I felt that strange sense of tension and even subtle despair beginning to rise again. My breathing again grew labored. I quickly looked back toward Killian again, saw his face across the mass of humanity between myself and the stage—and it was as if a hammer struck me.

For a moment I was no longer in Kansas, no longer in the midst of a camp meeting. I was instead in the midst of a familiar hell I had escaped from many years ago.

And as my chest closed up tight and sweat broke out on my brow, I stared at Killian's face and realized that it belonged there, in Andersonville. Realization overwhelmed me—I understood why he seemed familiar. I had indeed seen his face before, in Camp Sumter, another sad visage among thousands, another human phantom struggling to cling to hope.

Stricken hard by this realization, overcome by the terrifying feeling that Andersonville had arisen around me like a demonic phoenix, I scrambled toward the perimeter of the meeting ground, breaking out of the crowd and rushing into the darkness, gasping for air, bent over with my hands on my knees.

For two minutes I remained in that posture, my breathing gradually slowing, my racing heart slowing as well. And as that unexpected fit of panic passed, so also did my assurance that I had seen Killian at Andersonville. Unexpectedly, I chuckled. What a fool I was! The press of a crowd, an accidental similarity of appearance between a meeting camp and a prison camp . . . and suddenly I had thrust Killian from the present into the past, right along with myself. Even if he had been at Andersonville, would I have been able to recognize him now? The men I remembered from that place were drawn and hollow creatures, skin clinging to their bones, rags hanging on their stick-figure frames.

And there was no one with three crosses on his brow. Of that I was sure. Such a thing as that I would not have forgotten.

I looked back at the ongoing camp meeting and debated with myself whether to reenter it. No, I decided. This was enough. Perhaps I would attend again when Killian came to Bleeker County. Perhaps I would not.

In the meantime, I would consult a list I carried with me at all times. It was a document I had obtained through the federal government, which itself had obtained it as one of hundreds of thousands of records of the Confederacy seized at the end of the war. It bore the names of every known prisoner of Andersonville. If Edward Killian had been among the prisoners, his name would be on that list.

I went to my horse and mounted, ready to begin the rather long ride back to Starnes. That I was absent from the town tonight had not been problematic, or at least so I hoped; it was Broughton's night for duty.

Mounted and turning my horse toward the road that would take me to Starnes, I glanced back one last time at the camp meeting, an expanse of flickering torchlight and dark human forms out on the flatlands. Nothing like Andersonville, really. Why had it affected me so? I hoped sincerely that I was not going to become a man who could not abide a crowd, simply because of one earlier dark experience in life.

As I turned away, a rider passed between me and the assemblage. Once again my heart leaped up toward my throat as a shock of recognition struck. The form of the rider, silhouetted against the meeting ground torchlight, was that of Broughton! And he carried a long rifle.

I wheeled my horse and rode in his direction. But just as Killian had appeared on that stage so mysteriously, the rider vanished in like manner. Ridden off into the night, no doubt . . . Had it been Broughton? How could I be sure, with no more than a fleeting impression, the fast passing of a shadowed form?

But if Broughton it was, then Starnes was left unguarded by a lawman at the moment. It was Broughton's place to be there tonight.

Deciding that I had been as mistaken about the rider as I probably was about Killian and Andersonville, I rode toward Starnes, hearing the now distant voice of Killian becoming weaker and thinner the farther I rode, until at last I could hear it no more.

⇥ 18 ⇤

WHEN I ARRIVED BACK IN STARNES, BROUGHTON'S horse was not in the stable. This was in itself proof of nothing; Broughton sometimes made his patrols on horseback, especially since his wounding, or he might have been called out.

The jail was unoccupied, the office empty. Remembering that long rifle the rider had carried, I went to the rifle cabinet and unlocked it. My rifle case was still inside, and a quick check of its weight indicated the rifle was still inside. And I could feel the scope in its storage pocket.

That much at least gave me relief. I'd envisioned Broughton out there circling the camp meeting with my rifle and scope in his possession. I imagined him peering through that scope, drawing a bead on Killian as he spoke on the torchlit stage. . . .

What if Killian really had been at Andersonville? What if Broughton recognized him? Maybe he harbored some old bitterness toward Killian.

But if so, why wouldn't he tell me about it? I, of all people, would be likely to understand. I'd shared the same miseries as Amos Broughton. I would seem a natural ear for him to fill on a subject like that.

Words Broughton had spoken, seemingly insignificant at the time, came back to me, raising a chill: *If I was going to do a crime, something that would get me in trouble . . . I'd say nothing about it, not give a hint to anybody of what I was thinking. I'd make myself the last person anybody would suspect would do the act, and then, when it was done, the odds would be high that nobody would ever catch me.*

I went to my meager little store of personal possessions and removed the list of Andersonville prisoners. Lighting the lamp on the main desk, I spread the list out and scoured over it. No one named Killian.

Yet it meant little. Killian might be an assumed name. I put the list away, still feeling unsettled.

The bed was inviting to a weary man who had ridden many miles and had an active day. I crawled between the sheets and went to sleep very quickly.

The creak of the outer door being opened awakened me. Enough moonlight spilled through my window to let me see the watch beside my bed.

Four in the morning. I heard the door thump closed.

Someone moved around in the office. Rising, I opened the door of my room and stepped out. Amos Broughton, dimly visible there in the dark room, turned and looked at me.

"Well, hello, Jed!" he said. A match struck, illuminating his grinning face. He lighted the lamp and cranked it down low. "Didn't mean to wake you!"

He was drunk. Not falling down drunk, but clearly intoxicated. His speech had a certain slur, his grin a certain twist. "Have you been patrolling?" I asked.

"Yep."

"All around town, huh?"

"That's where I usually patrol. Where you been today?"

"I went over into Russell County."

"Did you? Why was that?"

"Actually, I was looking for Smith from the newspaper. He went missing for a night and his mother got worried about him."

"Did you find him?"

"I sure did. Found some other things too. I ran into Leroy. There'd been a bank robbery there, and his cousin, a guard, got stabbed by the burglars."

"Do tell! Not fatal, I hope."

"No. He'll be fine."

"Bank robbery, huh? How much they get?"

"I don't know."

"I guess Sheriff Pride is busy, then."

"He and the town marshal were waiting for the federal marshal to arrive while I was there."

"Where'd you find Smith?" Broughton pulled open a desk drawer and pulled out a cheap cigar. I caught a whiff of whiskey as he moved.

"In a doctor's office. He got himself stabbed."

"No!" Broughton fired up the cigar. "How the hell did he get stabbed?"

"He wouldn't say. He'd gone to meet a fellow and talk to him about the Rev Killian." I watched for a reaction as I said that name.

There was none. No twitch, no start, no flick of the eye. "Smith's writing about Killian, is he?"

"Not now. He told me there would be no story. He's scared to death. Whoever cut him put the fear of God in him."

"Ha!" He drew on the cigar, then ovaled his mouth and made a failed attempt to blow a smoke ring. "Never could get the hang of that," he said. "That's the one thing Smith can do well, blowing smoke rings. That and getting under folks' skin, the son of a bitch. I can see how somebody could get mad enough at that runty troublemaker to cut him."

Conversation lagged. My abandoned bed called

to me. I was about to say a good-night and return to it when he spoke again.

"Russell County, huh? So did you go to preaching while you were there?"

"Killian's camp meeting, you mean?"

"Yep."

"As a matter of fact, I did."

"Do tell!"

"That's right, I did. Didn't stay for the whole thing. For a minute, though, I thought I saw you there, Amos."

"Me? Not me. I've been patrolling all night, here in town."

"I noticed your horse had been ridden."

"I got a visitor just after midnight who called me out into the county to settle a little family problem."

"So you weren't patrolling in town all night."

"I was, except for the time I was called out."

"Where'd you go, exactly?"

"Over on Henry Creek."

"Who was it?"

"Nobody you'd know." A tension was creeping into his voice. He'd started this by asking if I'd gone to the camp meeting—a verification to me that he'd seen me there, just as I'd seen him—and now I was turning it into a cross-examination.

"I swear I saw you at the Killian meeting," I said.

"I wasn't there."

"While I was in Wallen, Sheriff Pride told me he'd seen you there the night before too."

"Hell, no!" Broughton's face went crimson and he started to make an outburst, then caught himself just in time. Swallowing, regaining control, he forced out a grin. "I swear, there's got to be somebody out there who looks like me. I hear people saying all the time they've seen me here, seen me there, when I ain't been those places."

"Speaking of looking like somebody, I thought tonight that I recognized Killian. From Andersonville."

This time Broughton failed to hide his reaction. It was subtle, just a kind of twitch, followed by a stare that lasted half a second too long. "Andersonville! You mean it?"

"I thought I recognized him. It was sort of strange, Amos. I looked at him across that crowd of people, all packed together like we used to be in the prison camp, and it was like I jumped back across the years and the miles. It was like I'd done that very thing before: looking across a crowd and seeing that same face. Then I decided I was wrong. When I got back here, I checked my list of Andersonville prisoners. No Killian."

"Funny that you'd have thought that."

"You haven't thought the same thing, have you, Amos? Does Killian remind you of anybody from Andersonville?"

"Can't say he does."

He was lying. I could smell it on him just like the whiskey. "Yeah, yeah. I guess we'd remember a man with crosses on his forehead, huh? Because that part isn't what seemed familiar to me. Just the face. But like I said, I was wrong. No Killians at the prison camp. Unless, of course, Killian is a false name."

Broughton pulled another cigar from the desk and put it in his pocket, then went through the motions of checking his pockets and so on, the acts of a man readying to leave. I don't think he liked the atmosphere my questions and comments generated. "I can't figure a preacher would lie about his name. Wouldn't be a preachery thing to do."

"Unless he was really a scroundrel. That's what Smith thinks, you know. Or at least he did. I don't know what he thinks now. He won't talk."

"Huh. Yeah. Well, got to go."

"Don't hurry off, Amos. It seems quiet tonight. Let's talk some more. Maybe about Killian."

He wheeled and looked at me, and I locked my eyes on his. More truth passed between us in that silent stare than had been conveyed in any of the cagey words passed between us so far.

"Why would I want to talk about Killian?"

It was time for total honesty. I stepped toward him. "Because I believe you know something about Killian that you aren't saying. I believe you've got

some kind of private reason to despise the man, and
I believe having him hereabouts nags at you, eats at
you, and has made you start drinking and being de-
ceitful to your wife and your friends."

"What the hell are you saying? I don't drink!"

"I smell it on you right now."

"I got whiskey spilled on me when I broke up a
brawl over on Bull Creek Avenue!"

"You didn't mention any such brawl earlier."

"Am I supposed to tell you everything I do?"

"You weren't on Bull Creek Avenue, Amos. And
you weren't out answering some call on Henry
Creek either. You were at Killian's camp meeting,
riding the perimeter out in the darkness."

"You're a damn liar! And you're calling *me* a
damn liar!"

"Callianne is worried sick about you, Amos. She
wonders what you're up to, what's eating away at
you, and she asks me about it."

"You been visiting with my wife behind my
back?"

"No. But we've run across one another, and she's
spoken to me about her concerns. They're the same
concerns I've got, Amos. And let me say this right
now: if you go back to her and give her any kind of
trouble because she's spoken to me out of love for
you, well . . . you and me will have some dealing to
do. That's all I can say."

"What the hell's wrong with you, Jed? You come

marching into town out of the blue, all the big famous writer, all the know-it-all fellow who has took the miseries we suffered and turned them into money, and now you're telling me how I'm supposed to live with my wife? You're calling me a drunk and a liar? I ought to beat the living fire out of you, Jed!"

"You're too drunk to do it, Amos."

He lunged toward me, but restrained himself. "I don't think I need you around here as a deputy no more. I think you've outstayed your welcome."

We were both angry just then. The words were coming out of me with little restraint, though a part of me wondered if I had already gone too far. I swallowed down what would have been a brutal barrage of criticism and accusations and forced myself to regain my composure. "Amos, I'm sorry if I've said things I shouldn't. I just want you to know that I'm worried about you, and your wife is worried about you . . . and I just don't know what to say or do about it. You know what, Amos? I'll just tell you straight out. Tonight, when I saw you riding around the perimeter of the camp meeting, you had a rifle. And the notion came to me that you might have it in mind to shoot the Rev. Killian. For what reason, I don't know. But the notion was there."

He gave me a look that was one of the ugliest I'd ever seen, and spoke through gritted teeth. "You're getting yourself mixed up with me," he said. "It's you who shoots people from hiding, remember? That's your role, sharpshooter. Not mine."

If he intended the words to hurt, he succeeded. "Amos," I said quietly, "I'll just leave it at this. If there's something, anything, about the Rev Killian that is making you like you've been, or about anybody or anything else, for God's sake don't close out your friends and your wife. You've already run off Leroy by how you've changed. Don't keep going that way. Tell me, or Callianne, or somebody, what's bothering you. Don't do something that you'll regret."

He didn't answer me for several moments. When he did, his voice was much quieter. "There are things a man just has to deal with himself," he said. "And he has to deal with them in his own way. You ought to understand that, Jed. It's just like you and Andersonville. You write about it, you visit folks who lost loved ones there, and tell them of their kin's fate. That's your way . . . that's how you deal with it all. Me, I can't do that. What I've got to do has to be dealt with in other ways. Maybe you'd understand, maybe you wouldn't. It don't matter either way. I still got to do my duty."

"I don't understand what you mean. Tell me straight out, Amos: do you have some intent of harming Edward Killian?"

He stared at me, then gave a cold chuckle.

"Harming Edward Killian? I'm a man of the law, Jed. I help folks. I don't harm them. I just do my duty, that's all. Just my duty. Whatever happens . . . you remember that. It's just Amos Broughton doing his duty, no different than you doing yours."

He headed out the door and into the night, leaving me wondering what had really just transpired, wondering if he had murder on his mind . . . wondering if I was still a deputy of Bleeker County. I suspected I was not. He'd seemingly invited me to leave.

Returning to my bed, I tried to go to sleep again, but it was hopeless. After half an hour I rose, took up pad and pencil, and began to write. But the words made little sense, had no direction.

I put down my pencil, bowed my head and prayed for my friend Amos Broughton.

LUCRETIA SMITH SHOWED UP AT THE JAILHOUSE AS I was leaving for breakfast. I quickly delayed my departure and invited her in. She seated herself on the chair beside the desk and laid out a copy of the telegram I'd sent her from Wallen.

"Thank you for this," she said. "I was surprised to receive it. I had no idea you would go to such trouble to look for my boy. When I learned he was alive, I broke down and wept right there in front of the telegraph man."

"Mark is home now, I hope."

"He is. He arrived home yesterday. He was stabbed. . . . It terrified me to learn of it. Stabbed! My very own son!"

"Did he say how it happened?"

"Yes . . . he was so ashamed of himself. He told me that he'd given into temptation and gone into a barroom over in Wallen. He saw a man bothering a young woman, and stepped in to help her. The man stabbed him."

Somehow I managed to keep my mouth from dropping open. I didn't know exactly how Smith got stabbed, but I would have been willing to bet my left hand it wasn't in any heroic manner remotely similar to the tale he'd told his mother.

"He's . . . quite a fellow," I said.

"Yes. But I'm worried about him. He's not left the house. He won't go to work, even though his father demands him to." She paused. "But his father is proud of him for what he did in that barroom. He says that it's the first time in his life that Mark has acted like a man instead of a boy. He even seems proud that Mark actually went into the barroom! I just can't understand that. I hope it's all right that I say that to you, it being a private family matter of ours."

"It's fine." I was back to pitying Mark Taylor Smith again. An overbearing father on one hand, a smothering mother on the other, and he was short besides.

"Anyway, I wanted to come and personally thank you. My family doesn't think much of Amos Broughton, but I can say he does have a fine deputy." She gave me a gentle smile.

"Thank you," I said. "By the way, did Mark say whether he ever got to meet that Hamm fellow he was going to interview?"

"He told me that Hamm never came."

"I see." I didn't really believe that. Smith's stabbing in some way stemmed from that planned meeting with Hamm. He sure hadn't taken a knife while defending a barmaid's honor. If he was ever in a saloon when a brawl broke out, he'd be found at the end whimpering under a table on his hands and knees, face against the floor.

"Mrs. Smith, may I ask you a question that you have the option of not answering if you don't wish to?"

She paused, then said, "I suppose so."

"I'm just wondering what the origins are of your family's dislike for Amos Broughton."

"Oh. That." She looked away. "It's not so much me, Mr. Wells. I don't know much about politics and so on. My brother-in-law, though, is interested in being sheriff. He doesn't believe Broughton has done a good job. Especially lately."

"How so?"

"People say he leaves the county when he's supposed to be working. Some say he has begun to drink."

"Will these things be printed in the newspaper?"

"Perhaps. Yes, I think they will, once they have people willing to say it in print, you know."

That probably wouldn't require a lot of looking. "Will Amos be given his chance to respond?"

"He always is free to respond. He never does. That's one of the things about him. He seems too private a man to be doing such a job of public responsibility. That's what Aristotle says."

"Aristotle?"

"My husband. Aristotle S.P. Smith."

"What does the S.P. stand for?"

"Socrates Plato."

I congratulated myself on an accurate private prediction. "Ma'am, is there anything else about Amos that causes a problem in the perception of your husband? Anything from his history?" I wasn't quite sure what I was fishing for, but it seemed a good question to ask.

"Well . . . I've heard him say that some people believe Amos Broughton might have beaten a man nearly to death a few years ago. It had something to do with something that happened during the war. I don't know the details."

"Somebody who had wronged Amos during the war?"

"I think so. I'm not sure."

I nodded. "Thank you for stopping by, Mrs. Smith."

"Thank you again for helping Mark."

"Glad to do it. Tell him I hope he heals up quickly, and that I wish he'd print a story in the paper about how he helped that poor girl in the saloon."

"Oh, Mark will never do that. He's too humble to

present himself so heroically, and too good a Christian to admit in public that he entered a saloon."

"We need more like your son, Mrs. Smith."

"Don't we, though? I'm so very proud of him."

"I'm sure you are."

I learned the news while having my usual lunch at the café: the camp meeting over in Russell County was over. The stage and other parts of the setting were being taken down, packed up, and would be under reconstruction here in Bleeker County by evening. It was anticipated that the first sermon would be preached as early as tomorrow night.

The news filled me with some dread. My conversation with Mrs. Smith had been troubling, particularly her mention that Amos had apparently already had an altercation with someone over something going back to the war. If true, that established a history for him of dealing violently with the ghosts of his past.

Ghost . . . the word brought to mind yet another recent round of words from Amos, words that took on a potential new and threatening meaning when I reflected upon them: *I know the war, and Andersonville, both left their ghosts to haunt you . . . but what you've done with them ghosts, Jed, is just feed them. Make them stronger . . . You know what I believe should be done with them ghosts? Kill them! Get rid of them! Sometimes there's ghosts*

*that are so bad that there's only one way to rid
yourself of them, and that's to kill them. Kill them
dead.*

What if he meant that more literally than I'd assumed? And what if one of those ghosts was Edward Killian?

As I lingered over my coffee and pie, I wondered
just what I should do, if anything. I didn't even
know my status right now. The badge was still
pinned on me, and I intended to keep acting as a
deputy until told clearly that I no longer had a job.
I'd done that already this morning, patrolling as
usual. But what was my duty as a lawman in this
situation, or for that matter, as a private citizen? I
had no solid proof that Amos was planning to do
anything rash . . . yet I knew he was. He had not
been riding around that camp meeting last evening,
rifle in hand, for no reason. He had plans for Killian. All the indicators were there.

I paid for my lunch and left the café, deciding it
was time to visit the Broughton house. If Amos was
there, I'd ask him straight out if I was still working
or fired. If he wasn't, I'd talk to Callianne and see if
I could make more sense of all this. And I'd warn
her of my suspicions and see if she had similar ones
of her own.

It was my fault, in a way. So wrapped up in my own
thoughts that I paid insufficient heed to what was

going on around me, I let myself be surprised by the pair that came out from behind a shed as I rounded through an alley and backstreet to get back to the jail.

"Hold it there, bluebelly," the bigger one said. He had an axe handle in his hands and a mean look on his pockmarked face. Beside him was a second fellow, much smaller, but with a bigger axe handle in his grip.

"Good day, gentlemen."

"Not for you, Yank. You damned Lincolnite scribbler! You're a stinking liar and we intend to have our say about it. With these." He hefted up the axe handle.

"Ah, I see. I'm faced with the pride of the Confederacy here. You may notice I've got a pistol. I'd advise you to toss those axe handles aside."

I should have known there was a third one, and I should have known he'd sneak up behind me. My first hint, though, was the crash against my skull of the hickory axe handle he carried. Fortunately, my hat crushed and scooted beneath the impact, softening it enough to save me from much damage. But it did drive me to my knees, and all at once my head felt about like it had when I woke up in the home of Murphy Wagoner and family.

It made me angry, and anger gave me strength. I put my weight onto my hands and kicked backward and up with both feet, my heels striking the knees of the man who'd pounded me. He fell, dropping his axe handle as he tried to catch himself. In a moment it was in my hands and I was on my feet, a touch woozy but furious enough to overcome it.

The bigger of the two who had stepped out before me looked shocked at the swiftness with which the situation had changed, but the smaller one with the bigger axe handle came at me quickly, swinging. I brought up my own axe handle and blocked the blow he aimed at me, then swiftly swung and caught him on the side of the head. He fell, stunned and already out of the fight.

The man I'd kicked behind me got up and came at me. I spun to meet him and expressed my warm greetings with the hickory in my hand. I aimed for his ear but got his temple instead. No matter. It did the job. He shuddered and collapsed.

I turned to see the first man still frozen in place, eyes wide. A look of realization that he was now facing me all by himself spread over his face like white paint.

"Well?" I asked. "Ready to strike a new blow for secession?"

His lips moved a little, but nothing else did.

"Glory, glory, hallelujah!" I said. "His truth is marching on. Maybe you'd better march on too. No point in you and me fighting a war already over, is there?"

He shook his head, turned, and was quickly gone.

I tossed down the axe handle, retrieved my hat, and went on my way, no worse off except for a headache that would linger for hours.

As I walked back toward the jail, planning to circle around to the stable in the rear and fetch my horse, Joe Reid, the new deputy, came out onto the porch, apparently having seen my approach through the window.

"Jed!" he said. "Have you been in the office this morning?"

"Not since I left for breakfast. I've been patrolling all morning. Why?"

"I came in to pick up my pocketknife—I'd left it in the desk drawer day before yesterday. I was surprised by what I found. Come take a look."

I walked in. Reid stepped back and made a sweeping gesture toward the desk.

Atop it sat a nearly empty whiskey bottle and an overturned glass. "Good Lord," I said.

"And look there," said Reid, waving toward the rifle cabinet. It stood open. I knew for a fact it had been locked when I left that morning after Mrs. Smith's visit.

"You didn't do any drinking last night, did you, Jed?" Reid asked. I didn't blame him for his forthrightness. Clearly somebody had been drinking, and I was the one here last night. And surely no one had been drinking here so early in the day . . . had they?

"No," I replied. "I swear, Joe, I never touched a drop last night. This bottle and glass have been left here since I went to breakfast."

"So somebody came into our office, drank at the desk, and broke into the rifle cabinet?"

"Has it been broken into, or opened?"

Reid investigated. "I'll be! No damage. I think it was opened with the key. Was it you?"

"No. I left it locked this morning. Amos has been here, Joe. He's done this."

"Amos told me he doesn't even drink."

"Amos tells people a lot of things these days. He does drink. Too much. He came in early this morning while I was still sleeping, and woke me up. He'd been drinking then. But if he came back and drank more this morning, right here in a public office . . . his problems run deeper than I thought."

"Nothing appears to be missing from the rifle cabinet. No, wait. There's some ammunition gone. Your cache of rifle ammunition, Jed."

I checked. Joe was right. Broughton had cleaned it all out. Yet the rifle case was still there, and when I touched it, I felt the rifle still inside. The scope was there too. I ran my hand over the pocket that held it.

Something felt different. I lifted out the rifle case

and knew right away that something was not right. The rifle inside was shorter than mine. I opened the case and pulled out a battered Henry I'd never seen before. Checking the scope pocket, I found the scope gone too, and in its place a light piece of pipe.

"He's taken my rifle, and my scope," I said. "Joe, last night I saw Amos at the camp meeting over in Russell County. He was riding around the outskirts of the meeting site, with a rifle visible. It was dark, but from the length of the rifle and such I thought it was mine. When I came back here, though, I felt this rifle in the case, and the pipe, and thought my rifle and scope were still there."

"So Broughton has traded one rifle for the other."

"Yes. And he did it in a way to make it less likely I'd discover it right away."

"Why would he want that rifle in particular?"

"Because it's a sharpshooter's rifle, with a scope. The kind of rifle you can use to kill a man at a distance."

"But what would Broughton want with that?"

"You and I need to talk, Joe. I've got some things to try to sell you that you might find hard to buy. But I hope you'll hear me out. I think Amos is about to do something he'll regret very badly, and it may be up to you and me to stop him."

"I'm listening."

← 20 ⇥

REID MADE A GOOD AUDIENCE. I LAID IT ALL OUT
before him: Broughton's strange behavior, his
drinking, his wife's worries about him, his obsession with Killian and his camp meeting.

"I've seen this kind of thing before," Reid told
me. "Men getting caught up in something out of the
past, making themselves useless . . . dangerous. It's
worst of all when it happens to a man of the law."

"We've got to find Amos," I said. "And we've
got to do our duty for the safety of this county.
Right now part of that means protecting Killian
from Amos . . . and protecting Amos from himself.
By the way, technically I'm no longer a deputy.
Broughton fired me. I intend to ignore that for
now."

"Good. And unless we can get this thing settled
out right away, I say we should ask Leroy to come
back for a spell," Reid suggested. "We could use
him, with Broughton out of the picture. I think he'd
do it."

"So do I. It's a good idea."

"What first?"

"I want to talk to Callianne Broughton. Maybe she knows where Amos is. Meanwhile, maybe you could go look around town, ask some questions, see if anybody has seen him. Try not to rouse suspicions."

"I'll do it. Tell you what: let's report back to each other as often as we can. We can leave notes under the blotter on that desk there."

We parted. I rode out toward the Broughton house, pushing hard, having a bad feeling about the situation.

Halfway there I saw a rider approaching me. From a long way off I realized it was Callianne, riding pell-mell back toward town. She slowed when she saw me, then spurred her horse, eager to reach me.

"Jed!" she said, her tone desperate. "Thank God I've found you—Amos is gone."

"I was afraid of that."

"I'm very worried, Jed. Look at this."

She handed me a note, scribbled on a torn piece of paper in an almost illegible hand. Making it even harder to read was the fact that something had been spilled on some of the letters, making the ink smear. A scent of whiskey emanated from the note, revealing what had been spilled.

The content of the letter was as raw and ragged as its form. Broughton had obviously been quite drunk when he wrote it. Alternately maudlin and angry, the letter rambled on for a page about his intense love for his wife, an admission that he had turned to drinking, as she'd suspected, a declaration of his regret at their years of childlessness . . . and then the letter turned very dark. Amos Broughton told his wife that he would be away for a brief time, carrying out a "duty" that he could not avoid, one whose obligation upon him he had been gradually realizing—and resisting—over the past month. It would be a difficult and saddening task, but he was obligated and sworn to God to fulfill it . . . "for the sake of Stephen and Kelly."

I read it, then looked up at her. "Stephen and Kelly . . ."

"Do you know those names?" she asked. "They mean nothing to me."

I pondered. "There's something familiar. Christian names, I think, not surnames. Men from Andersonville. Both from Indiana, I think. Neither survived. Of course, there are a lot of Stephens and Kellys in the world. He may be referring to someone else."

"There is a tone in that letter that frightens me, Jed."

"Me too."

"It sounds as if he might not be expecting to return from whatever it is he is doing. What is this 'duty' he talks about?"

"I'm not sure, but I think he intends to kill someone."

"Killian?"

"Yes. You should know, Callianne, that he took my rifle and scope. He replaced it in the case with a different rifle and a false scope so that I wouldn't immediately notice."

"Oh, God . . ."

"I'm going to try to find him, Callianne. And I'm also going to try to take temptation out of his path by persuading Killian to put off his camp meeting. It's pretty obvious that Amos may be thinking of shooting him from a distance, probably while he preaches. If Killian will stay out of sight and off that pulpit stage, Amos will have no opportunity."

"This is a nightmare . . . a nightmare."

"Yes, but one we may still be able to change before it comes true. Tell me: is there anyplace you can think of that Amos might go if he was trying to lay low? A friend, a hotel, rooming house, camp . . . anyplace at all."

She thought hard, then shook her head. "No . . . there are so many places. He knows this county like he knows his own face in the mirror. He could be anywhere."

"Callianne, I think you should go home. Stay

there. Keep your eyes open. Watch for Amos. He may sober up, get a fresh view about all this. And pray. Pray he doesn't do anything foolish before he has time to come to his senses."

"I'm so scared."

"Come on. I'll ride back home with you. Then I'm going to pay a call on the Rev. Killian."

The camp meeting set up outside of Starnes looked little different than it had when set up in Russell County. Apart from the landscape around it, the design was the same. Even the "street" signs in the flat area before the stage were identical. The stage was still under construction, its deftly fitted portions being pieced together by men who'd done it probably a hundred times before. Others were farther out from the main part of the meeting site, digging deep holes that would be covered by the portable privies.

I noted that, like the setting in Russell County, Killian's group had chosen a very flat area, for obvious reasons. But there was one difference: surrounding the flats here were low hills. Close enough, I noted, to provide refuge for a sharpshooter, giving him an easy shot at anyone on the stage. My military background had me picking out the most promising locales. Would Amos Broughton wind up at one of those places? Maybe. But then, he was not a trained sharpshooter. He might pick a poorer location. In short, it was hard to predict where he might go. A great sense of help-lessness overwhelmed me.

Killian's big, cleverly designed residential wagon sat, relative to the stage, exactly where it had in Russell County. I dismounted, tied my horse to a sapling, and walked toward his door.

"You, sir!" a man called to me. "Hold a mo-ment, please!"

I turned and saw the same fellow I'd helped es-cape from that barn loft.

"Who are you here to see?" he asked.

"Rev Killian," I replied.

He hadn't recognized me. It was hard to hold back a grin.

"You have an appointment with him?"

"No."

"He's busy with his Bible study. He can't . . ." The man paused, noting something familiar about me, I was sure. ". . . he can't see anyone just now."

"I think he can see me," I said, pulling back my coat enough to show my badge.

He knew me then, and gave me the oddest, wide-eyed stare. I grinned at him.

"Yes, sir," he said, face growing red. "I'll see if he is in." He turned toward Killian's wagon, hesitated, then turned back to me with a plaintive look on his face. "Sir . . . if you would . . . if you could perhaps not tell him . . ."

I learned something important right then: Killian

was not of the same moral character as this fellow. If he were, there would be no reason for this man to wish my silence. And if Killian was a morally strict man regarding the relations of his staff with women, it was hard to imagine him being lax about robbery and burglary.

"I'm here to talk to the Reverend about a different matter," I said. "I doubt I'll need to discuss anything beyond that with him. But I can make you no promises."

He looked dismayed. "Sir, if the preacher finds out what I did, there'll be no more work for me. He's a strict man. He doesn't abide somebody not following the rules."

"Is he that way about everything?"

"Yes, sir. He'll fire me if he knows what I did, sir. I don't fault him for it. I'm wrong to do the things I do. I just can't keep away from the women."

"I'll try not to cause you any problem," I said. "Just keep control of yourself while you're in this county. You understand? Next time I won't help you out of any barn loft."

"Yes, sir. I'll watch myself."

"It's very important that I see Killian now."

"I'll tell him."

"Wait a minute . . . let me ask you a question. And if I don't think you're giving me a straight answer, I'll tell Killian all about you and Beulah Gray."

He looked just then like a propped-up dead man. "What is it?"

"Do you know a man named Morgan Hamm?"

A pause. I could see he wanted to lie, but dared not. "Yes."

"He worked for Killian?"

"Yes."

"Why did he leave?"

"He was sent away by the Reverend."

"Why?"

The red face grew a little redder. He looked away. "He was caught with a woman."

"Is he the kind of man who would make false accusations against people he had fallen out with?"

A longer pause than before. I knew right away that he knew exactly what I was getting at. He answered with a little too much eagerness. "Yes, sir. He'd lie like a dog, that man would. In fact, he did lie. He made all kinds of libels against everybody he worked with. Told the Reverend all kinds of stories, but the Reverend didn't believe them."

I nodded. "I'm ready to see Reverend Killian."

A rolling library. That's how Killian's unusual mobile residence struck me. Shelves covered two entire walls and were built with wooden bars that held the books in place so they wouldn't fall off when the wagon was in motion. Many were Bibles; almost all the other titles I could read were on religious themes, classic theology, church history. Numerous books were spread open on his desk, piled atop one another, an open Bible in the center of it all.

To me, it was more evidence that Killian was no fraud. No fraud would feel the need to devote himself to this depth of study.

Killian looked tired, his eyes lined and red. He welcomed me with hospitality, however, and pulled back only a little when he recognized me as one of those present when Amos Broughton had so rudely refused his prayers after the shooting.

"Ah, you again! You are the deputy who told me I prayed over you after the train accident," he recalled.

"I am indeed, and you did indeed."

"You are still doing well?"

"Your prayer did its work, Reverend."

"Why have you come today?"

"I have something very serious to talk to you about, and I hope you'll take it as seriously as I intend it."

He frowned, intrigued. "Have a seat, Mr. Wells."

I did sit, perching on a three-legged stool that sat near his desk. He sat on the leather-lined chair behind the desk and rested his elbows on the pages of one of the open books. And at that moment I noticed something about Killian I had not noticed before.

The man was thin . . . beyond thin, really. Nearly skeletal. A broadness of the skull disguised the thinness in his face, but his body was as frail and delicate as that of an emaciated woman. It wasn't something all that evident when he was in his rather bulky garb, but he wore no heavy black jacket at the moment, and his shirt did not succeed in hiding his frailty.

I think I must have stared, because he moved, pulling back some, changing his posture and seeming to know what I looked at.

"What is it you wish to tell me?" he asked.

"I have to tell you, sir, that I believe your life is in danger."

He took that in, eyes narrowing slightly. He reached up and slightly adjusted the cloth covering his scarred forehead. "How so?"

"I believe that Amos Broughton, the same man who refused to let you pray for him, plans to kill you. His own wife believes that as well."

Killian's eyes shifted downward. I stared at him. My mind shouted at me: *I know him.* But I didn't remember how or where. Was it Andersonville?

"Why would he want to kill me?"

"I don't know. He's denied any interest in you. He's attended your camp meetings but refused to admit it. He's taken a rifle and scope designed to let a good marksman kill from a great distance. And he's left a letter for his wife, telling her he has a grim duty he must do. For the sake of Stephen and Kelly."

Something subtle flashed in Killian's eyes.

"Stephen and Kelly. Do you know those names?"

His lips moved, closed again, no words said.

I held his gaze. "Reverend Killian, were you a prisoner at the Andersonville camp?"

His lips moved again; the tip of his tongue slipped out, brushing over them nervously. "No," he said. "I was not."

"I ask you that for a reason, Reverend. I was at Andersonville. And from the first moment I saw you, there's been a sense of having seen you before. Watching you as you preached, seeing your face across a mass of crowded people, I had a sense of being back at Andersonville again . . . of having seen you before, at that place."

"I was not there." His answer was firmer this time.

"There were two other men I knew there. Stephen Morse and Kelly O'Brien. It came back to me tonight, at the same moment that I knew I'd seen you at Andersonville. They were men caught trying to escape, and punished severely for it, one in the stocks, another in a ball and chain. Neither had the strength to survive. I knew them both. So did Broughton. He was at Andersonville as well."

"I . . . I see." Killian reached up and adjusted the cloth covering his forehead. His hand was trembling.

"Preacher, I don't fully know why, but Broughton is determined to kill you. I'm sure of it. I want you to delay the start of your camp meeting. I want you to stay inside, out of view, until we can find him and persuade him to leave you in peace."

He rose and walked to a shelf, staring at the spine of a book and saying nothing. At last he turned back toward me.

"I cannot delay this meeting. I am a man called to preach the gospel, and that is what I must do, danger or no danger."

"You want to die?"

"No. But whether living or dying, I want to be doing what my Lord has called me to do."

"You love God."

"I do."

"Do you seek to obey his commandments?"

"Always."

"Do you believe that God wants those who love him to lie?"

His eyes flashed a little, with hurt or with anger, I could not tell. "No," he said.

"Then don't lie to me, Reverend. I am certain you were at Andersonville. Standing here, talking to you, I feel sure of it. Why would you deny it?"

"I was not at Andersonville!"

"I believe you were. Perhaps not under the name Edward Killian . . . but I believe you were there. And something that happened there has Amos Broughton persuaded that it is his duty to kill you. I'll protect you if I can. But you must be truthful with me. I have to understand what is going on."

"I was not at Andersonville," he repeated, almost a whisper.

I saw that I was getting nowhere. For a moment I toyed with the notion of changing my approach and asking him about the men who worked under him, airing to him Smith's suspicion that his associates used his meetings as a distraction that allowed them to commit crimes. But I'd hit this man with enough for now. He was trembling, nearly overcome with emotion. No doubt remained for me that he had in fact been at Andersonville.

"I'll go now, Reverend. I did not intend to upset you. But please delay this camp meeting. Let us find Amos Broughton. Then you can preach to your heart's content. Will you at least consider it?"

"I . . . I will consider it. I don't feel well in any case. Perhaps I can delay it."

"Have your men go into town and announce it, then. And take no more visitors. It's possible that Amos Broughton may decide to do his 'duty' in a more direct way than shooting at you from a distance."

He hesitated, then said, "I will not preach tonight. But I will not delay beyond that. God has called me to preach, not cower."

"He has also called you to tell the truth. If you know why Amos is so bitter at you, it would help me if you would let me know it too."

"I have said all I will say."

"Suit yourself." I stood and put out my hand. "I've spoken hard words, but not with hard feelings, Reverend. I'm glad you're delaying your meeting. And unless we can find Broughton right away, I hope you'll delay even more."

"One night. That is all."

We shook hands and I departed. My friend from the barn loft was outside and watched me nervously as I descended the portable staircase to the ground.

"Don't worry," I said to him. "Your secret is still safe."

He looked immensely relieved. I unhitched my horse, mounted, and rode away.

21

BACK AT THE OFFICE, I FOUND REID LEANED OVER
the desk, writing a note to be left for me under the
blotter. When I walked in he wadded the paper up
and tossed it away.

"Good—now I can tell you instead of write it for
you to find: Broughton was seen."

"By whom?"

"A fellow named Spencer, just a cardplayer I
talked to over on Bull Creek Avenue. He said he
saw Broughton out in the county, near Hankstown.
He was out on the plains, taking target practice
with a long rifle."

"My rifle, I'll bet."

"No doubt."

"Hankstown . . . if my memory is correct, that's
that little community some miles on down the
track?"

"Yes. A peaceful, quiet little place where nothing
happens, people describe it to me. Maybe a place

where Broughton figures he can stay out of sight until tonight."

"There'll be no preaching tonight. I persuaded Killian to delay it. And I've persuaded myself that he was at Andersonville, and whatever problem Broughton has with him goes back to that. Something to do with a couple of men there who died under some harsh punishment after trying to escape."

"What role did Killian play?"

"I don't know. I don't remember many details about their escape attempt. It was not a situation I was close to. All I know is that they died. If Killian was there, it was probably under some other name."

"I think at least one of us should head toward Hanksville."

"Let's both go. We can take a look around, and if we find nothing, come back here. I'm thinking one of us should try to be near that camp meeting site tonight. Killian is going to announce in town here that the preaching is called off, but they probably won't know that in Hanksville."

"So Broughton might still show up."

"That's my thought. Did you talk to Leroy?"

"Yes. He's willing to come back for a while. He's already out patrolling. When it comes down to it, he cares what happens to Broughton."

"Leroy is a good man. So is Amos, when he's himself."

"Let's hope we find him at Hanksville."

* * *

Hanksville was a community typical of so many spread across the American West—nothing but a conglomeration of houses, sheds, and barns, along with a handful of small commercial establishments, plus a church and a stumpy looking water tank. Hanksville was primarily a railroad stop, a place with a big café but no saloon. A sign at the edge of the community declared: WELCOME TO HANKS-VILLE, A CLEAN AND MORAL PLACE.

It seemed odd that Broughton, a man with a fondness for liquor, would come to a place with no saloons. But maybe that was the very point. He had a task in mind that would require a steady hand. It would be hard to shoot a preacher at his pulpit if you were drunk out of your head.

"What now?" Reid asked.

"We ask around, to start with," I said. "Maybe somebody's heard some shooting."

We rode around the corner of a stable and saw a little cluster of men seated on a storefront porch. One man was perched on a barrel, a white cloth pinned around his neck. A fellow with lots of oil glistening in his immaculately pasted-down hair was clipping at the locks of the seated man. As we neared, the barber handed his customer a mirror. A close inspection apparently gave satisfactory re-sults; the customer stood, took off his cloth, and paid the barber.

"I could use a trim," I said to Reid as we dismounted and tied our horses to a hitching rack one building down.

We were being eyed closely, but not warily, by the men on the porch. Our badges got their attention.

"Hello, gents," I said to the group. "This the local barber shop?"

"Nope," said the good-humored barber, who smelled heavily of scented hair oil. "The shop's across the street. But when your customers are too lazy to come to you, sometimes you got to go to them."

"Good common sense business, that," I said.

"You fellows are deputies?" asked a seated man who was whittling an aromatic cedar stick.

"We are. In fact, we're looking for the sheriff. Meanwhile, Mr. Barber, I'll have a trim, if you're still open for business." I was immediately waved onto the barrel seat. The cloth, shaken free of the prior customer's trimmings, was pulled around my neck and pinned.

"Broughton?" said the whittler. "Well, he's been around, I think. My wife said she saw him riding through town this morning, as she was opening the curtains in the kitchen. That's my house there." He pointed down the street at a little clapboard dwelling, plain as a box but neatly painted and clean.

"Is there a problem?" the barber asked, clicking his scissors a few times as if to limber up his fingers.

"No . . . just need to find him." I wondered how they would have reacted had I said we needed to find the sheriff before he murdered a preacher with a sharpshooter's rifle.

The whittler said, "Well, if my wife is to be believed, the sheriff was here. But I've seen not hide nor hair of him myself. He must have ridden in and ridden out. My wife wondered if he was hunting for a scofflaw."

"Well, a bank over in the next county was robbed very recently," Reid threw in.

"I heard that was the case," the whittler replied. "If the newspaper is to be believed, the scofflaws who did it are still uncaught."

"Are you saying the sheriff believes the bank robbers are hereabouts?" asked the barber, clipping away enthusiastically.

"I know of no indication that they are," I said, casting a glance at Reid. He'd brought up the bank robbery because we couldn't very well tell the truth about why we were looking for Broughton, but now he had these folks worrying. It wouldn't be long before a rumor was flying.

"Then why would the sheriff come here?" asked a third man, whose jaw was distended with chewing tobacco.

"I think he answered a call of some sort," I said. "Nothing serious."

"There's a stranger hid out in the woodshed behind the church house," said a piping voice from nowhere.

I looked around for the speaker, causing the barber to curse beneath his breath as my motion caused a snip to go awry. Over beside the tobacco chewer was a little boy, no more than eight or nine, sitting on the porch and mostly hidden by the man's chair. I'd not even noticed him.

"What was that, son?" I asked.

"There's a stranger hid in the woodshed behind the church. I seen him go in there early this morning. I can see it from my winder. He had him a big old long rifle."

"Why didn't you say nothing, Munsey?" asked the barber.

"Warn't no law here to tell. Not until now."

"A long rifle, you say?" Reid said.

"Yep. He went in there just about sunrise. I was up and looking out the winder when I seen him."

I unpinned the cloth around my neck. "Thank you, sir," I said to the barber, rising.

"I haven't finished the back yet, sir!" he said.

"That's all right. I like it on the long side back there." I fished out money and handed it to him. "Keep the change."

"I hope that's no scofflaw in the woodshed," said the whittler. "My wife fears a scofflaw. If she is to be believed, there are scofflaws hiding behind every tree. I would hate for there to prove to be one in the church woodshed. It would only make her all the more fearful."

"Thurston is educated," the barber told me in a low tone. "You can tell it from how he talks, can't you!"

"Yes, sir." Reid and I stepped down from the porch and headed toward the church.

"He'll be in there drunk as a backslid deacon," Reid said.

"Better that than out trying to draw a bead on Killian," I said. We reached the church a few moments later and headed around the far side of it. The woodshed was off in the back lot, sitting diagonally to the back of the church.

"I'll pull open the door, then we'll step back a moment, just in case he's so drunk he panics and shoots," Reid said.

I didn't expect Broughton to shoot. I expected to find him passed out. Hoped to, in fact. Men tend not to be argumentative when they are passed out drunk.

"We may have to put Broughton in his own jail, you know," I said. "I've been thinking about that. It might be the only way to keep him under control.

I even thought about arresting Killian for one thing or another, then I realized I'd be locking him into Broughton's own jail. He'd be a rat in a cage."

"Well, here goes," Reid said, and yanked open the woodshed door.

Nothing but a darkly shaded interior. Then from out of the gloom a figure emerged, slashing a knife in all directions, roaring, and holding a battered old muzzleloader by the barrel.

It wasn't Broughton. I'd never seen this fellow before. Reid and I danced back, avoiding the blade, and reached for our pistols.

With another roar, the man slashed at Reid and managed to bury the point of the knife in the woodshed wall. His hand came off the handle, and at the same moment he stumbled over his own feet. He fell onto his rump, bounced up again like he was made of rubber, then began swinging the rifle like a club.

Somehow, in all the furor, I noticed there was a red stain spreading on his left side, soaking through his shirt.

Reid leveled his pistol. "Drop that rifle!" he demanded.

The man gave a deft swing and batted the pistol right out of Reid's hand. It flew fifteen feet and landed in brush, out of sight. I had a strong impression the swing had been pure luck.

It was bad luck for Reid. He grabbed at his hand, making a face of great pain. I hoped a finger or two hadn't been broken.

I could shoot this man, or I could try to bring him down in some drastic way. Opting for the latter, I waded in, ready to pistol-whip him in the back of the head. He was faster than I thought. He ducked and swung, and the rifle caught me across the belly. I folded, breath driving out of my mouth and nose, and he lifted a foot and kicked my back.

"You'll never get me!" he hollered, his voice a slur. "I'll talk to the law, I will!"

"We are the law!" Reid hollered back.

The man bellowed, "The hell!" Then he must have noticed our badges, because he calmed all at once, looking puzzled, then said, much lower, "The hell! You *are* the law!"

I staggered to my feet, leveling my pistol. "Drop that rifle!" I demanded.

He instantly complied. The whirlwind of a moment before now was quiet and docile, just a small-framed fellow with narrow shoulders and eyes that revealed the shadows of some very hard living.

"I'm mighty sorry," he said. "If I'd knowed you was law, I'd never have done that."

"Reid, are your fingers broken?" I asked.

Reid was shaking his hand about, frowning. "No . . ." He wriggled his fingers and winced. "No . . . but it stung me just right. Like hitting your elbow on something, but all the way up my arm."

"Mighty sorry," the man said again.

"You're bleeding," I said to him.

He looked down. "Aw, durn. Durn . . . I broke open that cut again."

"You've been cut?"

"Stabbed."

"By who?"

"I don't know his name. Just his face, and that missing ear." He was clearly drunk, but didn't sound quite so slurred now. I suppose the agitation must have contributed to it some.

"Missing ear," Reid repeated, still frowning at his stinging fingers.

"Yep."

"Were you in a brawl?"

"Not one I wanted to be in. I got attacked. Just because I was going to do the right thing and tell the truth about something."

An intriguing possibility had just come to mind. "You didn't get stabbed over in Russell County, did you?"

"As a matter of fact—"

"And the man you were going to tell the truth to . . . a newspaperman, named Smith?"

"How did you know?" He tensed up. "Them badges ain't fake, are they? You really are law, ain't you?"

"We really are law, Mr. Hamm."

He looked like I'd just pulled off an amazing card trick. "How do you know me?"

"It's just something I figured out. I know Smith, and what happened to him when he tried to talk to you."

Reid looked interested in all this, but remembered his pistol and went over to look for it in the brush.

"Who are you?" Hamm asked.

"My name is Jed Wells. I'd like to talk to you, Mr. Hamm."

"Mister. I don't get called that much anymore. Not since the demon in the bottle took hold of my soul."

Reid said, "Here it is!" and came up with the pistol. He began brushing it off, picking dirt out of the end of the barrel with his little finger.

"You had anything to eat yet today?" I asked him.

"Not a bite. Nothing but liquid hellfire, if you know what I mean."

"Come on. Let me buy you a meal over at the railroad café. I'd like to talk to you while I've got the chance."

"You ain't going to arrest me? I'm drunk. I tried to whup two lawmen."

"You have a choice: a meal, and telling me what I want to know, or jail."

"I'll take the meal."

Reid returned with his pistol. "Jed, I'll keep poking around town, seeing what I can find out."

"Good, Joe. I won't be long."

22

FOR THE FIRST FIVE MINUTES I SIMPLY WATCHED Morgan Hamm eat. He seemed nearly starved, eating big bites, eyes narrowed in concentration, jaws working hard and fast. At length he slowed down.

"So let me get this right," I said. "You were stabbed by a man with one ear because you tried to talk to Smith."

"Yes." Another big bite.

"The same man stabbed Smith too?"

"That's right. Scared him so bad that Smith fainted. I think the knife man thought he was dead. He left Smith alone and came at me."

"Does this one-eared man work for Killian?"

"Nope. He works for Brother James."

"Who's that?"

"Brother James Boucher. One of Killian's bunch."

"You were one of his bunch too. What happened?"

"Killian let me go. I don't blame him for it."

"The drinking?"

"Yes. He had to fire me. A preacher can't have a drunk helping him out. People kind of notice, you know."

"It sounds like he's got worse than drunks working for him."

"He does. But he don't know it. Brother Killian is a trusting man. He thinks the best of folks until they prove to him that they can't be trusted. And it's hard to prove that to him."

"Wait . . . are you telling me that Killian doesn't know about the robberies and so on?"

"No. It's Boucher and Malone who are behind all that. Brother Timothy knows about it, but he has no part of it himself. He keeps his mouth shut, though. If he speaks up, they'll tell Killian about the way he dallies with the women."

I took a guess at who Brother Timothy was, and described to him my friend from the barn loft.

"That's him," Hamm said. "Can't keep away from the females. Killian has no idea."

"What's Malone's first name?"

"Lamar."

"So James Boucher and Lamar Malone work for Killian, have his trust, but rob banks and so on behind his back."

"They don't generally do it themselves. They have folks hired. One of them is the same one who stabbed me and Smith. I don't know his name. He's a hellion. He'd kill a man as soon as look at him—I'm convinced of it."

"He convinced Smith too. Smith is too scared to talk, much less write. Did you tell Smith what you've told me?"

"Didn't get the chance. We'd just sat down to talk when old one-ear showed up with his knife."

"So Smith knows nothing."

"Nothing from me. I don't know how much he knew before."

"I do. He had suspicions, but he believes Killian himself is involved."

"If he ever prints that, he'll be hurting a good man. I respect Killian. I wish I could be the kind of man he is."

"Why did you agree to talk to Smith?"

"Because I respect Killian, and it ain't right for him to be used the way that Boucher and Malone do. They need to be exposed."

"Why not just tell Killian?"

"I tried once. He didn't believe it. Told me it was the liquor talking. He's a . . . I can't think of the word. Gubbli . . . gubba . . ."

"Gullible?"

"That's it. He's a gullible man. But a good one. A true Christian, that man. I admire him a lot."

"Even though he cut you loose?"

"Partly because he *did* cut me loose. It shows he's serious about doing what's right, and he wants his people to do what's right too."

I weighed my words carefully at this point. "Mr. Hamm, I take you at your word that the Reverend Killian is a good man. But have you ever had occasion to believe he wasn't telling the truth about something?"

He frowned. "No. Not a time I can think of."

"Do you know what his history was during the war?"

"I know he was a Union man. He's never talked about any details, not to me, anyway."

"Has he ever said anything about being captured and held as a prisoner of war?"

"Was he?"

"Yes, I'm nearly sure he was."

"He's never said a word about it."

"Has he ever mentioned the name Amos Broughton?"

"Lord, I don't know. I don't recall it."

I sat back, pondering it all. I'd learned a lot from Hamm, but little about Killian, and nothing about what might have prompted Broughton's hatred of the man.

"Do you have any specific evidence that the one-eared man robbed the bank in Russell County?"

"No. Not court-of-law kind of proof. Some things you know but can't prove."

"Right." I stared at the cup of coffee before me, the only thing I'd ordered.

Off in the distance, not very audible, I heard a popping sound. A faraway gunshot. It could have been any hunter.

A few moments later, the same sound. I lifted my head, listening closely.

Mothers know the sound of their own children, hunters the bay of their own dogs. And a sharpshooter the crack of his own rifle.

I stood, digging out money and tossing it onto the table, signaling to a waiter to show him the money, because I wasn't certain I trusted Hamm not to sneak it for himself.

"You leaving?" Hamm said.

"I am. Where are you staying, Mr. Hamm?"

"Any woodshed I can find. Hiding out from one-ear. He put a scare into me too. That's why I came out to this no-whiskey backwater town. Nobody'd expect to find old Hamm here. I brung my own whiskey, of course."

"You can find me at the sheriff's office in Starnes. You come to see me . . . I'd like to talk to you some more."

"I'll do it."

But as I left, I strongly doubted Hamm would come around. He seemed a drifting type; he would go wherever he could find food, a few drinks.

Out on the street, Reid was heading my way.

"Gunfire, north of town . . . it has the sound of somebody taking target practice."

"More than that—it has the sound of my own rifle. It's got to be Broughton."

We headed for our horses, mounted up, then headed out of town, riding onto the plains.

North of town the flatlands were broken by low, wooded hills and huge outcrops of rock. We'd followed the sound of the gunshots for ten minutes, but then they ceased.

"He saw us I'll bet," Reid said. "He's probably been up in those hills, where he has a view of the land all around."

"Wait . . . I saw something move there in the trees."

"I don't see anything. . . . Hold it . . . yeah, I saw it too. Animal or man, though, I couldn't say."

"Let's go take a look."

Exploration revealed that the hills were laid out in a kind of roughly rounded ring, encircling a little hollow in which a small house and a few outbuildings stood. These were rugged structures, rundown and now seemingly abandoned. Reid and I crouched in the hillside brush, our horses now left behind us, tied safely to some trees on the other side of the hill behind us.

"Well, Callianne said that Amos knows this county like his own face in the mirror," I said. "I'll bet he knew about this spot and has made a refuge of it for himself. Hidden, empty . . . a good place for a man to go if he doesn't want to be found."

"Think he knows we're here?"

"I'm not sure he's even down there. It looks empty. No horses or anything, no smoke from the chimney. And it sounded to me like the shots we heard were coming from out on the flats. But I wouldn't be surprised if he is staying here. Let's go take a look and see if we can find evidence anybody's been living inside."

We rose and quietly descended toward the little cluster of unpainted buildings, all of them made of rough barn lumber. No sound or movement gave indication that we were seen, or that any living beings other than ourselves were even present. As we drew closer to the structures, the less sure I was that Broughton was here or had ever been here.

Reid expressed the same feeling. "I think we may be on a cold trail," he said.

"Maybe. Tell you what—you go around toward the back and I'll go to the front. Once we're in place, I'll give a holler, just in case he or anybody else is inside. I don't want to surprise anyone."

"What if he's here but won't come back with us?"

"Then I guess it will be up to us to be good men of the law and make him comply. Somehow."

We separated. I waited a couple of minutes, watching Reid circle down and around toward the rear, where the outbuildings stood. I lost sight of him among the structures. At that point I circled down myself, heading to the front.

Positioning myself behind a tree to afford a little protection in case things turned strange and dangerous on us, I put my right hand to the side of my mouth and called, "Hello the house! Looking for Amos Broughton!"

No one replied. The little house looked empty, the single front window dark and closed. The front door was shut tight.

"Hello! Anybody home?"

Still only silence. Then, around the back of the house, I caught a faint glimpse of movement. But it was only Reid, moving in closer from the rear. From my side, I did the same, coming out from behind the tree and advancing toward the house. Though I had no evidence the place was occupied, I was tense, and subtly slipped the tie-down strap off my pistol, just in case.

"Hello the house!" I hollered again. "I'm coming in—looking for Amos Broughton!"

I reached the front door, touched the latch, pushed the door open . . .

Gunfire exploded without warning. I leaped back, drawing my pistol, convinced someone had just fired at me. Then a second shot blasted and I realized it came from behind the house.

"Reid!" I yelled, and burst into the house, running straight through and out the rear door, which stood ajar. As I passed through the house I was vaguely cognizant of a saddle dumped on the floor in the corner, a jumble of blankets on the floor, some canned food, a scattered deck of cards, and a corked bottle of whiskey, half empty.

Outside again, I looked about wildly, pistol up and ready. No one. Not Reid, not Broughton, nor anyone else. Then something thumped against the back of a nearby shed, and Reid came around from behind, blood on his right shoulder, his face white as milk.

"Jed . . . I'm . . . I'm . . ." He collapsed.

I went to him, found him breathing but passed out. There was no time for a real examination, but it appeared he'd been shot through the lower part of his shoulder, at a slightly upward angle. It did not seem likely anything vital had been damaged; his unconsciousness was probably momentary, from the shock.

But he was bleeding, and I would have to deal with that. Suddenly, though, I heard someone moving in the trees behind us, very close. I would be in the same fix as Reid at any moment, or worse.

"Amos! Is that you? Amos, it's me, Jed Wells! You've just shot Joe Reid, Amos! You just shot your own deputy!"

I heard him running, scrambling away. Fury overwhelmed me. At that moment I had no regard for Amos Broughton, no sense of pity or friendship. If he'd let whiskey and bitterness get such a hold on him that he'd turn lethally upon his friends and fellow lawmen, I could only despise him.

I ran into the trees, caught a brief sight of him moving into a rocky area. Not good . . . If he found cover back there, I'd be hard-pressed to get to him without being gunned down. But just then my fury was at such a peak that I pressed on, determined not to give him time to position himself and develop any strategy.

A shot rang out; a bullet thumped into a tree three feet from me. I ducked behind that tree, then circled out around the other side, making for the boulders. Another shot. This bullet struck stone and sang off into the sky.

Reaching the rocks, I paused and debated with myself for about three seconds. Continue, or go back to get Reid's bleeding stopped? I decided to continue. The bleeding was not so severe that he was in immediate danger. I had a brief span of time in which I could eliminate the threat and work on him without getting my own head blown off, which would do neither Reid nor me any good.

Moving through those rocks, I fully expected to either kill Amos Broughton or be killed by him. My feelings, my pulse beat, my focus and determination—all these aspects of myself were momentarily concentrated, and familiar. I had felt the same way many times before, during the war. Having it all come back again had me in states of living contradiction: invigorated and numbed, fearless and terrified, all at the same time.

He was still moving, scrambling through the rocks. I wondered if maybe he wasn't seeking cover at all, but trying to get away, out onto the plains. If so, that meant he was scared, running in fear, because leaving the cover of the stones would put him in an exposed position, easy for me to gun him down.

If he was afraid, that gave me an advantage. My courage and determination intensified.

Reaching a narrow pass between two rocks, I pushed through, but my foot slipped and was caught tightly for several moments in a hurting pinch. Suddenly trapped, I tugged and twisted and tried to free myself, and at last did so, but my boot remained wedged between the rocks. I was hampered now, less able to run and scramble. Reaching down, I grabbed at the boot, tugged it free . . .

The world exploded at the back of my head. Pain tore through me in a fast, lightning jolt, and for a second I knew, just knew, that the back of my skull had been shot away. In that brief moment I felt a sense of cold irony, of a universe dispensing an appropriate recompense. How many men had themselves felt bone and flesh blown away by bullets I had fired from the relative safety of a hidden position? How many had been living one moment, destroyed the next, because of me? I had lost count long ago.

If I died here and now, gunned down by an unseen assailant, I had no right to voice any complaint. It was only the great balance of life at work, doling out to me what I had doled out to others.

Going down hard, I blacked out for perhaps a couple of seconds, then opened my eyes and stared at a smooth expanse of stone inches from my face. An important realization came: there was no blood. If I'd been shot, the blood should be pouring like water, down the sides of my head and onto the rock before me . . . but there was none.

I'd not been shot, only struck.

Rolling onto my back, I looked up and saw a huge, looming figure above me. Not Amos Broughton, but Cleve Miller, cousin of the late Jimmy, and a man I'd already danced one waltz with back on Bull Creek Avenue.

"Got you now, you son of a bitch!" he yelled down at me. "I'm going to shoot your damn finger off before I kill you, just like you done to Jimmy! Hell, I'll shoot off your whole damned hand!"

He raised the pistol he'd hit me with, clicked back the hammer, took aim . . .

His head exploded into an ugly red mist about half a second before the sound of the shot reached me. That familiar crack—my own rifle. He fell away to the side and went down heavily, dead before he struck ground.

I passed out, eyes closing, darkness descending, one last realization rising and then fading: Amos Broughton was out there, with my rifle, and he'd just saved my life.

⊸ 23 ⊸

I HAD JUST DOZED OFF WHEN THE DOOR OPENED and she entered, walking through the dark outer office to the door of my little quarters. Joe Reid, asleep at the moment, lay on my cot, his shoulder bandaged. Before falling asleep he'd berated me for sitting up with him, hovering over him like an old grandmother, as he put it, when I should be resting myself, taking care of my injured head.

The pistol blow I'd taken had struck me hard, but so flatly that it hadn't even broken the skin. I figured there was a hideous bruise back there, but my hair hid it, so it didn't matter. Apart from a headache, I was fine.

Callianne stood in the doorway, watching Joe sleep. "How is he?"

"Fine," I said. "The wound was hurting him some, so the doctor gave him a small dose of laudanum. Knocked him out. The wound is clean, just a straight-through shot. He'll heal up fine, according to the doctor. He may have shoulder pain for a year or two."

"How about you?"

"I'm just fine. Not even a bandage."

She stared silently at Reid. "I don't fully understand what happened," she said.

"Well, I'm not sure I do either. All I can do is try to piece it together. The dead man, I'm told, is Bob Henry Miller, a cousin of Jimmy Miller and true to the family form in character. He was holed up out there in that shack for God only knows why. He's in trouble all the time, always has somebody or another after him, so probably he was just hiding out for a time. Amos had been out there, taking target practice, learning to use my rifle and scope, so Miller was bound to have had his nerves on edge from hearing that shooting going on. If he investigated, he might have even realized it was Amos doing it—the local sheriff, out squeezing off shots almost in the shadow of his hideout. So when Reid and I showed up, looking for Amos, we probably scared him good. Scared him, but also put an opportunity before him. He had his chance to even the score for me shooting his cousin's finger off. What he didn't know was that Amos was close by, with my rifle. I guess the commotion and shooting drew him. He saw Miller about to do me in, and did Miller in first. He's turned into a good sharp-

shooter, Callianne. He killed him with one shot . . .
a clean head shot. I don't know how far away he
was, but it was a good shot at any distance, by any
standard."

She shuddered. "It's dreadful. I hate to think of
Amos shooting off another man's head."

"He saved my life."

"Yes. I'm glad for that. I only wish he'd come
back in with you."

There'd been no chance for that. I'd not even laid
eyes on Amos Broughton. As soon as he'd dis-
patched Miller, he vanished. With Reid in need of
help, I'd had no opportunity to go looking for
Broughton. I managed to patch Miller up some and
get him back to Hanksville, where that barber
who'd clipped my hair proved to be a good ama-
teur medical man and completely stanched Reid's
bleeding. Then the train rolled in, heading back toward Starnes, and Reid, myself, and our horses
caught a ride in a boxcar. Back in Starnes, a real
doctor examined Reid and dressed his wound.
We'd ensconced my fellow deputy here in my jailhouse quarters so I could keep an eye on him, just
in case he did something to get the bleeding started
again. Now the day was past and night had fallen.

"This day didn't turn out a bit like I expected," I
told Callianne. "I'd hoped we'd find Amos at Hanksville and talk him into coming back home. Short of
that, I'd anticipated being out at the camp meeting

grounds, looking for him to show up. I doubt he had any way to know that preaching was called off tonight."

"Maybe he did show up."

"Maybe. Very clearly he is serious about killing the preacher. And very clearly he's developed the marksmanship to do it. I'm going to talk to Killian again tomorrow and try to persuade him to not even hold a camp meeting here. He should just move on elsewhere. As long as he's close by, Amos is going to feel it is his duty to kill the man."

"Do you know anything more about why Amos hates him so?"

"Nothing specific. Something to do with Andersonville, and the two men whose names Amos left you in his note. The only thing I can figure is that Amos must hold Killian responsible for their deaths. But I don't know why. Killian denies he ever was at Andersonville, but I'm persuaded he's lying."

"What if Killian refuses to stop preaching?"

"Then I have another card to play. I encountered a man in Hanksville who used to work for Killian. The preacher is apparently an honest but gullible man. He's surrounded by scoundrels, some of whom are involved in crime and take advantage of the distraction his meetings create. Killian doesn't know it. If I reveal the truth to him, he might be persuaded to cease his meetings for a time to deal with the problem. If not, I might consider arresting him on some charge or another, just to get him off the street."

"You can't lock him up. Amos would have access to him."

"I know. I haven't figured it all out yet."

The door opened and Leroy entered. He looked like a walking dead man, having been on duty all day and now into the night, given Reid's injury and my own aching head. The doctor had ordered me strictly to stay off duty at least until the next day, meaning that Leroy's thank-you for his voluntary, temporary return to the force of deputies was an immediate double shift.

But he was in a surprisingly decent mood, or at least did a good job of feigning one given the presence of Callianne. He came to the door, nodded a greeting to her, then looked in at Reid. "How's the sleeping petunia?"

"Opiated into blissful slumber," I replied. "Is it quiet out there tonight?"

"So far. Thank God for that."

"I'll do a double shift myself to make up to you for all this, Leroy."

He waved it off. "Unusual circumstances. Nothing to get riled over. Things just happen sometimes. But you ought to go to sleep yourself, Jed. Two shifts I can handle, but if you expect me to work tomorrow after you sit up all night, it ain't going to happen."

"I'll sleep right here in the chair. The doctor wants somebody close by Joe tonight in case he starts to bleed."

"I'll do it," Callianne said. "You go to my house and sleep. I'll stay here and watch Mr. Reid."

"I can't ask you to do that."

"You didn't ask. I volunteered. Now go! Take my buggy. It's parked outside. The kitchen door at home is unlocked, so you can go in that way."

The prospect of a night's rest in that comfortable guest bed was too enticing to turn down. "Thank you."

"Think nothing of it. Just keep trying to find my husband, and stop him from doing something he'll regret."

"I'll do my best, Callianne. I promise it firmly."

Gathering a few items, I left the jail, climbed into the buggy, and traveled to the Broughton home.

The bed was even better than I'd anticipated. My aching head sank into the pillow, and in moments I was deep in sleep.

Noises in the night, subtle but audible . . .

A door opened, closed gently. Footfalls whispered across the hardwood floor downstairs. A floorboard creaked.

I rose in silence, creeping to my gun belt, which hung over the back of a chair. The cherrywood grip was cold in my palm as I gripped it and edged toward the door of my room.

Whoever was below moved toward the downstairs master bedroom. I softly opened my own door, praying the hinges would make no sound. They did not; the door opened in silence, giving me entrance to the darkened upper hallway.

I heard the master bedroom door open, creak just a little.

Then a voice: "Callianne?"

I lowered the pistol to my side, leaned over the rail and looked down the staircase. "Amos," I said.

He moved quickly, startled, bumping some piece of furniture in the dark.

"Who the hell—"

"It's me, Amos. Jed."

"Jed . . . what the hell . . ."

"Callianne's not here. She's at the jail, keeping an eye on Joe Reid. She invited me to come sleep here tonight so I'd be rested for tomorrow. We've had to operate the sheriff's office without a sheriff, you know." The sarcasm came out despite my attempt to stifle it. But equally strong was my sense of gratitude to this man. He'd saved my life that day.

I descended the stairs quickly, wanting to confront him before he could simply leave. He stood there in the darkness, visible only in the very dim moonlight that managed to penetrate the mostly curtained windows. There was that familiar scent of whiskey about him.

"You're drunk again, Amos."

"Maybe I am."

"You weren't drunk today when you shot the head off a man who would have killed me not two seconds later."

"No. I was stone sober then. It was a good shot, huh?"

"I couldn't have done better."

"How's Joe?"

"Is that what brought you home? To ask about Joe?"

"Yes."

"Joe will be fine. He'll be inactive for a spell. Leroy's come back to help out, though. Seems he's concerned about you, even as disgusted as he's been with you over the last month or so."

He moved; I caught a glimpse of a familiar rifle held against him, stock resting on the floor.

"My rifle. And you've got the scope on it."

"Yes. I ain't stole it, Jed. I've just got it borrowed. This was the rifle that I used today."

"Yeah."

"I never shot a man in the head that way. I was . . . amazed, I guess you'd say, at what it did to him."

I'd seen many times before what a well-placed

shot did to a man's head, and had nothing to say about it now.

After a moment or two of tense silence, he said, "There's one thing I'm sorry about. . . . I should have come out today and helped you get Joe back to town. I could see it was a struggle for you."

"I could have used the help."

"I knew that if I came out, you'd try to stop me from doing what I have to do."

"I might have."

"I couldn't let that happen. Still can't."

"Callianne let me read the note you left. Stephen and Kelly. Men from Andersonville. They died while under punishment for attempted escape."

"That's right."

"What does that have to do with Edward Killian?"

He stared at me through the veil of darkness. The big clock in the next room ticked loudly, then chimed three times.

"There's things best left unsaid about this. This ain't your matter, Jed. It's mine. I'd as soon leave you out of it, for all kinds of reasons."

"I was at Andersonville too, Amos. I'd understand if anybody would."

To my surprise, he grew snappy, angry. "Yes, you were at Andersonville, and you'd think they gave you a deed to the place, the way you act about it. Just because you collected a bunch of stories and wrote them into a book don't mean that there ain't others who have their own stories and memories . . . some they may not want to go jabbering about or writing down in storybooks."

"You mad at me, Amos?"

He stared at the barely visible pattern of the wallpaper. "No. Mad at myself because I find it so hard to do what I should. Mad at myself because maybe, just maybe, if I'd done some things different when we were prisoners, I might have been able to stop something bad from happening to two good men."

"I wish you would explain this to me. I wish you'd tell me what Killian has to do with this and why you hate him so."

"Jed, the less you know, the better. There could be things that come of this that could get a man in bad trouble. No reason for you to share that. Just leave me to what I have to do, and be glad this is one Andersonville story you missed out on."

He sighed loudly. "I was ready to do it tonight. I'd have done it . . . but there was no preaching. I couldn't believe it. Just went off and got drunk. That's all I did."

A sense of despair was rising inside me. I could see that he would not be dissuaded from his intention. "Amos, I've talked to Killian. I think he's a good man. I hear from most everyone that he's a good man. And Smith, from the newspaper . . . he'd thought that Killian was involved in crime. He was wrong. Some of Killian's people are, but he has nothing to do with it, no knowledge of it. If you kill him, you're killing a good man. I truly believe that."

"There's things you don't know, Jed."

"Amos, if you're determined to do this, you know I have to stop you. Kind of a funny thing . . . when you swore me in as a deputy, I vowed to uphold the law. That means I have to intervene to stop the very man who swore me in from violating the law. The law of man, and the law of God too. It's not right to murder a man like that."

He laughed. "You say that? You, of all people, sharpshooter?"

"The acts I did were acts of war, done at the command of my superior officers."

"And the act I intend to do is an act of justice, done at the command of God almighty."

"You believe that God wants you to murder a preacher, before his congregation?"

"I believe He wants me to do justice."

"Amos, damn it all, tell me why you think you have to kill Killian? What did he do?"

"The sin of Judas. That's what he did. I'm no saint, Jed, I got my faults, my drinking . . . but I don't betray. I don't betray."

Persuasion would not work. But perhaps I could at least make his killing task harder to achieve.

"Amos, if you're determined to do this, I have one favor to ask of you. Don't use my rifle. I don't want it put to that purpose."

"It's the purpose it was made for, Jed."

"It wasn't made for murdering preachers. Especially ones who as far as I know don't deserve killing."

"He deserves killing."

"I can't believe that until you tell me why. Who did he betray?"

"I'll say no more to you of it. The less you know, the less anyone can say you were an accomplice."

"If my rifle is used, then there's trouble for me right there. Don't use it, Amos. I demand you give it back to me now."

I could feel the coldness of his stare even though I could hardly see his face. "Very well, then. Take it and be damned. I'll kill him with my bare hands if I have to."

He shoved the rifle to me, then roughly yanked the ammunition pouch off his shoulder and dropped it at my feet.

I picked up the rifle and put it behind me, leaning against the wall. I kicked away the ammunition pouch and from behind me produced the pistol that had been in my hand all along.

"You know I have to stop you, Amos," I said. "I owe it to the law, to Callianne . . . and to you."

He shook his head. "I figured as soon as I saw you here tonight that you'd try something like this. Good-bye, Jed. I got to leave."

"Can you not see this pistol, Amos?"

"I see it. You want to use it, use it. I'm close enough that even somebody who wasn't an expert shootist could hit me. Go ahead and shoot." He turned and headed toward the door.

"Amos, stop where you are!"

He went out the door, and I went after him.

"Amos!" I hollered into the night, as he vanished. "Amos, come back here, or I'll shoot!"

He didn't come back, and I didn't shoot. We both knew all along it would go that way.

"Damn you, Amos!" I yelled after him. "I'm not going to let you do it! I'll protect him from you! I vow it!"

He said nothing. I could barely hear his receding footfalls.

"You're loco, Amos!" I yelled. "Plain loco! You're going to destroy yourself, your wife, your whole life!"

I might as well have been shouting at the moon.

⊱ 24 ⊰

SLEEP WAS NO LONGER A PROSPECT. I COULDN'T have slept if I'd wanted, and besides that, it didn't take long to realize that Broughton's last words might indicate an immediate threat to Killian. Ironically, in reclaiming my rifle, I might have reduced the threat of Killian being shot while preaching, but now Broughton might just go to him where he lived. Even tonight.

I readied myself, booted the rifle, dropped the hated scope into the saddlebag. I rode through the night to the campground. No activity, the place sound asleep. A few tents and covered wagons sat along the various "streets," people settling in for a long-term revival under the powerful orations of the Reverend Killian.

I made a sort of temporary camp within view of Killian's house on wheels, and spent the remainder of the night watching for any evidence that Amos Broughton was sneaking about. I saw movement, a figure crossing near Killian's dwelling, but it proved to be only someone heading to a privy.

Morning came and found me underrested but glad that Broughton had not showed up.

Going to the nearby stream, I washed my face and splashed water through my hair. Too bad I couldn't shave; ever since Andersonville, where my beard had grown long and shaggy, I'd been a stickler for shaving.

Killian probably hadn't had his breakfast yet, but he was about to get a visitor. I walked across the dewy grass and up to his door, and rapped hard on it.

There was no immediate answer, so I knocked again. This time the door opened a couple of inches and Killian's right eye peered out through the crack.

He opened the door when he saw who I was, and stepped back to wave me in. He wore a long nightshirt, no shoes, his hair matted from sleep. His skeletal frame looked even thinner than the last time I'd seen him, and I was reminded anew of the living corpses of Andersonville.

"I got you out of bed," I said.

"No, actually I was up," he said. "I rise early for prayer. An old habit."

"And no doubt a good one," I replied. "But I've come to tell you something not so good. You are in need of protection." As quickly as I could I laid all the details out for him about my nocturnal confrontation with Amos Broughton, including his final threat. "You must take him seriously," I said. "I am convinced he will try to kill you. Initially he planned to shoot you from a distance. Now, I don't know what he will do. Suffice it to say, you can't remain here. You should go, far away, and right now."

This was much for him to take in before whatever meager repast this man considered breakfast, but that was my intention. I wanted the truth of the situation to hit him hard.

"Why didn't you stop him when you had the chance?" he asked me.

The question hit rather hard. How could I justify to this man that I'd simply let Amos Broughton walk away? On the other hand, how could I have done violence against the very man whose well-timed shot had saved my life only hours earlier?

"I should have stopped him. I'll make no excuses. But the point is, he's out there, and you should go."

"The sheriff of the county, determined to kill me," Killian said, running his hands through his hair and staring at the floor. "Astonishing."

"It's the strangest situation I've run across," I admitted. "Preacher, I don't know what happened to cause all this. You say you weren't at Andersonville, and Broughton says you were. He accuses you of the 'crime of Judas.'" At this, Killian flinched before he could hide it. "I believe as well that you were at Andersonville, but I'll not push you about that matter just now. All I want you to tell me is that you will break down this camp and leave. I demand it for the public safety. I don't believe Amos Broughton will pursue you if you leave this region."

He frowned at me, like a man thinking several thoughts at once. He shook his head. "I can't do that."

"Why not?"

"I've said I'll preach here. People have come. I can't just run away because some madman threatens me."

"Preacher, there are lost souls everywhere. Not just here. Go help them."

"I'll not run, deputy. I won't do it."

"You're a stubborn man."

"Persistent in righteousness."

"In foolishness."

"You are a man sworn to uphold the law. You do it. I'm sworn to preach where God plants me. I'll do it."

It seemed to me that it was the Reverend, not God, who had chosen this campground, and I said as much.

Killian seemed to be growing weary of me. "I've said what I've said, deputy. I'll not flee this madman who you let go. I appreciate your concern for me, but my life is in God's hands. If He wishes me to die, I will die. If He does not, then nothing this madman sheriff can do will harm me."

Weariness, tension, frustration at the stubbornness of men—all combined at once to make me lash out at this willful man. "Listen to me, Preacher. You stand here and put some sort of spiritual mask on everything that comes up. You preach in one county and move to the next, and say God did it. You refuse to protect yourself and expect God to do it for you. You act like a man cloaked in righteousness, yet the very men who surround you and work for you are crooked as broken-back snakes."

"What?"

Anger made the words pour out. "You heard me. You may be a sincere man, Preacher, but you are surrounded by men who are anything but good. I personally saved the hide of one of your men who was sporting with a loose girl and almost got himself shot by her father. Over in Starnes there is a newspaperman who is now so scared he's probably hiding behind his mother's skirts right now. He's scared because he was stabbed by a ruffian under the hire of one of your men . . . stabbed because he was about to expose in print the fact that your own men use your camp meetings as a cover for robberies in whatever town is nearby."

"That's a lie!" The preacher's face went bright crimson. I found myself imagining how white and

distinct those crosses on his brow would look at
this moment if he didn't have that cloth across his
forehead.

"No lie. It's a fact. I've talked to Morgan Hamm.
I know what goes on. You're about the only one
who doesn't."

"This is a slander!"

"It's the truth, and you should know it and face
it. Boucher and Malone . . . both of them criminal.
Both of them using you."

"Those are two of my most trusted associates.
Good Christian men, both of them. How dare you
voice such lies!"

I stared at his face. The more I saw this man, the
more I spoke to him, the more clearly I saw these
wan features in the setting of Andersonville. Just
now, something almost fell into place in my
mind . . . yet it remained just out of reach, as always.

"Why are you staring at me that way?" he demanded. "You are an intrusive and rude man, sir,
and it is time for you to leave!"

"I'll leave . . . but I'll be back. I'll be here tonight, watching the crowd, riding the perimeter
while you preach. If I can, Preacher, I'll save your
life. In the meantime, keep yourself out of sight,
locked up. You're in danger as long as you are in
Bleeker County . . . probably as long as you are

in this region. If I were you, I'd go preach the word in Missouri a few months."

I turned and went out the door, down the rickety portable staircase. During my brief visit the campground had stirred to life a little; I saw two of Killian's men talking to one another while taking drinks from a big water barrel strapped on the back of a wagon. I heard one call the name "Brother James." Immediately I veered over to the pair.

"Is one of you James Boucher?" I said.

The taller of the two, a lean, mortician-looking type, eyed me with small eyes that peered down over a beaklike nose. "I am James Boucher."

"My name is Jed Wells. I'm a deputy for Bleeker County. I must tell you that your friend the Reverend in there is in danger. A man named Amos Broughton has determined that it is his duty to kill the preacher for something that happened years ago—I don't know just what that was, but the important thing is that the threat is real. You should look out for him if you care about him. Keep watch."

Boucher frowned at me. "Are you being serious with us, sir?"

"Very serious. Look out for him. And another thing: don't try your usual acts while you're in Bleeker County. I know what you do, the robberies and such. The local law has its eye on you. Tell your one-eared friend he'd best lay low and not show himself in this county. I'd like to question him very closely about a stabbing incident or two he was involved in."

Boucher's face had gone white while I spoke. "Sir, I have no notion as to what you mean."

"You're a liar, Boucher. And I'm fast losing my patience with liars. No robberies while you are in Bleeker County. You understand me? If anything happens, I'll have a shotgun stuck up that plug-cutter nose of yours quicker than you can holler 'Amen.' You understand me?"

He glared at me, so surprised to hear all this from a man with a badge on his shirt that he could find no words. No doubt he'd believed his schemes were all deeply secret.

"Keep watch over the preacher," I repeated in conclusion. Touching my hat, I nodded at them. "You two have a fine day and stay out of trouble."

I mounted up and rode out, leaving them staring after me.

Callianne was still at the jail, looking very tired, but as polite and appealing as always. I smiled a good-morning to her and thought how fortunate a man Amos really was, and how foolish he was to risk throwing it all away for the sake of whatever vengeance obsessed him.

"How's Joe?" I asked.

"Still asleep," she said. "He rested very peacefully. I suppose that laudanum must be quite a strong thing."

"I suppose. You look tired."

"It's hard to sleep in a chair. But I can go home and rest."

"Speaking of your home, Amos made a call on it last night."

"Amos!"

"He came looking for you, so he was surprised to find me there instead. I managed to get my rifle and scope back from him. But I don't know that it makes much difference. He's still determined to kill the preacher, and there's plenty of other rifles around he could use. Or he could do it some other way."

Her eyes filled with tears. "What is wrong with him, Jed? This isn't the Amos I married and have known all these years."

"It's Andersonville, Callianne. A place and experience like that does things to men that affect them the rest of their days. It leaves wounds that won't heal. Something happened there, involving the preacher, and now Amos believes that God wants him to settle whatever old score it is. He believes it is his divine duty to kill the man."

"I wish you could have arrested him last night."

"I tried. He just walked away. I couldn't shoot him, Callianne. You know that. So did he. And shooting him is all I could have done to stop him."

"Do you know where he's staying? Maybe an entire posse of men could bring him in."

"I don't know where he's staying. He may be moving around, just camping here and there, out of sight. He knows what he's doing is against the law, so he's laying low."

"If he comes back, I'll plead with him not to do this."

"Do it. Though I don't think he can be persuaded at this point. But maybe I'm wrong. He's had this obsession growing and festering in him for some time but still hasn't acted on it. He was attending Killian's meetings even over in the next county, for days. And he hasn't killed the Reverend yet. At heart Amos is a law-abiding man. It's his very role in life, upholding the law. This drive he feels to commit a murder is bound to have him torn up inside, different parts of himself at war with one another."

"I hope that the better side wins."

"God help us, and Amos, if it doesn't. And now, Callianne, I need to talk to you about something. There might be a way to make it difficult for Amos to do what he's planning . . . but it would ruin his career to do it."

She blanched to hear that but after a moment

said, "I'm listening. Better a ruined career than a destroyed life."

"Let's sit down and have a cup of coffee. I'll tell you what I have in mind . . . and I won't do it without your permission."

The newspaper office reeked of cigar smoke, most of it drifting out of the glass-walled office occupying the front left corner. Though the office walls were all windows, it made little difference because of the incredibly tall and precarious stacks of paper filling it. I could barely see over the tops of the shortest ones. Inside that office, rampaging around among his heaps of yellowed papers, was a man who could be no one else but the senior Smith, publisher and editor. He was sawed-off, stumpy, bald on the top, with white, wild hair around the ears, a stinking cigar jammed into his wide mouth. In all, he was just as I'd expected him to be, the kind of unpleasant man who probably had single-handedly molded Mark Taylor Smith into the pitiful specimen he was.

The elder Smith was ranting on to an ink-stained fellow about some problem with the printing press and did not notice me enter. I slipped around past a couple of desks and made my way toward the rear corner of the big room, where I saw Mark Smith laboring away on a tablet of paper.

"Writing a great masterpiece of American journalism, Smith?" I asked as I approached his desk.

He looked up, startled. His eyes widened when he saw who I was. "Hello," he said weakly. Right away I saw that he was still the battered, cowering poststabbing Smith, not yet back to the obnoxious strutting gander he'd been before.

I removed a couple of old newspapers from the chair beside his desk and sat down. He laid aside his pad, which I could see held an obituary in progress.

"Smith, I'm here to make you a proposition," I said. "How would you like a story that will make your father grin from ear to ear?"

He looked cautiously intrigued. "What story is that?"

"A story that will probably end the law enforcement career of Amos Broughton . . . but which might save him from doing something rash to a man who probably doesn't deserve it, and destining himself for the hangman's noose at the same time."

A new glitter was coming into Smith's piggy eyes. The phoenix was starting to rise from the ashes.

"Where am I going to get this story?"

"From me, and from Calliane Broughton."

"His own wife is willing to give me a story that will ruin her husband?"

"From her viewpoint, she's saving her husband."

He grinned. "I'll take that story, Mr. Wells."

"Good. You want to tell your father about it?"

He mulled that over a moment. "Not yet. Just let

me have it, and I'll show it to him. When can we talk? Now?"

"An hour from now. The Broughton house. But listen to me, Smith: if I see you start strutting and being rude and obnoxious and arrogant with Callianne Broughton, I'll spread all over this town about how you backed off that other story because you got stabbed. I'll describe you as the biggest, most pitiful coward to ever walk the hallowed halls of American frontier journalism. I'll put a character in my next book that will be you in the thinnest of disguises, and I'll make that character so sniveling and miserable and laughable that you'll never get so much as a flicker of respect anywhere you go for the rest of your days."

He swallowed. "That's a bit . . . unethical, don't you think, to threaten me that way?"

It was, and I'd never actually do it, but he needn't know that. "All you have to do to avoid that fate is behave yourself and act like a good little gentleman. What Callianne Broughton is going to do will feel to her like she's putting a knife in her husband's heart. I swear, if you start grinning and crowing about it all, I'll render you one castrated rooster, ethical or not. You understand me?"

His wide, pallid face nodded up and down. "I'll be polite," he said.

SMITH WAS AS GOOD AS HIS WORD. HE SAT LIKE A perfect gentleman in the front parlor of the Broughton home—a place whose interior he'd probably never expected to see—and took notes quietly as Callianne Broughton did the bravest and most difficult task of her life. When he asked questions, he did so without a trace of his habitual smugness, and if he was inwardly dancing to hear laid out before him the coming downfall of Amos Broughton, he didn't let it show. In an odd way I was actually proud of him.

Her words, supplemented by mine, were all given for quotation. We had carefully chosen those words in advance, limiting as much as possible what details we could, especially those involving the nature of Amos Broughton's hostility toward the Reverend Killian. We did not mention the Andersonville connection, given Killian's staunch denial of ever having been there. We simply told the newspaperman that Broughton and Killian had some unclear and apparently unfortunate earlier connection, which sparked whatever current bitterness drove Amos Broughton's actions. We didn't reveal that it was Amos who shot my attacker in the hills above Hanksville. Should that question ever come up, I'd already decided to speculate that the shooter was probably some unseen hunter who saw a man about to kill another and intervened. We did not mention Amos's drinking or let Smith see the rambling letter Amos had left Callianne before he took to the plains or wherever he was right now. We told Smith the letter was destroyed, because we did not want him to see it and detect the obvious: it was written by a very drunk man.

Though I was no newspaperman, I could see that this was indeed a barn-burning story even absent some of the more lurid side details. A local sheriff abandons his job and tells his wife and associates that God has called him to kill a famous and beloved traveling preacher. It was a story to end the career of a better man than Amos Broughton. Yet it would have beneficial effects otherwise. The entire population would become aware of the threat against Killian, which would act as a protection for him. Broughton would be unable to show his face before a knowledgeable public. Attenders of the camp meeting would be on the lookout for Broughton's presence and would deter him from any rash actions.

By giving this story to Smith, we were saving Amos Broughton from himself. Amputating his sheriff's career like a gangrenous leg, to be sure, but through that amputation giving the man a second chance.

The story would be out that night. Smith assured us of it. Though his father did not yet know what we were doing, there was no question that he would rush this story into print in a special edition. And Smith himself would take copies, fresh from the press, to the camp meeting. They would be passed around . . . and life would not be the same thereafter for Amos Broughton.

I wondered if we were doing the right thing, and if Amos would ever forgive me. What else could we do, though?

The interview ended, and Callianne bowed her head and wept. "I've just destroyed my own husband," she said. "It means so much to him to be sheriff. Now it will all be taken away."

"Callianne, it's Amos who has taken it away, by his own choice," I said. "He's neglecting his professional duty, planning a murder that he doesn't see as a murder. But the law will. If we don't stop him, Amos will probably end his life on the gallows. Losing his career is a small price compared to that."

Smith stood. "I've got a lot of writing to do, very quickly. Mrs. Broughton . . . I know your husband despises our newspaper. He has every reason to do so, and he'll despise us all the more after this is published. But I promise you this: whatever I can do to take the sharper edges off it, I'll do. I have no desire to cause you pain, ma'am."

She nodded, and I found myself thinking that maybe Mark Taylor Smith should get stabbed a little more often. It seemed to do his personality some good.

It wound up that I wrote as much of the story as Smith. It was a lot to put together, and easier if the task was divided. We wrote, compiled, edited, and set it all in type with Smith's unpleasant father all but leaping about in joy to finally have a story that would end the career of his nemesis. I felt like a traitor to Amos all the while and had to remind myself repeatedly of why we were doing this.

Mark Smith did himself proud one more time. His father, eager to twist the knife in Broughton's side, prepared a multidecked headline that declared the sheriff to be little more than the devil himself, a murderer of the lowest sort, and a "Hater of Those Who Proclaim the Gospel."

Trembling like a leaf in the wind, Mark Smith stood up to his father, challenging the headline, threatening to do damage to the press if he tried to print it. I could hardly believe it. Yet another new and better side of young Smith was revealing itself.

And he won the fight. The headline was removed, and replaced by one much more restrained.

I waited until the printing began before I left, and took some of the first copies. My first stop was at the office, where I let Joe take a look and left a copy on the desk for Leroy, who was out in town doing the normal work of a lawman, work that for me seemed to be too much pushed aside by the oddities of the present situation.

Then I went to Callianne, and watched her weep as she read the story. But when she was finished, she nodded and handed the newspaper back to me. "It is done as well as the assassination of a man's character and work and dreams can be done."

"I'm very sorry it came to this," I said.

"We did what we had to do. Now let's just pray that it is sufficient to stop anything worse from happening." She paused. "He'll not forgive me, you know."

"He will. You're too great a treasure not to be forgiven. When Amos is himself again, he'll understand, and be grateful."

I said it, but even as I did, I wondered if it was true.

The campground was full, packed with people, wagons, tents, and arbor shelters. There were nearly twice as many people as I'd seen the night I visited the camp in Russell County, and I wondered what drew them so passionately to this preacher. Perhaps he truly was a godly man with a divine gift. But if so, why would he lie about his past?

Perhaps I would never know. All I knew was that it was my duty to help keep him alive. I rode the perimeter of the big encampment, watching the darkness beyond the great circle of light spread by scores of campfires and torches and lanterns. Was Amos out there? I had to believe he was, and that he would draw in nearer the darker the night became.

He no longer had my rifle. It rode in its boot on my saddle. But there were rifles aplenty to be had. And plenty of other ways to kill a man besides shooting him.

I drew little attention as I moved about in the dark. The music began, swelling beautifully toward the patchily overcast sky, which only occasionally let through moonlight enough to let me look about for Broughton. I saw nothing of him.

But I did see Smith, at last, entering the crowd bearing a big stack of newspapers. With him were two boys with stacks of their own, and the three of them scattered out across the camp, handing out papers to all who would accept them. Seated in my saddle, unseen by most, I watched as people began to read first the headline, then the story. Conversations began, the music now carried by fewer and fewer voices—and eventually Killian's men on the stage noticed what was happening. Boucher descended, took one of the papers, looked at it. He quickly gathered other copies and vanished off behind the stage, probably looking for Killian.

A deep sadness overcame me. The act was done. Amos Broughton's career had just been drowned in printer's ink. But at least the word was out. Everyone now knew of the threat against Killian, and for that reason alone the threat was lessened.

Was Broughton out there, close enough to see what was happening, wondering what were those papers being spread about, what was the cause of the visible tumult of the crowd? The spirit of worship was giving way to excitement and bewilderment. I could guess the questions flying around the camp. Could it really be true that the very sheriff of the county was spoiling for the murder of the very preacher they'd come to hear? It said so right there in the newspaper, the information attributed to Broughton's own wife and to one of his deputies—me. Was this a hoax or real?

At length the hymn ended, just faltering away as the crowd's attention shifted. The songleader looked defeated and confused, then obtained a copy of the newspaper for himself. As far away as I was, I could detect his shock in the way his posture and manner changed as he read it.

A few moments later Killian was on the stage. No dramatic magician's appearance this time. He simply walked onto the stage, a copy of the paper in his hand, and went to the pulpit. The crowd hushed its chatter; someone called up, "Preacher, don't stand up there, all visible that way! It ain't safe for you!" Others joined in with calls of agreement.

Killian raised his hands for silence, and looked around the huge crowd. I had a strong impression that he had not a clue about what he should say.

"Beloved brethren and sisters," he finally began, "I stand before you as a man bewildered. Never in my experience of service with the Lord have I encountered such a thing . . . as this." He held up the newspaper.

"Is it true?" someone called.

"I cannot say," Killian replied. "I received a warning. . . . How seriously that warning deserved to be taken, I don't know. Now I find this printed in the local paper, and I am still unsure whether there is any credence in it. But this I can tell you: I have come to this place to preach the gospel, and nothing will stop me from it! No threat, no newspaper story, no idle words!" With that, he dramatically wadded the newspaper into a ball and tossed it behind him.

This act handed the crowd something they could grab hold of, set a tone with which they could harmonize their own responses. Several score of people followed the preacher's lead and wadded up their own papers, throwing them to the ground or into the nearest fire. Cries of "Amen!" and

"Glory!" echoed across the camp. Smith, standing off to the side near the stage, suffered some verbal abuse and flinched visibly, the messenger, as usual, taking the brunt of anger over the message.

This kind of response wasn't universal, though. Many continued to read their copies and to talk among themselves. A couple of men near the back edge of the crowd, having noticed my presence, came back to me.

"You're the deputy Jed Wells quoted in this article?"

"I am."

"Is this true?"

"It is. The Reverend Killian is in danger. I admire his courage in going on despite it, but it's not wise. If these worshipers care about him, they'll persuade him to close this meeting down."

It was just at that moment that the shooting broke out up at the stage.

⇥ 26 ⇤

It happened so fast that it was almost impossible to take it in. The gunfire came in rapid pops; Killian flinched back, fell, landing on his rump. The cloth came off his forehead, exposing his scars to those close enough to see them. Boucher leaped off the back of the stage, and my old friend from the barn loft prostrated himself on the stage, hands covering the back of his head.

The crowd nearest the stage pulled back, people falling over one another, trying to get away. Farther out the reactions were more mixed. Some people ran, others ducked for cover, others simply froze or threw themselves in front of their children.

I leaped off my horse, drawing my pistol, and ran up "Glory Avenue" toward the stage. People poured out in pandemonium, crowding in front of me, forcing me to dart this way and that as I headed for the stage area.

How could Broughton have done it? How could a man so well known have gotten so close to the stage without being recognized and pointed out—especially considering that the newspapers in the crowd's possession indicted him by name?

When I finally broke through and reached the front, others had already wrestled Broughton to the ground and disarmed him. He was currently trapped under a huddle of five or six men, and probably very nearly crushed to death by their combined weight.

"Let me have him!" I said, thumbing out my badge. "Get off him!"

They did, as quickly as they could, and I took him by the arm and jerked him to his feet.

It wasn't Amos Broughton. This was a stranger.

"Who are you?" I yelled into his face. "Answer me!"

"My name is Tom Dewitt," he said.

"Why did you shoot the preacher?"

"I didn't. I missed him."

I backhanded him across the jaw. "You answer me straight—no jesting around! Why did you shoot at him?"

"I don't apologize for it. I only wish I'd killed the sorry traitor!"

Traitor. The sin of Judas.

Tom Dewitt . . .

Another piece of the puzzle found its place.

"Come on, Dewitt," I said. "Let's pay a visit to the jail. We've got some talking to do."

* * *

I took him back into a cell, had him sit on the bunk,
and stood looking down at him by the light of a single lantern burning out in the hall between the cell
blocks. Shadows of the bars lay across his face,
which bore a look of terror that was trying hard to
hide beneath a feigned confident defiance. I suppose he thought I was going to strike him some
more.

The jail was empty. After his long and opiated
sleep, Reid had gone home to continue his recuperation. Dewitt and I were alone.

"Where are you from, Dewitt?" I asked.

"Illinois. Just moved over into Bedford two
months ago."

"Why did you come to the camp meeting? To kill
the preacher?"

"No. I came to hear him. Everybody talked
about what a fine preacher he was. But then, when
I seen who he really is . . ."

"What do you mean?"

"That man ain't no Edward Killian. Not by a
long shot. He's made that name up. His real name
is Skelly."

It clicked. I remembered. "Edward Skelly," I
said.

Dewitt stared at me, frowning. "That's right. Edward Skelly."

"You were at Andersonville. And so was he."

His eyes widened, then narrowed. "I was. How did you know?"

"Because I was there too. We ran across each other there a couple of times, Dewitt. My name is Jed Wells."

"Good God! The same who lived for a couple of months in that shebang over near the dead line?" The "dead line" to which he referred was an invisible line that circled the prison camp inside the stockade walls, crudely marked at most places by a kind of small fence. Anyone who stepped across that fence into the area between the dead line and the stockade walls was subject to being shot to death by the guards.

"You shared your rations with me one day when I was sick, Dewitt," I said. "I never got the chance to thank you. And it makes me feel mighty bad right now that I struck you."

"It's all right. Most of the blow glanced off."

"I need to learn some things from you, Dewitt. Did you read the newspaper that got passed out at the campground?"

"Yes. Enough of it. Is the Amos Broughton who is after Skelly the same who was imprisoned with us?"

"Yes."

"Then I say more power to him. I hope he does better than me and kills the bastard stone dead."

"Why, Dewitt? What did the preacher do?"

"He betrayed some good men, that's what. Told

the guards about their tunnel. You remember what happened to them? Punished by Wirz so severe that two of them died."

"Stephen Morse and Kelly O'Brien."

"That's right. I'll never forget what happened to them. I'll never forgive it."

"Broughton hasn't forgotten either."

"Then bless him, I say. Bless him."

"You're sure that Killian—Skelly—was the one who betrayed them?"

"I'm sure. He did it to get extra food from the guards. They'd use it to bribe for information about escape attempts . . . you'd know about that, I guess. But what you might not is that Skelly paid a price." With that, Dewitt touched his brow.

"The cross scars . . ."

"Just one of them, to start with. And not really a cross. Just the letter T, standing for traitor. I helped hold him down while they cut it into his flesh. Cut it deep so the scar would be big and white for the rest of his days. I wish now we'd just cut his throat."

"But there are three marks now."

"Yes. You know what he's done, don't you? Ain't you figured it out? He's took the mark that was put on him to show his sin and turned it into something to make him look righteous." Dewitt's face went dark, and he turned and spat on the floor in pure contempt. "Damn him . . . damn his Judas soul! I wish I'd not missed him. I don't care if I'd have hung for shooting him. I'd kill him without a flinch and dance my way to the gallows. I hate the bastard. Hate him."

I looked at Dewitt sadly. I pitied him, pitied the pain that his lingering bitterness must surely bring him—but at the same time I understood him. I carried some of the same myself, the remnant that had not been excised through the healing scratch of pen on paper. Even now, hearing at last the Andersonville secret of Edward "Killian" Skelly, I found myself hating the preacher too.

At Andersonville there was no lower form of life than a traitor. The maggots that squirmed in the filth of the latrine swamp were more exalted beings in the eyes of Andersonville's lost souls than were those among that sad number who would betray their companions.

"So now I know," I said. "Broughton wouldn't tell me. He didn't want me to know, because he was protecting me. He knew that if he did something to Killian and was caught for it, the more I knew about his motives, the more suspect I'd be too."

"I hope he gets Killian. I hope he's getting him right now."

"Good Lord," I whispered. Rising, I left the cell, locking it behind me. I fetched up my rifle again, returned to my horse outside, and rode at top speed toward the meeting ground.

* * *

As I drew near I realized I was already too late. A great flow of humanity came toward me, people fleeing the campground with pallid faces, mothers shielding daughters.

I reached down and grabbed a fleeing man by the collar; he almost ran his feet out from under himself.

"What happened?"

"Another shot fired at Killian . . . and this one struck him!"

"Is he dead?"

"I don't know—I saw him go down, and then everyone just broke and ran! Let me go!"

He jerked free and ran on.

What a fool Killian was! He should never have tried to continue that camp meeting after the first incident. No doubt he'd felt compelled to prove his courage to his faithful—and Broughton had gotten his opportunity.

Not all those at the campground had fled. A good number remained, most of them in a great cluster at the center of which I expected to find the preacher.

Pushing my way through, I discovered Killian on the ground, Boucher tending to him. I knelt beside him.

"How is he?"

"Clipped him across the side of the neck. Not

life-threatening." Boucher glanced at me as he spoke, and I felt his resentment of me radiating off him like heat. I wondered if Killian had questioned him about the robbery accusations I'd revealed.

Killian looked pale as milk, but pushed himself up. "Don't do that, Reverend," one of the remaining faithful admonished. "You need to wait for the doctor to get here."

"Here he comes now!" someone else announced.

The doctor had no patience for the crowd and forced everyone back. Most remained and watched him begin his preliminary examination. I took advantage of the time to ask questions. Any witnesses? From where and how far away had the shot come?

No one had seen or heard anything particularly helpful. The most I could learn was that the shot had come from the darkness beyond the camp, that two people had seen the flash of the shot, and that no one had caught a glimpse of the gunman. From the sound of the shot and the distance it was fired, it was assumed that the weapon was a rifle.

Leroy joined me and told me he'd done little better. "After the shot, I headed out in the direction it had come from," he said. "No good. Whoever it was was long gone, and it was too dark to see anything."

"Broughton?"

"Who else could it be?"

"Let's break up this little party, Leroy."

"Let's do."

We began dispersing the crowd, sending home all those who had come from town or nearby areas, and urging back to their individual campsites those who had taken up short-term residence at the campground. Then Leroy went back to town himself, while I lingered.

Meanwhile, the doctor continued his work, and at last stood.

"How is he, Doctor?" Malone asked.

"A very superficial wound. More blood than anything else. Simply a deep graze along his neck. He'll be fine."

Killian stood, looking woozy but regaining a little color now that he'd been tended and knew he had no serious damage. "I'll be back behind the pulpit tomorrow," he declared.

I stepped forward. "Killian, you and me need to talk."

He wheeled and glared at me. "What was the meaning of distributing those newspapers in this meeting? You intruded on a sacred occasion, disrupting all we were trying to achieve!"

"The purpose was to protect you, sir. The more people know the danger you're in, and that Broughton is out to get you, the less likely Broughton is to succeed. He can't show his face now."

"It wasn't Broughton who attacked me the first time, now, was it?"

"No. And I need to talk to you about that."

"I have nothing to say to you."

"Yes, Mr. Skelly, you do."

It was as if I'd kicked him. His eyes did something very strange, and he moved his lips but made no noise.

"What'd you just call him?" Boucher asked.

"Any further conversation needs to be between me and the preacher, in private. Right, Reverend?"

Killian nodded. His color was gone again. He looked like he might pass out, but didn't.

"Come on," I said. "Let's go to your wagon and talk."

He lit a lamp with trembling hands, then sat down and stared at me by its light, saying nothing, looking like a man expecting any number of tragedies to immediately befall him.

I stared at him a long time, heightening his misery. At last I spoke softly. "I want you to pack up this camp meeting, take your criminal associates, your fancy house wagon, your 'Glory Avenue' signposts, and your traitor scar and get out of this county. And I don't want you ever to return. You understand me, Skelly?"

He licked his dry lips and decided to give lies another try. "I'm Edward Killian. My name isn't Skelly."

"Don't lie to me, Preacher. I know you now. I was reminded of who you really are when I talked to that first man who tried to kill you. I almost wish he'd succeeded. Tom Dewitt, late of Andersonville, reminded me not only who you are, but what you are. I was right. You were at Andersonville. And your name was Edward Skelly. I remember you. But what I didn't know about you until now was that you were a traitor, betraying a tunnel's existence and the men who'd dug it. And because of you, two of them died."

"I'm . . . not Skelly."

"You are. And those marks on your forehead, there's nothing holy about them. That center one started out as the letter T. For traitor. The others I guess you added on your own. Took some grit to cut your own forehead that deep, no doubt. That I'll give you credit for. Beyond that, I have nothing but contempt for you. Get out of this county. Be gone by morning."

"You have no authority to order that. You're just a deputy."

"If you don't go, I'll turn Tom Dewitt out of the jail and tell him to finish the job he started. I'll have Smith print your whole history in his newspaper. You're leaving, sir. Tonight."

I stood to go. I was no longer concerned about this man's welfare. I would still seek to keep Broughton from killing him during the time he remained here, but it would no longer be in any way for his sake. It would be for Broughton's.

Killian rose. "Listen to me!" he said, stepping between me and the door. "You're wrong about me! I was no traitor!"

"So you're admitting at last that you were at Andersonville?"

He paused, then said, "Yes. I was there." He actually looked as if it physically hurt to say the words.

"You were there . . . you were recognized by others as the traitor who betrayed the tunnel, and you even bear the scar on your forehead that was put there for punishment. Yet you persist in denying that you were that traitor! How can you expect me to believe you?"

"I cannot give you a good reason. All I can do is tell you the truth: I was not that traitor."

"Then why the scar on your forehead? Why are those who actually saw that traitor, and dealt with him, so certain that you are that man that they're ready to kill you?"

"I am not free to explain."

"But there is an explanation?"

He paused. "Yes."

"I don't believe you."

He bowed his head. "God knows the truth even if you don't."

"The same God who commands that we not tell lies? That God? How can you stand in the pulpit, claiming those marks on your head are a sign of God's favor, knowing that it is a lie? How could you have denied so persistently that you were at Andersonville, when all the while it was a lie, and you knew it?"

To my surprise, tears welled up in his eyes. "I cannot turn aside your accusation. I have indeed been a liar. I have lived a life inconsistent with the very things I preach regarding truth and honesty. I can't and don't deny it. All I can tell you is I had no choice. In all things, I've done what I had to do, and had I done otherwise, much worse things would have come about. But, God help me, how I wish some things could have been different. Small turns along the way, little decisions made in a different manner . . . everything could have changed."

"You talk in riddles. Self-serving riddles. I have no regard for you, Preacher. You are a hypocrite and a liar, and I have no use for such."

He looked intently at me, through his tears. "Are you without sin yourself, sir? Is there nothing in your past that you wouldn't change? Is there nothing in your own mind and heart that haunts you? Are there no things you have done that you have sought to justify to yourself time and again, even though you know there is no justifying them? Have you made no mistakes?"

I stared at him, struck dumb. My heart pounded hard.

"You condemn me, and I understand that. But all I have done, even the lies I have told, I have done because—God forgive me—I could see no other way. I bear the scar on my forehead for a reason. I can't tell it to you. But there is a reason. Please believe me."

I turned to leave, suddenly eager to be away from him and this place. The questions he had asked pricked something painful deep inside me, and I wanted no more.

I shoved open the door and stepped out onto the top stair.

"Deputy," he said.

I turned, glaring back at him.

"This is all I can tell you: there is a great principle at the heart of the faith I profess and teach. It is the principle born at the place these scars represent." He touched his forehead. "It is the principle of substitution . . . the innocent taking upon themselves the guilt of those not innocent. Bearing their punishment for them. Bearing the scars they should have borne themselves."

"I don't know what you are talking about."

"And perhaps, sir, you never will."

"Get out of the county, Killian . . . Skelly."

He did not reply, only closed the door and left me outside, alone.

I saw Boucher and Malone standing together, talking, now looking at me as I emerged. I strode up to them.

"Hello, lawman," Boucher said in a contemptuous tone. "Still stirring up problems, I see. Do you plan to have the accusations you made printed in the newspaper?"

"If you're talking about your sideline criminal enterprises, you should be aware that the newspaper already knows about them. And I've had a few words with somebody who knows it all."

"Hamm, no doubt."

"I'll not say who it was. You might send a one-eared murderer to try to shut them up. But listen to me: that preacher in there, you'd best keep a watch on him. Two different men have tried to kill him tonight, and only one of them is locked up. The other will keep trying until he succeeds. You'd best keep Killian alive, or you'll be losing that convenient cover you've got for your bank robberies and such."

"We'll watch out for him, lawman. You can count on that. But maybe you ought to do some watching out for yourself. Sometimes folks who come along stirring up trouble get stirred themselves."

"Is that a threat?"

"Just an observation."

"You want to mess with me, Boucher, you come on. Anytime you want. You may find me a tougher apple to bite into than you think."

I went to my horse, mounted, and rode away.

GHOSTS RODE WITH ME AS I LEFT THE CAMPGROUND and returned to town. Ghosts were always with me because they were part of me, but more visible now than before.

The preacher's words had given them fresh life. I suspected he knew about ghosts too . . . and had plenty of his own.

I stared straight ahead but spoke to the heavens, in my mind. Why had there been a war? Why had I been drawn into it? Why had the skills that I'd originally developed to help keep my family fed been perverted for use in killing men?

Killian's words came back: *God help me, how I wish some things could have been different.*

Amen, Preacher. Amen.

I found Callianne waiting on the porch of the jail. Her eyes were red, her face streaked with the marks of tears not fully wiped away.

"I heard, Jed. I heard. Is it true?"

I tied my horse to the rail. "Amos shot at him,

yes. We assume it was Amos, in any case. He hit the preacher, but there was no serious wound."

She bowed her head and wept. "What a nightmare this is! Jed, did we do the right thing, having all that printed in the newspaper?"

"I think so. Callianne, listen. I know now what this was all about. I know why Amos is doing all this. Come inside. Let me fix you a cup of coffee, and we'll talk."

We entered the jail. I pulled up a chair, built up a fire in the stove, readied coffee for brewing. There was no noise from the cells on the far side of the rear office door. I figured Dewitt was sleeping.

As the coffee began to brew, I sat down at the desk. "Killian is an imposter," I told her. "And Amos has known it. He didn't tell me, or you, probably because he didn't want us drawn into any kind of legal difficulties as accomplices. And I'm sure he also didn't want us to try to stop what he meant to do."

"What do you mean, Killian is an imposter?"

"His name isn't Killian. It's Skelly." I went on to tell her the full story, as far as I knew it. She listened in rapt attention.

"I'm astonished," she said when it was over. "No wonder Amos has been so obsessed! But if this man is so hated, why did the other prisoners not kill him at Andersonville after they found he was a traitor?"

"Probably because commission of murder could

get a prisoner in serious trouble. Besides, it was considered quite a torture to force a marked man to go on living among those he'd betrayed. He had to live in peril of his life every moment."

"But why do Amos and this other man, Dewitt, want to kill him now, so many years later?"

"I think it is the fact that Killian has found a way to hide his shame. It eats at them. The three crosses mask his scar, and turn it from something to shame him into something that causes people to view him as far holier than the average man. I think it was that that drove Amos so mad." As I said those latter words, I wondered how they struck her. I'd just called her husband a madman. But she did not disagree or look offended. I think she believed he'd been driven mad as well.

"Jed, if Killian is what you say, I don't much care what happens to him. But I don't want Amos to become a murderer in the eyes of the law. What happened at Andersonville would not excuse him from the consequences if he kills the preacher."

"No. So we have to stop him."

"You'll guard Killian?"

"As much as possible. And I've told Killian's people to guard him too. I think they will. They have a strong interest in keeping him alive and preaching."

"Jed, if Amos comes home, what should I do?"

"Do this: pretend to be sick. Very ill. Collapse.

Act like you're passed out. Bite your tongue until it bleeds and then cough the blood for him to see. Make him bring you into town for medical care. Then we can get him, and lock him up."

"It would shame him so much, being jailed in his own prison."

"Better a cell than a hangman's noose."

Callianne didn't remain for coffee. Worried, tired, desirous of being home in case her husband made another unexpected appearance there, she left before I poured the first cup.

I sat sipping my coffee alone, thinking over all that had happened, and about the person of Edward Skelly.

Skelly . . . what was it about that name? Something I had not yet remembered. I went to my store of personal effects and removed my list of Andersonville's prisoners, scanning down it until I found the Skelly name. But not just one . . . two. Edward Skelly's name was there, but above it was that of Bartholomew Skelly.

Now I remembered! Two Skelly brothers had been there. Captured independently, and sent to the same prison by chance or destiny. I'd not known either of them well, but did recall seeing them. But only once did I see them together. I remembered that someone had told me the pair were at odds, estranged. One of those stray little details that lingered in my mind for no obvious reason.

I put down the list of names and pondered very deeply for a few minutes, and an intriguing theory began to take form.

Substitution. That was what the preacher had said. The key to the truth.

Remembering that Dewitt was back there and might be able to contribute some of his own knowledge of the Skelly brothers, I headed back into the cell area . . .

. . . and found it empty.

I stood in disbelief, gaping at the open door of Dewitt's cell. How the devil had he managed to open it?

A note lay on his bed. I went in, picked it up, read it . . . and swore out loud.

I had to find Leroy, right away.

The arrival of a camp meeting outside of town had done nothing to sanctify the lives of those who loved Bull Creek Avenue. I found Leroy busy trying to quiet a rowdy drunk who didn't like the notion of visiting the jail, despite the fact he'd just urinated across a bar because somebody bet him he wouldn't. He'd filled most of a row of empty glasses sitting on a tray behind the bar, and from the general character of this particular saloon, I doubted those glasses had ever had a better cleaning or ever would again.

"Leroy, come with me!" I said while the drunk

bellowed and made big, wild swings with his fists. Leroy ducked each time, though the fellow never really came close to him.

"I'm busy right now, Jed," Leroy said, moving in and trying to get a knee into the man's groin.

"Leroy, Broughton has broken a prisoner out of the jail. The one who shot at Killian from the crowd. He must want to team up with him to get the preacher."

Leroy was still too busy to answer. Tired of the distraction, I moved in and slammed the drunk's jaw with three fast jabs, elbowed the back of his neck, and kneed his stomach as he fell.

Leroy looked down at him, panting hard. "Showoff," he muttered.

"Come on, Leroy. We've got to get to Killian. Broughton has an ally now. This is now a two-man job."

"What about this one?" He pointed at the prone man at his feet. "We need to lock him up."

"Leroy, do you not understand what I'm saying? I locked up the man who shot off his pistol at Killian before I headed back to the camp meeting, when Broughton took a shot at Killian too. After you left, and while I was there talking to Killian, Broughton circled back to the jail, freed my jailbird, and very kindly left me a note telling me he'd done it. Admitted to shooting at Killian too. Amos is loco, Leroy. He's not even trying to hide anything anymore . . . nothing but himself, anyway, until he can get the job done."

"What are we supposed to do?"

"Go to Killian, Arrest him if we have to. We'll make up a charge. Lock him up in the jail and then guard the jail so that Amos can't get to him. Then we'll arrange to escort Killian away from here and make sure he doesn't return to this county."

"You going to get a court to order that?"

"I don't know. Yes, I suppose. You're the one who has the real deputy experience. I'm just a writer playing make-believe, remember?"

"I don't know that you can get Killian ordered out of the county without a reason."

"We'll worry about that later. Right now let's just go get him."

We went out of the saloon, onto the dark street. Leroy's horse was tethered a block up the street; he trotted down the boardwalk toward it. I headed for my own horse, a few yards up the street in the opposite direction.

I saw a movement in the shadows, a figure stepping out from a recessed doorway onto a boardwalk. Something about him drew my attention; I glanced his direction.

A match flared, rising toward his face to light a cigar. I saw broad, plain features, a head bald as an egg . . . and a bit of mangled scar flesh where one ear had been.

There was threat in how he looked at me. Just as there had been threat in the words Boucher had spoken to me earlier. I knew now that the arrangement had already been made. I was a troublesome deputy, talking too loudly and too much about the secret little crime network of the unwitting Killian's associates, and one-ear the bank robber was ready to silence me.

I couldn't worry about him now. There were more pressing matters afoot.

Leroy rode up to my side as I mounted. "Ready?" he asked.

"Ready," I said. We rode off down the garish and rowdy avenue.

I glanced over my shoulder. One-ear had stepped down off his porch and was watching me depart. He did not try to hide his stare when I looked at him.

We approached a corner, started to turn. One more glance back. One-ear was gone.

I felt an odd, creeping feeling in the middle of my back. A feeling of endangerment . . . the kind of sensation I'd always felt before pulling the trigger back during the war, when the target was clear in my sights.

But this time I felt like the rifle was trained on me. I glanced back yet again.

"What are you looking for?" Leroy asked, sounding cross.

"Nothing," I said. "Just a man I saw, that's all."

"Who was he?"

"Just a man."

⇌ 28 ⇌

OUTSIDE OF TOWN, BROTHER TIMOTHY, LATE OF the Gray family barn loft and now inexplicably covered in blood, staggered toward us as we rode toward Killian's house on wheels. I came down off my horse and headed for him, catching him as he collapsed. We were still a quarter mile from the campground. He must have staggered that far.

"Timothy, what happened?" I asked. "Are you cut? Shot?"

"Took him . . . they took him away!" he said. "Hit . . . me . . . when I tried to stop . . . them."

He was close to passing out. "Who has been taken?" I asked. "Killian?"

"Yes . . . Killian . . ."

I glanced up at Leroy. Too late! It was becoming a common state for me.

"Who took him?"

"Same man . . . who shot at him . . . and another man . . ."

"Broughton and Dewitt," I said.

At that point, Brother Timothy passed out. I shook my head in disgust.

"I can't believe they had this one guarding Killian," I said. "He's weak as warm water, this one is."

"Jed, if they've got Killian, he's probably already dead."

"I know. Leroy, can you get Timothy here back to the campground? I want to ride ahead."

"Why you?" Leroy asked sharply. "Since when did you take over the Bleeker County sheriff's office? You bark orders like God came down and tapped you on the shoulder."

"Sorry I irritate you so, Leroy. But if you recall, you walked away from the sheriff's office, and right now you're only back on a temporary basis."

"No more temporary than you."

This was wasting time. "Fine, then. You ride ahead. I'll get Timothy back to camp."

"He probably should go to a physician."

"I'm not riding back to town with him. Not with Killian already taken."

Leroy rode off at a gallop, quickly going out of sight.

Annoyed, very nearly panicked by fear of what we'd find at the camp, I considered simply leaving Timothy where he lay. But I couldn't do it. If he died out here, I'd always consider myself responsible.

I gave him a quick examination and found, as

best I could tell by the light of one match after another, that the only injury he possessed was a sound knock to the back of his head. The skin was broken, accounting for the blood, and his skull probably had a crack, but my own opinion—untrained except by what I'd learned in Andersonville, where all men were doctors for all others—was that he was probably not seriously injured.

I managed to get him onto my horse, somehow, and tied him in place with a short length of rope I habitually carried coiled on my saddle. Then, frustrated by my slowness, I led him to the camp.

Boucher was there, with Malone and a few others of Killian's entourage I didn't know. Also present were some men of the camp itself, apparently trying to clumsily organize themselves into a search party.

"Where is Deputy Fletch?" I asked as I began untying the now half-conscious Timothy from the saddle. "Somebody help me here."

"He's gone off that way," answered Boucher. "That's the way they took him off." He came over and with reluctance began tugging at the bonds holding Timothy in place.

"Two men?"

"Yes. One was the man who shot at him from the crowd, the other a man I didn't know. They held us at gunpoint and forced the Reverend away with them. I thought you locked up that first one, deputy!"

"I did. The other one sprang him free. He's the sheriff and he's got the key." I waved down at Timothy. "How did he, of all people, happen to be guarding the Reverend?"

"We were all guarding him, deputy. Timothy just happened to have the misfortune of being too close when the ruffians sneaked in, and got himself a blow on the topknot besides. It addled him so he wandered off."

"Keep an eye out in case they return for any reason," I said. "I'm off to follow Deputy Fletch."

"How fortunate for us we have such fine lawmen on the job," Boucher said with the deepest of sarcasm.

I loped off into the darkness, hoping I could manage to pick up Leroy's trail.

It proved far easier than I'd thought. The moonlight spilled out through clouds now breaking up and revealed a road before me. In the momentary stark brightness, I saw fresh prints of horses that had passed, even the lingering clouds of dust kicked up by their hooves.

It could have been the dust of any traveler, but instinct and likelihood spoke in favor of it being Leroy. I wished he'd not ridden off ahead of me.

As I advanced I began to wonder if I was wasting my time. Clouds covered the moon again, making the road almost invisible. Still, I found sufficient evidence of Leroy's passage. But did he know where he was going? Was he sure that Broughton had come this way?

Several times I considered stopping, turning back. But each time, the bright moon sailed out and revealed the road and dust clouds ahead of me, so I continued.

Maybe Leroy knew something I didn't, or had some notion about where the kidnappers were taking their victim.

Another hour passed, and still I had not caught up with Leroy. I stopped, about to give up.

At that moment I became aware that I was not alone. Someone else was here. Behind me.

I turned, wondering if someone from the camp was trailing me just as I was trailing Leroy. This certainly was not that posse that was in formation while I was there; I'd seen no sign of them at all.

At most there were two people, though probably just one.

Some instinct warned me, and I turned my horse off the road and into the brush. The rider behind me—for now I saw it was only one man—advanced slowly. Looking for me, I thought. That warning instinct was all the stronger now.

He advanced until he was just in front of me on the road. There he stopped. And my horse gave a small whinny.

The moon sailed out and I saw him looking back

at me. He wore no hat, and the brilliant moonlight shone off his bald pate and illuminated the nub that once had been an ear.

He'd followed me all the way from town. Boucher and Malone's man, the thief, the blades-man who had stabbed Smith and Hamm . . . the man who no doubt had come after me to kill me here out on the plains, in the dark, where no one would know.

"How much they paying you for this?" I asked him.

He shook his head. "Ain't them I'm doing this for. I'm doing this for me. Boucher says you know about what we do. They say you talk about it all threatening. We can't have that, now can we?"

"So you decided all on your own to shut me up?"

"That's the long and short of it." His hand moved, fast, and came up with a pistol. "Sorry about this, Marshal."

I drew my pistol and shot him out of the saddle before he could even tighten his finger on the trig-ger. He fell with a grunt, staring up at the sky. The moon went behind a cloud, then sailed out again. He stared up at it with a look of disbelief.

"I'm a deputy, not a marshal," I told him.

His eyes shifted over to look at me, and he grunted.

"You lied to me. They did pay you to do this, didn't they?"

He nodded and closed his eyes.

"Sorry it had to be this way," I told him.

He grunted again, very softly, and died.

I watched him die, and wished that it bothered me more to see it. I realized the depth of what had just happened here, that a man was gone because of me. Sure, it was self-defense; sure, he was an evil soul. I had done only what I'd been forced to do. But still, shouldn't it hurt more to watch a man die?

That depth of feeling was one of the things that had been stolen from me during my days of looking through a sharpshooter's scope, and when I was trapped behind the walls of the Andersonville stockade.

I had lost a little of my humanity in those times. I no longer believed that what I'd lost would ever fully return.

More noise on the road . . . someone coming my way. But from the opposite direction.

It was Leroy. He rode up with rifle in hand. He halted his horse and stared down at the corpse on the road.

"I know him," he said. "I've seen him on Bull Creek Avenue."

"He works with Killian's bunch. Robs for them and so on. They sent him after me to kill me. He followed us all the way from town."

"He drew on you?"

"Yes. There's nobody's word about that but mine, though."

"What will we do with him?"

"For now, leave him. Nothing else to be done. What matters now is finding Killian before they can kill him."

"I've lost them, Jed. I thought I was right on their trail . . . I think I truly was, but then I just lost them."

"So what now?"

"I don't know. I think we'll have to just go back. There's no finding anyone at night, even with the moonlight bright. I think they must have left the road." He glanced down at the dead man again. "Should we take him on back?"

I didn't get the chance to answer. Far out on the plains we heard two fast shots. We glanced at one another, and without a word turned our tiring horses in that direction.

There was no road as such. Just a horse trail, and that was hard to see except at those moments the moon and clouds were cooperative. We rode into more rugged country, hilly by the standards of Kansas, and came upon a stream that meandered into a thick stand of trees.

"Listen!" Leroy said, raising a hand.

I'd already heard it. Voices on the other side of the hill, carried on a gust of wind.

"Sounds like Broughton," Leroy whispered.

"It does," I agreed. "I wonder what the shooting was about?"

"Can't you guess? They've gunned down Killian. What else could it be?"

We were off our horses now, moving on foot, weapons in hand. I had little hope for Killian. Those two shots surely had marked the end of his life. And that meant as well the end of the life of Amos Broughton. He would hang for this.

There might be another sad twist to this as well. I believe that just maybe I had figured out Killian's secret, and why he claimed so adamantly that, despite all the evidence to the contrary, he truly had been no Andersonville traitor.

I prayed that by some miracle he was still alive.

"I smell smoke," Leroy said.

"So do I."

Leroy and I topped the low hill, dropped to our bellies, crawled forward a few yards, and looked down into a shallow valley. I had a sense of having done this before, and realized it reminded me much of the little hollow Reid and I had entered north of Hanksville. But this time there was no little shack house and spread of outbuildings. There was nothing but moonlight and the faint flicker of a campfire, revealing . . . what? I was too far away to see.

"Can you tell who it is, Leroy?"

"No. Not enough light down there."

"It might be them . . . we can ride on in. . . ."

"Jed, I swear, I believe they may have a man situated for a hanging. It looks like there could be a man astride a horse."

We had to get down there. But if we went barreling in, would they not just more hurriedly send him swinging, hanging him before we could interfere—or even shooting him?

"You got that rifle scope of yours?" Leroy asked.

"Yes. In my saddlebag."

"Take a look through it, then. Like a telescope."

Odd, how my heart hammered against my ribs so violently. Strange, how the simple prospect of putting that device to my eye, nestling it against my crescent scar, breaking a vow I'd made to myself, filled me with such a terror.

"I . . . I can't do that, Leroy."

He gaped at me. "What?"

"Leroy, I can't look through that scope again."

"You're as loco as Broughton, then! Damn it, man, they're about to hang somebody!"

I forced myself up, back to my horse . . . and fetched out the scope. Pausing a moment, I drew my rifle from its boot as well, and returned to where we were.

"You look through it," I said, handing him the scope, embarrassed that my hand trembled.

He yanked it away from me, put it to his eye. The clouds sailed clearer of the moon; light spilled across the land.

Even without the scope, I could see what happened at that moment. A horse, stepping forward, a man swinging off its back, dangling and kicking in midair . . .

"It's Killian . . . they've hanged him!"

"Dear God . . ."

"The limb, Jed . . . shoot the limb!"

He shoved the scope at me. I stared at it.

"Damnation, man! You're the sharpshooter! Put the scope on the rifle . . . shoot the limb!"

I had to do it. I grabbed the scope, put it in place . . . lifted the rifle . . .

The scope touched my eye, cold as the finger of Satan, electric as a lightning jolt.

The clouds were moving back over the moon, light fading. . . . The campfire alone did not provide sufficient light by which I could aim my shot. I had to take it now. I peered through the scope, such a familiar thing to do even after so long, and saw the frail form of Edward Killian kicking, flailing . . . Broughton standing nearby, just watching . . . Dewitt beside him.

"Help me, God," I whispered. "Guide my shot this time to save a life, not take it."

In the last moments of clear moonlight, I peered

through that scope, leveled the rifle, squeezed off a shot as I'd done so many times before . . .

The limb splintered, bent, sagged down, broke.

Killian fell to the ground. The moon went behind clouds, and Leroy came to his feet and raced down toward the place they were.

It was a smart move. Get down there before they could see us coming, while they were still confused by what had happened. Before they could pull themselves together and put a bullet through the head of the man they'd just failed to hang.

But I couldn't rise for a moment. I was frozen. I'd just done a thing that I'd sworn never to do . . . but as I had prayed, my shot had given life, not death.

Or so I hoped. Killian had not dropped far enough to break his neck, but he had hung there several moments, swinging and choking. But maybe, light and birdlike as he was, he'd not hung long enough to crush his throat.

Rising, I ran down after Leroy. The moon came out again as I reached the little hollow.

Killian was alive, on his knees, mouth hanging open, eyes bulging, chest heaving for breath the rope had denied him. The noose still encircled his neck, the rope still draped over the broken-down limb. And the preacher was still in danger. Broughton had a pistol out, pressed against the side of Killian's head, as Dewitt watched, a few feet away.

"Don't do it, Sheriff!" Leroy said. He had his own pistol drawn, leveled at Broughton. "I don't want to shoot you, Amos! But I'll do it, I swear, I'll do it!"

Broughton saw me and grinned darkly. "Well! The sharpshooter is back at his old tricks! Limbshooting this time, though? But did you put that scope to your eye, Jed? Did you break your vow?"

"I saved you from murdering an innocent man."

"It's not murder. It's justice."

"Not if he's innocent. And he is. I know he is. I know the truth."

I didn't know the truth, though. All I had was a theory, hints that were as skeletal as Killian himself, fleshed out mostly with surmise and guesswork. But I believed my theory valid . . . and under these circumstances, I might be able to get Killian to verify it.

"I've got to kill him, Jed," Broughton said. "He's a traitor. He betrayed the tunnel to the guards, and good men died."

"No, Amos. It wasn't him. He isn't your man."

"The hell he isn't! Why do you think those scars are on his head? I know who he is, Jed. I know a Judas when I see one. I know betrayal . . . I saw it tonight, in print. I read that newspaper Smith brought to the camp meeting, Jed. You've betrayed me, and what's worse, you've had my own wife do the same! Right there in print, Jed! Damnation! Do you know what that does to a man to see that? You know what that newspaper story is going to cost me?"

"It'll cost you your job, Amos. And it should, because you've cast aside the right to hold that job. What you're about to do here is take the law into your own hands, and that's not the role of a lawman. And what's worse, you're about to hang a man not guilty of what you believe he is."

For the first time I noticed blood on Killian's thigh. "Amos, why is there blood on his leg?" Leroy asked.

"He tried to run. We had to stop him."

That explained the two shots that had drawn us here.

"Amos, Edward Skelly didn't betray that tunnel. Isn't that right, Reverend?"

"Yes," he said, his voice weak and trembly. "I swear before God, I did not do that!"

"Then who did?" Dewitt shot back.

I laid out my theory, hoping desperately that I was right and that Killian would confirm it in a persuasive way. It would be the only chance, most likely, to save his life. "It wasn't Edward Skelly who betrayed the tunnel. It was his brother, Bartholomew."

I glanced at Killian. He stared at me in an odd way, a look that told me I had found the truth. A grain of it, at least. My hope was to prompt the preacher to fill in the gaps.

I went on. "Bartholomew Skelly and his brother spent most of their time apart at Andersonville. I remember that. Why it was, I don't know. Brothers fall out sometimes. Family arguments. Maybe that was it. But I've got a notion that whatever drove them apart, it wasn't enough to keep Edward Skelly from doing something noble for his brother when he had to. When Bartholomew betrayed the tunnel diggers, Edward took his brother's place. He let them cut the traitor's mark onto his forehead instead of Bartholomew's. And ever since then, he's born the guilt of his brother. Substitution. Right, Reverend?"

Killian nodded. Tears were in his eyes. He opened his mouth as if to speak, but something held him back.

"Is this true?" Dewitt demanded of the preacher.

Killian hesitated. When he spoke, his voice sounded different, altered by the squeeze of that noose around his neck while he was hanging. There was blood on his neck too, that rope having torn and worsened the bullet furrow that Broughton's bullet had put into his flesh. "I made a vow never to reveal—"

I spoke quickly. "Preacher, your life is on the line. You owe it to yourself, and to the truth itself, to finally say what really happened."

Killian took three deep breaths. He trembled, his head bumping the pistol Broughton still held jammed against his temple.

"Yes," Killian said. "My brother betrayed the tunnel. It's true. But it was my fault. *My* fault. Not his."

"How so?" I asked.

"He should never have been a soldier. He wasn't fit for it. He suffered a terrible beating when he was a boy . . . a drunken uncle of ours. It damaged him in body and mind. He was impossible to control, impossible to get along with. I . . . I didn't like him much. Shunned him, really . . . even in the prison camp, when I should have been there to help him through. If I'd been with him, he'd never have told the guards of that tunnel. He only did it for the food. That's all. He didn't understand that what he was doing would hurt anyone. He was just hungry, that was all. There were others there who preyed on him because he was weak of mind. They took his rations much of the time, leaving him with barely enough food to survive upon. He was hungrier even than the rest of us. No wonder the guards were able to bribe him into talking!"

"I remember things like that happening there," Dewitt said. "Guards, offering extra rations to those who would betray escape attempts."

Killian went on. "Bart was easy to push, to manipulate. . . . He didn't grasp what he was doing.

He never understood the concept of consequences. Then, later, one of the guards let out the word: 'Skelly did it. Skelly betrayed the tunnel diggers.' But he didn't say which Skelly. When those seeking vengeance came looking, they came to me instead of Bart."

Perhaps unconsciously, Broughton moved the pistol a little farther away from the preacher's head. "Why didn't you just tell the truth? Why didn't you tell them it was Bart they wanted?"

"Don't you see? Because he was my brother! What other reason did I need? We weren't close, Bart and I . . . no one could be close to Bart. But I should have protected him. I'd vowed to our mother that I'd always protect him, and I didn't do it. I left him alone in that prison camp hell most of the time. If I'd stayed near him, I could have kept him from having his rations stolen so often, or shared my own with him when they were. I could have kept the guards from bribing him. I could have saved his life. When the angry ones came looking for revenge, telling what the guard had said, I would not defend myself. If I'd denied guilt, they would have gone to Bart. I couldn't let that happen. So I accepted his guilt, and bore his punishment."

Broughton said nothing for a few moments, then asked, "So where is Bartholomew now?"

"He's dead. His health was bad after Andersonville. Ironic . . . the starvation did something to him that he never could overcome. For the rest of his time on earth he was not able to bear food well . . . he was able to eat barely enough to sustain himself."

I did not speak the thought aloud, but I understood something further about Killian just then. His thinness, his own lack of eating . . . maybe he suffered himself from a condition similar to what he'd just described. Or maybe it wasn't physical in his case, but mental. Feeling responsible for giving his brother insufficient protection in Andersonville, and watching him waste away and die even when it was all over, Killian now punished himself by eating only enough to live.

He went on, "I took care of Bart about a year after we were freed, and he died. And I was left with a scar on my forehead and my name associated with treachery . . . all this along with a clear call to preach the gospel. But how could a man with a ruined name, and a traitor's T carved onto his flesh, ever be a preacher? So I did what I had to do. I changed my name, and changed my scars. . . . I know it was wrong to live a lie while preaching the word of God, but what else could I do? No one would have come to hear the preaching of the 'Traitor of Andersonville.' I had no choice but to lie. No choice." He bowed his head and wept, the heaving of his shoulders making the rope around his neck move.

"Preacher," Dewitt said, "why didn't you tell us that before we whipped that horse from beneath you?"

"I vowed at the grave of my brother never to reveal what he'd done. It wasn't really his fault, you know. He didn't understand. He wasn't able to understand."

I spoke to Broughton. "I believe him, Amos. There is the ring of truth in what this man says."

Amos nodded slowly, and holstered his pistol. "I believe him too."

The rope was gone from Killian's neck, and Dewitt had crudely bandaged the bleeding bullet furrow with a bandanna. Amos stood before Killian, who was seated leaning back against the same tree they'd hanged him from, and forced himself to look into his face. His eyes flicked up, studied the three crosses on Killian's forehead, then down into Killian's eyes again. I could tell it was hard for Broughton to do what he was doing, and I was proud of him for it.

"I owe you a great apology, Preacher. The greatest of apologies."

Killian said, "You didn't know."

"I'd have killed you, sir, if not for Jed intervening. And it was me who fired the shot that wounded you."

"I know. But God has been gracious. I am yet alive."

Broughton came to me. "That newspaper . . ."

"We did it to protect the preacher, Amos. We had to. Somehow people had to know what you were doing, for we couldn't dissuade you."

"Did Callianne really say them words that story put in her mouth?"

"She did. And wept to do it, because she knew what it would cost you."

"My work, Jed. I can't be sheriff anymore. Not after this." His eyes moistened. "I need a drink."

"You need Callianne. You need your home. You need anything but a drink."

He nodded. "Yeah. Yeah. But a drink is what I want."

Dewitt approached me. "I guess I'm in your custody, deputy. I've busted a lot of laws all to pieces this night."

"Just get on your horse and go home," I said.

"You mean that?"

"I'm not a lawman. I'm a writer. All I've been trying to do all along is help out Amos."

"Then . . . I truly may go?"

"Yes."

He turned and walked away into the night.

I approached Killian. "Reverend, there's something you must know. When I told you before that some around you have involved themselves in crime, I spoke the truth. Boucher and Malone are involved, working with a one-eared fellow who tried to kill me tonight."

"Tried to kill you?"

"Yes. I had to kill him instead."

"Merciful heaven!"

"Your house needs cleaning, Preacher. In the worst way."

"I'll see it is done."

"Your man Brother Timothy was struck on the head tonight when you were captured. He's addled but I think he'll be all right. I don't believe he's involved in the robberies, but he has some habits with the women that may not be what you want from people who work with you."

"I'd suspected as much."

"But Timothy was concerned enough about you that he was heading for town to get you help, even though the back of his head was pretty well pounded. I think the man probably has some good in him."

"I'll keep that in mind, sir." The preacher stuck out his hand. "You have saved my life today. I thank you."

"I'm sorry for some things I said to you, sir. At the time I didn't know all the truth."

"Think nothing of it."

*   *   *

The horse that Edward Killian had straddled with a rope around his neck was now his mount as he rode back toward the campground. The clouds had dissolved completely, leaving the moon shining so brightly that the edge of the landscape was completely visible.

We traveled up the horse trail and reached the main road. Leroy spoke up.

"Jed . . . he's gone."

At first I didn't take his meaning, but then it became clear: the one-eared man I'd shot was no longer on the road. Who could have moved the body?

We rode up, a sense of great caution and mystery giving me a prickly feeling on the back of my neck.

There were bloodstains on the road where he had been, darker shadows on the shadowed way. I dismounted, knelt, and looked at the ground. No footprints, no sign that anyone else had been here.

Something loomed up from the roadside brush. I saw it only a moment before the gunfire broke out. Something slammed hard into my leg and it buckled out from under me. I went down, hard.

I rolled, looked up, and saw him. Back from the dead, it seemed. Bloody, ugly, but alive.

I'd not killed him after all. He staggered toward me, pistol out. . . .

Multiple shots rang out, fired by Leroy and Broughton. They hammered the man's big body and drove him back and down. His pistol went off one time, fired off randomly, unaimed.

No question this time. He was gone. I rolled over, looked up at the blue-black of the sky and the stars now visible, then turned my head back toward the others. Just before I passed out I saw Edward Killian roll slowly off the side of his horse and fall in a heap on the road.

My eyes closed and I knew no more.

When I woke up, I thought I was back in Bedford, in the house of Mayor Murphy Wagoner. The same kind of ceiling, the same angle of light spilling through the window . . .

A look around revealed I was wrong. I had never been in this room before. It was a long, narrow place with three small beds, one of which I occupied. The other held Reverend Killian. Leaning over him with a look of concern was the same doctor who had tended to Amos Broughton after the shootout with Miller.

I sat up slowly, wincing as pain shot through my leg. My motion made the doctor look up at me.

"Ah! Back with us, I see. Don't try to rise, Mr. Wells. You need to keep that leg still."

I sat up anyway. "How is the preacher?"

"Bad. The bullet went into his stomach. Nothing I can do for him."

The doctor moved slightly, and I noticed others behind him. There was Brother Timothy, his face ashen and his head bandaged. And Morgan Hamm, looking a little drunk.

"Hello," Hamm said, coming over to me. "You going to make it?"

"I'm hopeful of it. Leg hurts, though."

"At least you still got it. The preacher ain't going to pull through. It's a shame. He's a good one."

"Yes."

"All the bad ones are gone. Boucher and Malone and some others all cleared out last night. The talk was they believed they were about to be exposed."

"They were right."

"Damn shame, when bad men go free and good ones die. Why do you reckon things happen that way?"

"I couldn't say. How long have I been passed out?"

"A day and a night. The doc loaded you up with laudanum."

Just like Reid. The doctor here loved his laudanum, no doubt about it. Kept the patients quiet. I couldn't believe I'd been out for so long, though. No wonder my tongue was thick, my head filled with soft cotton.

Feeling dizzy, I lay back down again and slept, the aftereffects of the opiate still lingering.

*   *   *

It was the strangest dream I'd ever had. Surely it was the drug that caused it, but forever after, a part of me would ponder over it, and wonder.

When I opened my eyes next, the light in the room had changed and no visitors were present. The preacher must have been doing better, though, because he was leaning over me, praying like he had that day after the train crash. This time he was touching my brow, because I could feel the cool weight of his hand. But as real as it all seemed, I knew it wasn't in fact real, because he looked different. No marks on his forehead now. No cloth across the brow.

"Thank you for praying for me, Preacher," I said to this phantom vision.

"I must go now," he told me.

"No," I heard myself reply. "I don't think you should. There's still work for you to do. I think you should stay."

I closed my eyes a moment, or maybe longer, and he was gone when I opened them again. Rolling my head, I saw the preacher was back on his bed again. And the crosses were back on his brow.

The doctor appeared sometime later. "More laudanum?" he asked. "No reason to suffer pain that I can see when there's laudanum to be had. Makes a man sleep, and sleep is the heart of healing."

I wondered how much of the opiate the man used himself. "No more," I told him. "I want to feel like myself again."

Looking over, I saw the preacher still breathing.

"He decided to stay," I said. "I'm glad."

The doctor laughed. "He didn't have much choice but to stay, considering his condition."

"He'll live?"

"I think so. He'll be back spouting fire and brimstone again. It may take a few months for him to heal, though. The poor devil seems about starved, for some reason. Hardly any flesh on him at all."

"Where's Amos Broughton?"

"Home. With his wife. A bit of scandal about that fellow. Had to quit as sheriff. They say he went out of his head. That's a kind of sickness I can't cure."

"He'll be all right. He's with the one who can make sure of it."

I stood at Amos Broughton's side, looking across Killian's campground. The stage remained, and most of the wagons and such. The street signposts were there, standing somewhat askew now. All in all, it was a dejected-looking scene.

"Are you bitter, Amos?"

"Only at myself."

"I feel some responsibility, Amos. It was my idea to have that newspaper printed."

"And it was a good idea. No way could I get close to Killian with everybody knowing I was after his hide. It was a good strategy on your part."

"But a costly one for you. That's what I regret."

"Ah, I think it's for the best. I don't know that I'm cut out for sheriffing. Not for forever, at least. I believe I'll go back and do some ranching, like I used to. I've missed it."

"I wish you much success."

"You going to write up this story in one of your books, Jed?"

"I don't think so. Not every story demands telling. This one has too much hurt attached to it. Too many . . ."

"Ghosts?"

"Yes. Ghosts."

"You stopped me from hanging an innocent man, Jed. I'll never be able to repay you for that."

I shrugged. What was there to say?

Callianne's voice called. We turned to see her rolling up in her buggy.

"Right there is the greatest treasure you'll ever own, Amos. Don't you ever let go of her. If you do, I might just come collect her for myself."

"She ain't available, Jed. God, I almost threw it all away! Now it's time to recollect and rebuild. I'm glad we'll have more time together. And what about you? What's next?"

"There's some more people I need to find. More

information to give them about those they lost at the prison camp."

"Yours is a holy calling. Just like the preacher's."

"Maybe. But it's a hard calling sometimes. It's hard to live a life that keeps looking back on what you'd rather forget."

"We can't forget it, Jed. We must not. If we forget it, it will happen again."

We turned and walked toward Callianne. The wind was rising and the sky was clear. If the ghosts were out today, they were lost in the bright sunshine. It was good to be here, and good to be alive.

Catch the riveting new hardcover from
New York Times bestselling author Tony Hillerman
as Leaphorn and Chee join forces to solve a
puzzling new mystery, from the discovery of a
murdered man with no ID to covert activities
on a big game ranch.

TONY HILLERMAN
THE SINISTER PIG

ISBN: 0-06-019443-X
Price: $25.95/NCR

ON SALE: 5/6/03

Available wherever books are sold
or call 1-800-331-3761 to order.

HarperCollins*Publishers*
www.harpercollins.com   SP 0403